THE DEVIL IN THE DARK

JAMIE JOHANSSON FILES
BOOK 4

MORGAN GREENE

ALSO BY MORGAN GREENE

<u>Standalone Titles</u>

Savage Ridge

A Place Called Hope

The Trade

THE DEVIL IN THE DARK

CHAPTER
ONE

The woman was in her mid-forties. She had blonde hair and blue eyes. She was average height, not overweight, and she had absolutely no idea why she was blindfolded and bound, her hands above her head, her arms bearing the weight of her entire body, her feet just touching the ground. Enough so she wouldn't swing.

When she came around, she had no sense of how long she'd been asleep, or unconscious, or whatever it was. Though she didn't rouse of her own accord, it was the sound of a door opening and someone entering the room.

She all but held her breath, waiting, listening, hoping that this was all some big misunderstanding. Some sort of grave mistake. Who would want to hurt her? She was a mother, a wife ... she had never done anything to anyone! And she would have screamed that too, if she hadn't been gagged.

She couldn't see where she was, either. There was a bag over her head, she guessed. She couldn't feel anything pressed to her eycs, and yet she was completely blind. The place she was being held felt cold and dank, so she guessed it had to be underground. But how did that help her? It didn't.

Jesus, what the hell is going on? She mumbled through the gag, but the person in the room with her – she could sense them there just standing, watching her – didn't approach or move. She squirmed under their gaze, shuddering, but not from the cold.

It stayed like that for what seemed like an age, until she broke, until she whimpered and cried.

And then the stranger without a face sighed. 'I'm sorry,' he said, his voice soft. 'I'm sorry you're caught up in all this. It's not even about you, honestly ... it's not your fault you're here, and it's nothing you did that's to blame for what's about to happen.' He paused, as if collecting his thoughts, or building up to something. Perhaps building the courage for something. 'This is about someone else,' he muttered. 'Someone who needs to pay for what they've done. Someone who thinks they can do whatever they like, hurt people without conse- quence or remorse. But they can't. So you have to die.'

The woman cried out through the gag, the mewling sob stifled by the fabric pulled tight between her teeth. She felt the warmth of tears cut lines down her cheeks.

Every part of her wanted to run, to tear herself free of her bonds and escape. But she knew she couldn't. Her wrists were locked together, her muscles weak and exhausted. She knew it, the truth: she was going to die here.

Unless ... unless she could somehow—

But before she even formed that desperate thought, she felt a sudden sensation of cold in her gut.

She gasped, choking on the gag, and then pain exploded through her stomach.

A hand gripped her shoulder, pulling her body forward, deeper into the blade in her gut.

She convulsed, the coldness spreading across her torso.

Her fingers tingled, the blood roaring in them. She felt woozy, sick, faint, all at once.

Her world rocked and span, her heart beating fast and erratic.

More pain rippled through her as the knife was jerked upwards, right below her sternum.

And then there was nothing.

In seconds, the pain faded to a strange and distant ache, and then that subsided ... dying like a match that had burned itself out.

The hand, tight on her shoulder, loosened and softened, moving to the nape of her neck. The grip was soft, warm even, cradling her head.

'Shh, shh ...' the voice said softly. 'It's okay. It's over now. You can sleep.'

She whimpered softly, the breath leaving her body but not returning.

She couldn't hear her heart anymore.

Everything was growing faint, but she still felt it when he laid her head softly on her chest and receded into the darkness, soothing her as he went.

'Just sleep,' he said. 'Just sleep ... it's okay ...' And with the last semblance of consciousness, she swore she heard just one more word before the darkness took her, though she didn't know what it meant. The footsteps faded to nothing, his voice echoing in her mind as it shut down. Leaving her with one final thought before she died: Who is "Jamie"?

CHAPTER
TWO

T he wall clock was positioned such that Jamie couldn't quite see the numbers unless she obviously leaned to the side to look. Which she did once, and promptly felt judged for.

The armchairs were bright green. Comfy enough, but the sort that didn't really want to be sat on. They sort of tipped you forward out of them, and the throw cushions meant that you couldn't quite sit all the way back unless you moved them. And then you were either stuck clutching them like a teddy bear, or putting them on the floor because there was nowhere else for them.

The psychologist sitting opposite Jamie shifted her position slightly and adjusted her glasses, crossing her legs the opposite way to the way they'd been crossed for the last ten minutes.

'Would you like me tell you what time it is?' the woman asked. Her name was Dr Dumont, though Jamie felt it best not to get acquainted. She had no intention of coming back.

'No, that's fine,' Jamie said. 'I'm not counting.'

Dumont smiled easily. She was probably ten years Jamie's senior, a tall woman with fine features and keen eyes. She was wearing brow-line reading glasses and had both hands on the arms of her chair, making no effort to disguise the way she was studying Jamie.

'You feel rather on display sitting there, don't you?' she asked.

'I don't much like therapy,' Jamie answered. And it was true. She did not like therapy. And she did not want to be there. And she certainly wasn't there by choice. 'Radcliffe is forcing me to do this. That's the only reason I'm sitting here.'

Dumont smiled a little more. 'You know that's the third time you've mentioned his name.'

'I've got an axe to grind with him, clearly,' Jamie answered coolly.

'It appears so.' Dumont leaned forward. 'I understand your trepidation, even your discomfort being here. But, from my understanding, your operational status hinges on my approval. It's not an unusual thing for people in your line of work to require psychological support.'

'I don't need psychological support,' Jamie said firmly.

'Right. I thought exactly the same thing after reviewing your previous case files. It's perfectly natural to want to run headlong into mortal danger with complete disregard for your own safety.'

'Sarcasm isn't really befitting a person of your profession, is it?'

Dumont shrugged. 'I'm meeting you where you're at. You don't respect me, so why should I respect you?'

'Who says I don't respect you?'

'Where to begin? If you thought my profession or my time was worth something, you'd be at least reasonably receptive to this process. But you're not. You're counting the minutes, hoping that sitting here in silence will somehow lead to a faster conclusion than doing the work,' Dumont said, sitting back and getting comfortable.

'And that tells you I don't respect you?' Jamie asked lightly.

'Well, there is another alternative.'

'Which is ...?'

'That you're terrified. Terrified of what might come out if we prise open the door even a crack.'

Jamie remained quiet.

'I find it highly interesting, actually. You've breezed through prior psych assessments, haven't you? I know you have, there's no point asking. But I read their notes, the transcripts of those sessions, and it seemed to me like you were simply saying what needed to be said, what you *know* needed to be said, to get them over and done with and get your approvals. Which further reinforces my assessment that you lack respect for this profession, that you'd prefer to deceive than do the work.' She eyed Jamie carefully. 'But it also means you're smart enough to make an astute appraisal of the situation at hand, and of the person sitting in front of you. And I would think that had your appraisal of me been the same as that of those who came before me, you'd be feeding me the same rhetoric you still no doubt have memorised to dupe us head-shrinks. Which means that you don't think I'm as easily duped, or at least intelligent enough and experienced enough not to fall for the same script you've performed before. Which means that, actually, you *do* have some respect for me. Which means that my other guess is probably far more likely to be true. You're scared, Jamie Johannsson. Scared of what I'll find if I crack your head open. And most of all, afraid that I won't let you be you anymore.'

Jamie stared back, keeping her poker face.

'At this point, can you even extricate your sense of self from your work?'

'Do I need to?' Jamie asked quietly, trying not to sound too angry.

'Depends. What does your life look like if I tell Radcliffe you're not fit to be in the field, or to carry a weapon, or to be … you anymore?'

'I honestly hadn't thought about it.'

'Frightening to consider, isn't it?'

Jamie sighed. 'Is that what this is going to be? Mind games?'

'If you're not willing to meet me halfway, it's the

only way we'll make any progress. So, it's entirely up to you. Put in terms you might appreciate, we can strafe about each other on the mat, waiting for an opening to slip in a jab. We can feint and change up our stance, throw a low kick here and there to weaken each other's defences, and then strike a killing blow when an opening presents itself. But that entire premise predicates itself on this being a competition that can be won or lost, that we are opponents, each seeking victory. Mine, presumed, to strip you of your operational status. And yours, to trick me into approving it. But what if I told you that it's not the case? That we *both* want the same thing. That we're on the same side, not enemies.'

'If that's the case, tell Radcliffe I'm good to go.'

She smiled again. 'You know it's not that simple. And I have too much integrity to compromise myself in such a way that would endanger you and your team mates.'

'Then we're at an impasse, it seems.'

'Perhaps,' Dumont said slowly. 'There is another, much simpler way through this. I ask a simple question, you give an honest answer. And we go back and forth like that until I'm satisfied.'

'Satisfied as to what?'

'That you're not trying to manipulate me or lie to me to get me to sign off on you.'

Jamie processed that. 'And in the meanwhile ...'

'You'll have temporary operational status,' Dumont said, 'but I want you to know something.'

'What's that?'

'That I'm apprehensive to do it. There's more than enough in your file to concern me, and to suggest that I shouldn't. And I want you to recognise that, and appreciate it. I'm taking a little leap of faith, but more than that I'm offering you my trust. Once you walk out that door I'll call Radcliffe, and I'll tell him one of two things: I think she's fit to keep working in the meanwhile and I'll give you my full assessment at the end of our twelve weeks, or I don't think she's fit to keep working in the meanwhile, but I'll give you my full assessment at the end of our twelve weeks. So I'm asking you, which do you want? The easy way or the hard way?'

'Is it bad that I can't tell which is which?' Jamie asked dryly.

She was amused by that. 'The easy way is to take my show of trust, and not to spit in my face. Come back next week and talk to me. It will get easier. I promise.'

It wasn't talking that Jamie was afraid of. It was what would come spilling out if they cracked the door, as Dumont had said. Jamie was well aware that she wasn't quite *normal*, and it was likely that her status would be denied once plausible diagnoses started flying. Which meant that she needed to be both careful and honest here. She needed to keep working, so she'd have to take Dumont's easy way. Which at least bought her another week to figure out her next move. Because actually showing her what was behind that door was not an option.

'Is that it for this week?' Jamie asked, in as relaxed a way as she could force herself to appear.

Dumont took time to answer. 'Sure, if you'd like. I think there's plenty for you to think about.'

'And Radcliffe ...?'

'I don't have much to go on so far. So, you tell me. Do you want to build a little bit of trust here, a little bit of mutual respect?'

Jamie paused as if to consider it, and then nodded. 'Yes,' she said softly but affirmatively. 'Thank you.' That's it, show a little humility. Be guarded, she's smart. Don't overplay it.

Dumont regarded her for a few seconds. 'Alright then. You're free to go.'

Jamie gave her a nod, thinking that offering a handshake would be too much, and then got up and headed for the door.

'One more thing, though,' Dumont called from the armchair.

Jamie stopped and turned back.

'I'm not stupid, Jamie, and don't presume me to be. I didn't get to where I am, doing what I do, without being very good. I deal *exclusively* with people in your profession and those adjacent to it. People who are trained to lie, to deceive, to be other people. People who are ready to kill and ready to die every day they step out of their front door. Radcliffe and I have worked closely for years, and we have a very open, and very clear line of, communication. If you try to lie your way through this I will know, and I will tell him, and then all of this goes up in smoke.'

Jamie stared back at her.

'I just wanted you to know that. My trust is given freely, but it's also easily broken. And I don't give second chances. So don't underestimate me and, perhaps more prudently, Jamie ...' she said, taking off her glasses so Jamie could meet her eyes fully, 'don't overestimate yourself.'

CHAPTER
THREE

Jamie arrived back at the farm tired. The drive hadn't been particularly long, but she was still strung out. Dumont had an office in Cardiff, though it was lifeless enough that Jamie was able to guess with some confidence that she was just using it for drop-in sessions. Radcliffe had asked her to come and check Jamie out, make sure she was fit for this line of work, but where she was coming *from* to do that, Jamie didn't know.

All she wanted to do when she got back was have a cup of tea and relax. Just for a little bit. But as she pulled into the yard in front of the farm, she knew that wasn't going to be the case. Hallberg's black Mercedes and Radcliffe's silver BMW were both parked where Jamie normally parked so, with a huff, she pulled her little VW into the space next to Elliot's old pick-up and got out, heading towards the house.

The air was frigid now. Christmas had come and gone quickly, and though the new year brought brighter weather, it came with a bite, settling in for the long haul it seemed. Though Jamie didn't mind, it reminded her of home.

She and Alina had taken a trip just before new year back to Sweden, and Jamie had shown her around the city. They explored the streets, went by Jamie's old house – which was now a cleared lot, the ground still blackened from the fire – and then to her father's grave. She told Alina all about him, about her childhood and growing up there, and then they went north. To the lake he'd always taken her to. She stared out across it from the shore, remembering what had brought her back here what seemed like a lifetime ago. The Angel Maker.

They did not stay long.

And then it was north, to Kurrajak, so Jamie could finally tie up that loose end. So she could collect what few belongings she had – namely a few photographs, her father's old peacoat, along with his Remington R700, and a few other things of course. Mostly guns. While she certainly was a fan of the Glock family, she did have a soft spot for the SIG Sauer P226, her standard-issue pistol while she was working in Sweden. And while it would no doubt garner plenty of outward criticism from both Hassan and Church – if she ever saw him again – she didn't really give a shit. She could shoot the eye out of a gnat at twenty metres with her SIG, and she thought that might just come in handy with the kind of work they were doing. It was a matter of pride, in the end, of having your own gun. The loaners she'd been working with from Interpol were fine ... but having your own was special.

Alina seemed to think so too, and when Jamie opened the lid to her case, showing off the P226 and P229 Compact, her eyes lit up wider than they had on Christmas morning.

She licked her lips without realising, staring at the guns, and Jamie was a little concerned, but more thankful than anything that they were able to find more and more common ground.

Elliot's purchase of a rifle for her birthday had initially rubbed Jamie the wrong way. She wasn't keen on bringing Alina into their world if she could help it. But with everything she'd gone through, she was already deeper than Jamie ever would have wanted, and she knew that wrapping her in cotton wool would only hurt their relationship.

So, along with teaching her to fight, to know when to fight and, more importantly, to know when to run ... she was now teaching her to shoot. The air rifle that Elliot got her was a beautiful piece of machinery, accurate to almost a hundred yards, which was impressive considering it ran on compressed gas.

Though these – the weapons in front of them, and the rifle waiting by the door to be taken home – they weren't practice weapons. They weren't for learning, and they weren't for fun. They were serious devices of death, and all three weapons had spilled blood.

Jamie made sure Alina knew that, and to her surprise – and relief – Alina nodded slowly, acknowledging, understanding. Jamie never forgot that the girl had already claimed lives with her own hands, but she often overlooked the fact that she carried that weight with her every day. That she knew the burden, and wasn't keen to add to it.

She was just so sweet, it was hard to believe sometimes.

It wasn't easy getting the guns into the UK, but there were strings she could pull, and did. So she boxed everything up, and on the way back, after listing the house for sale with the local(est) estate agent, she stopped off at the national police headquarters in Stockholm, and dropped the crate, plastered with fragile stickers, to the Interpol office there, ready for special courier to the UK. Recipient: one Julia Hallberg.

And Jamie couldn't call in there without stopping in to the Violent Crimes department and calling on Anders Wiik. He wasn't exactly *happy* to see her. But then again, Wiik was never happy. About anything.

Jamie was just glad to hear that no other major serial killers had re-emerged in the city of late, and that his hand was now fully healed. It was still stiff on cold mornings, he said, but it didn't hurt anymore and he had full use of it. Even the scarring had faded.

After being introduced to Alina, and having – as

expected – barely any reaction to the fact that Jamie had all but adopted a teenage girl, Alina made no attempt to be polite when asking what had happened to his hand.

And Wiik made no attempt to be polite about the fact that it was Jamie's fault.

'Jamie took me five hundred miles out to sea, and then smashed it with a steel pipe,' he said flatly.

Jamie scoffed a little. 'It was four hundred and eighty miles, thank you. And it was a crowbar. Also,' she added, lifting a finger, 'it wasn't me. It was a six foot four inches tall Serbian named Sasha Kravets.'

'To-mato, to-mahto,' Wiik sighed. 'Is there anything else? I'm quite busy.'

Jamie smiled at that. Five minutes was enough to catch up after two years of not seeing each other. But she didn't mind. It was Wiik, after all, and she'd be sadder if he changed, rather than staying the same. So, she bid him goodbye. Told him if he was ever in Wales to look her up – to which he said he wouldn't be – and forced him into a brief and awkward embrace.

Following that, they left, heading straight for the airport. Alina, exhausted from all the driving and travelling, slept on the way. Jamie, on the other hand, queued through city traffic deep in thought, thinking about the one person she'd wanted to see, had thought about going to see, but didn't have the courage, or the stupidity maybe, to.

Kjell Thorsen had been her partner since Kurrajak. Jesus, that was a fucked-up case. She still couldn't look at a crow the same way. They'd been friends, and almost more than that. They'd lived together, travelled together, did everything except *be* together. And ... what might have been, Jamie didn't know. For a moment there, she was out, she was happy, whiling away her days, hopping from Greek island to Greek island with someone she thought she could have stayed with forever.

But that wasn't the life he chose, or the one he wanted. And answering the call for help from an old colleague, and dragging them back into a world of death and evil once more ... it had been his salvation. But also his end.

He nearly died, and whether Jamie was responsible or not, she could never quite say. But either way, though he'd survived that day on the water off the coast of Gotland, the man she'd known - and been too afraid to love - had died. Now, he was nothing but a stranger. One she couldn't speak to or visit. She'd been told not to call, not to come, not to contact him.

He needed to heal.

He needed to live his life.

And he couldn't do either with Jamie there.

What was that bullshit about setting something free if you love them?

Jamie shook her head, rattling that thought away, and dragged her knuckles across her cheeks to wipe away the forming tears.

She rolled the window down then to get some air on her face, and Alina stirred.

'What's wrong?' she asked, looking over at Jamie through one eye.

'Nothing,' Jamie said, 'just ... this was home for a long time. And now ...'

'Now you have a new home,' Alina said, closing her eyes once more and drifting back to sleep. 'Wake me when we get there.'

Jamie just smiled at that, and drove on.

And now, a few weeks later, here she was, back at the farm, standing in front of the building, a veritable Swedish bite in the air, staring at Radcliffe and Hallberg's cars, wondering what awaited inside. Inside her new home.

Alina was with Hassan, walking Hati somewhere in the Beacons. Which meant that the only ones here were Hallberg and Radcliffe.

Jamie walked in, trying not to sigh too outwardly at the fact that her two guests had seen fit to let themselves in. They were sitting at the kitchen table, drinking coffee.

'Make yourselves comfortable, why don't you?' she said, homing in on the pot and grabbing a mug from the drying rack.

'The door was open,' Radcliffe said. 'Looks like the lock's broken.'

'Well, that's what happens when someone kicks it in,' Jamie said, pouring her cup. It had been nearly eight weeks since Seda Petrosyan's men had come for Alina, breaking down her door.

'You intending to fix it?' he asked lightly. He sat there looking very comfortable, his pale skin and dark hair giving him a slightly vampiric appearance.

'It's not up there on my list.'

'Why not?'

'Because someone's probably just going to kick it in again if I do. And anyway, I have a much simpler solution to stop burglars and home invaders.'

'Which is?'

'The SIG Sauer P226 in the top drawer of my bedside table,' Jamie said coldly, taking a hot sip of her coffee.

He smiled at that, amused.

Hallberg gave Jamie a smile too. 'How are you?' she asked from next to Radcliffe.

'Fine.'

'How was your session?'

It was no secret that Jamie was being forced into therapy, and Hallberg was making no effort to disguise how happy she was about it. She'd harboured for a long time the thought that Jamie probably needed it, but had never said anything because she knew how Jamie would react if she did. Now, Radcliffe got to be the bad guy and she got to be the supportive friend. A good deal for her - not so much for Jamie.

'Fine,' Jamie answered.

'Just ... *fine?*' Hallberg fished.

'It was just their first session,' Radcliffe said. 'Feeling each other out, Dumont said.' He eyed Jamie carefully. 'That sound about right?'

'Something like that.'

He stared at her like he was peeling her skin off layer by layer in his mind. Maybe he was. Jamie didn't like the slightly sadistic look in his eye. Though to go far in his profession, she suspected you probably needed to take some pleasure in the suffering of others. He lifted his hand then and brought it down on a fat manilla file sitting in the middle of the table.

'What's that?' Jamie asked.

'This is your prize. Dumont says you're fine, for now. So this is what you get.'

Jamie sipped a little more coffee, seeing Radcliffe's white knuckles and splayed fingers pressing into the unmarked cover of the file. She sensed the graveness in his posture, and Hallberg's faded smile told her that whatever was inside wasn't anything happy.

'And what exactly am I getting?'

'Your favourite,' he answered. 'A serial killer.'

'Oh,' Jamie replied with a sigh. 'Tantalising. Anything special about this one, or are you giving me something easy for our first go around? Have the training wheels come off already?'

'You could say that,' he said, turning the file and sliding it towards the edge of the table. 'A new player, it seems. Notched up a few kills already in just the last few weeks. Though the number isn't the concerning part.'

Jamie came to the table slowly. 'Serial killer?' She glanced up at him from the file. 'Don't you have *actual* detectives with badges and all that official stuff to deal with this kind of thing?'

'*This* kind of thing? No.' Radcliffe shook his head. 'This kind of thing is ... well, you could say that I've got a feeling you're the right person for it.'

Jamie set her coffee down and reached for the cover. When she lifted it, her first thought was why the hell was there a picture of her in this file?

Her second thought was worse – that's not me, but it's damn close.

A woman stared up at her. Mid-forties. Blonde. Blue-eyed. High cheek bones.

Jamie stared back. Mid-forties. Blonde. Blue-eyed. High cheek bones.

Her heart beat more quickly. 'What the hell is this?' she asked, her voice barely above a whisper.

'This,' Radcliffe said, 'is Julie Johns. Found two weeks ago in a river in Yorkshire. Drowned, with ligature marks on her wrists.'

Jamie clenched her teeth, reading the bullet points beneath the photo as Radcliffe spoke.

'Turn the page.'

Jamie already knew what was coming, and she wasn't looking forward to it. But she had to turn the page.

Another woman stared up at her. Blonde. Blue-eyed. Her age.

'Judith James,' Radcliffe said. 'Found in a bedsit in Manchester. Single gunshot wound to the chest.'

Jamie remained silent, trying to calm her breathing. But before Radcliffe could reel off another, she had already turned the page, seeing the thing she hoped not to.

A third woman. Blonde. Blue-eyed.

'Jana Jelinek.'

Jamie lifted the photograph that was clipped to the page, seeing crime scene photos. She was in a rubbish heap, and her hands had been cut off.

'Any of this feeling familiar?' Radcliffe asked.

Jamie closed the file and rested her hand on it, as though pressing it closed would prevent the details from leaking out, from becoming real.

'They're my cases,' she said, her voice a little shaky. 'Someone's recreating my cases.'

He nodded. 'Yes, it seems someone's got an axe to grind. With you. There's no mistaking the message here, is there? Three women that could easily be mistaken for you in a line-up, bearing your initials, killed in ways that mimic your first three murder cases.'

'No,' Jamie said, 'I suppose there's no mistaking it.' Her mind reeled. Who would want her dead?

'This is a ... warning, a message, I don't know,' Radcliffe said. 'But that's why the case is in front of you, and not me.' He drained the last of his coffee. 'He's done one a week,' he went on, 'and you've solved more than three murders, so if the pattern holds ...'

'He's going to keep killing,' Jamie said.

'The women have no connections to each other, and

the kills are all clean and confident. They have no hint of a novice finding his style. This is deliberate, and it's aimed at you.'

'So, what do you want me to do?' she asked, watching as he pushed back from the table and stood up.

'Isn't it obvious?' he asked, buttoning his suit jacket and pushing his hands into his pockets. 'I want you to catch him.'

'And then?'

Radcliffe let a slow smile spread across his face. 'Cuff him. Read him his rights. Take him in ...' He began walking towards the door, pausing at the threshold. 'Or, there is another option.'

'Which is?' Jamie asked, hand still on the file.

He chuckled softly, opening the broken door. 'You know you really should get this fixed. There's a draft coming in, and it looks like it's going to be a cold winter.'

CHAPTER
FOUR

J amie bid Hallberg goodbye and called Elliot. He picked up quickly, as usual.

'Jamie?' he asked. 'Everything okay?'

'Uh-huh,' she said slowly, hunched over the table, staring at the pictures of the victims spread out in front of her. 'I, uh ...' she started, losing her train of thought.

'What's going on?'

She spoke softly, her voice small in her ears. 'We've got a case.' She wasn't rattled easily, but there was something twisted, unsettling about seeing your own face staring back from victim photos. It was hard to distance yourself from the reality of the crimes when that happened. It was something Jamie hadn't experienced, and it was throwing her off her game already.

Elliot waited, taking as much from the silence as the words.

When she didn't say anything else, he said, 'I'm on the way.'

'Okay, thanks,' she replied, almost automatically, running her fingers across the photographs, every detail of her own cases coming back in gristly, bloody waves.

They pulled Oliver Hammond out of the Lea River. His hands had been bound at some point, bearing ligature marks. His finger nails were broken, fingers bloody from where he'd tried to claw his way out of wherever he'd been trapped.

The body staring up at her was practically a perfect re-enactment. Julie Johns had been bound for long enough that the marks on her wrists would last. She'd been held somewhere flimsy enough that she thought she could escape, so she'd scratched until her fingers were raw. And then she'd been dumped into a freezing cold river and left to drown.

Jamie closed her eyes, her breath rattling in her chest, the phone still to her ear.

'You want me to stay on the line?' Elliot asked, already moving on his end.

'No,' Jamie replied, almost bitterly. And then she hung up.

Her relationship with Elliot was complicated to say the least. And when she wasn't staring at crime scene photographs that depicted a crime that Elliot had committed, it was easier to forget what he was capable of, and what he'd done.

Because she wasn't just staring at her case, she was staring at Elliot's too. He was the one who'd kidnapped Oliver Hammond and imprisoned him. Like he'd done with a dozen others. And though he hadn't killed Oliver, the fate that awaited him was arguably worse. He was going to sedate him, and then harvest his organs.

Jamie grimaced, seeing it all too clearly even with her eyes closed.

Oliver Hammond wasn't a good person, by all accounts. He was a thief, a drug addict. He wasn't a good son to his parents. But he was also a kid. A kid who'd made some bad choices. And though we all have to pay for our actions at some point ... Elliot wasn't God. And he didn't get to make that call. Oliver Hammond could have ended up overdosing on heroin and dying on the street. And if he had, that would have been the consequences of his own actions. But at least it would have been *his* doing.

Jamie shook her head, reckoning with it. That was Elliot's argument. That he knew the boy, knew what future lay ahead for him. Knew what he was into, and who he was into it with. And that taking his life would save ten others.

Jamie felt sick.

Could the cosmic scales be so easily balanced? Could taking lives be justified if you saved others?

It was a question she had to ask herself over, and over, and over. Elliot killed with full knowledge and honesty about that. He took from those who didn't deserve, and gave to those who did.

And Jamie did the same, didn't she? She killed people who deserved it, to save those who didn't. Was she so different from him because she hid behind a piece of metal? A meaningless badge in the grand scheme. Not enough to justify those trigger pulls, was it?

And now here she was, sitting four feet from a pistol strapped to the inside of the bottom drawer on her left where she kept the tea towels. And if someone burst through the door to hurt her or Alina, she'd kill them. Hell, that's what she was doing here. Looking at these photographs. She was looking for leads to hunt a man with the intention of killing him. Wiping him from the face of the earth.

She couldn't sit here alone anymore. Her mind was going to work against her. She needed perspective.

Hassan would be back soon, and Elliot would arrive within the hour. She let out a long breath and clenched her hands into fists. A fight was coming, she knew that much.

There was no doubt in her mind that a storm was on the way, and she needed to be ready. So instead of sitting there and pouring over the files in front of her, she got up, got changed, and went out to the shed to hit something.

. . .

THE HEAVY BAG WAS STILL SWINGING BY THE time Hassan pulled into the courtyard. He was still staying at the farm. Though the immediate danger of the Petrosyans had passed, he'd settled in nicely. Jamie remained in the room Elliot had prepared for her when she'd got out of the hospital, and Hassan had been glad to trade up from the couch to Elliot's old room when he moved home.

In time she thought she'd want her privacy, and no doubt Alina would too. For now though, it worked. She liked Hassan, and he was a good housemate. She was used to living alone, but a house with some life in it was growing on her. Plus he was clean and tidy, a good cook, and great with both Alina and Hati the dog too. And he made for a mean sparring partner. Jamie liked that he had a few stone on her – she didn't feel so bad slinging body-shots at full strength.

She figured he'd move on eventually, but for now it worked, and she wasn't ready for things to change yet.

She emerged from the shed slick with sweat and began unwrapping the tape from her wrists and knuckles.

Hassan and Alina climbed out of the car, both splattered with mud from a good day in the mountains, their walking boots thick with it. Both looked tired but happy, and Jamie had to admit that the area had that effect. The only noise in the air was the distant bleat of sheep, and here, protected by the hills, it was easy to forget the shit happening beyond.

But as though that very thought was tempting fate, Elliot rolled down the road and through the gates. And just like that, the case came crashing back.

He exited the car and approached quickly, his apprehension rubbing off on Hassan immediately.

'What's wrong?' he asked, his gaze moving from Elliot to Jamie.

Alina brought Hati out from the back seat and fussed with his gnarled ears, watching silently.

'Case,' Elliot said.

'Oh,' Hassan replied, looking at Jamie. 'New one?'

She just nodded, unbinding her hands.

'Something bad, I'm guessing,' Elliot said.

'You could say that.'

'Huh,' Hassan offered, trying to read Jamie, more waiting for her to expound than trying to have an input.

'Shall I pop the kettle on?' Elliot asked.

It was times like these that Jamie almost wished she drank. She felt like she could do with something stronger, something to tone it all down a notch.

'Sure,' she said, forcing herself to smile at them. They were here. Here for her. Here to help. And she should be glad of that. 'And as for the shower,' she said to Hassan, 'you have time, but ...'

He narrowed his eyes a little at her. 'Don't you dare.'

She cracked a real smile then, darting for the door.

'I'm soaked!' he called after her. 'Jamie! Oh, for fu—'

But she was already inside and kicking her boots off.

She headed up, trying to hold on to that small flicker

of glee for as long as she could. But as she reached the shower and turned it on, holding her hand under the water, it seemed to slip away just as fast as the droplets running through her fingers.

Before she even climbed in and let it wash over her, she was already back to thinking about the case, and all the horrors sure to come – as well as those that had already faded into memory.

And though she did her best to keep her focus on the road ahead, she couldn't help but feel that maybe, just maybe, her past was finally catching up with her.

CHAPTER
FIVE

She stayed in as long as she could, but knew she'd eventually have to venture downstairs to face it all again. She had hoped there might be some simplicity to her life, finally. She thought there was enough here to keep her occupied, and maybe even enough that she could allow herself to be ... happy. Not that she knew what that'd even look like.

She wasn't even sure anyone was home as she went downstairs. Things were quiet, and that was never a good sign.

Jamie stepped back into the kitchen, sponging water from her hair with a towel, and paused, looking at the two men in front of her, their expressions grave. They had the files and pictures spread out across the surface of the table, their eyes moving over them slowly, taking in the brutality there.

They both looked up briefly as she entered, but

Elliot turned away surprisingly fast. It was unlike him. Usually his MO was unflinching, unnerving eye contact. But now, he wouldn't seem to look at her. Perhaps because he *was* looking at her. Dead. Three times over on the table in front of him.

'Well?' was all she could ask as she stepped around to the other side of the table and braced herself on the back of one of the chairs.

Hassan let out a long breath, then stretched out and put his fingers on the two photographs in front of him; one showing the gunshot victim in the apartment, and the other showing the victim with no hands at the rubbish heap. 'These two.'

'The two cases we worked together,' Jamie said, nodding. 'The Jane Doe from the trafficking case, and Alyssa Doran from the Aaron McElroy case.'

Hassan licked his lips. 'We found Doran's hands severed, laid in a bin. And then it was—'

'Rachel Bartlett's hands that were posed,' Jamie finished for him.

'So, this ...' He pointed to the picture of the body again.

Jamie sighed. 'It's not a recreation, no, but if he just left her hands for us—'

'Then we wouldn't know she looked like you.' Hassan shook his head.

They hadn't discussed the particulars, that this case was handed to them because these women looked like Jamie. But they hadn't needed to. The reasons, and what they were expected to do, were pretty clear to all of them.

'And this one?' Hassan looked at the pictures of the first kill, the drowning victim with the ligature marks. 'You worked this before we partnered up.'

'Yeah, with Paul Roper,' she said, glancing at Elliot. He didn't look back at her, and she felt it unnecessary to bring up the fact that he was responsible for the original death. 'Oliver Hammond was the victim that this crime is recreating. My first murder investigation.'

'He's going way back, then,' Hassan said. 'I hope I'm wrong, but ... one, two, three?' He pointed at the pictures in order.

'My first three murders, yeah,' Jamie sighed, keeping her voice relatively low. She couldn't hear Alina, and she didn't want her eavesdropping.

'She's upstairs,' Elliot said, still looking at the photos, but seemingly hearing Jamie's thoughts. That was, unfortunately, all he offered though.

'So, what was the fourth case?' Hassan asked. 'What are we expecting next?'

Jamie's mouth went a little dry. 'The Angel Maker,' she muttered, hoping she'd never have to see another scene like that one. The brutality, the artistry. It made her shudder to think about it.

How much Hassan knew about it, Jamie couldn't say, but he seemed to know enough. 'Well, let's make sure that doesn't happen, shall we?'

'That's the plan.'

He leaned forward, spreading his arms wide so that he was leaning over the table. 'There's a lot here.' He bit his lip. 'Not perfect recreations, but they're homages, right? They're some sort of message, clearly to you, but what are they saying?'

No answer came from either Jamie or Elliot.

'Is it a straight up threat?'

'I hope not. I'm getting tired of sleeping with one eye open.'

'Me too,' Hassan said quietly. 'Could be an admirer.'

'Of me?' Jamie was *also* getting tired of serial killers taking special interest in her. Present company included.

'Or of the killers.' Hassan shrugged. 'These are recreations of your cases. All cases you solved, right? Maybe it could be a challenge for you to *re*-solve them. Or it could be someone telling you you're next. What happens once he's all caught up? The only kill you can't figure out would be your own.'

'Mm.' Jamie made a displeased groaning noise.

'You don't like the theory?'

'Mainly because I end up dead at the end of it.' She let out a long breath and closed her eyes. 'It's as good an idea as any though.'

'What about these things?' Hassan pushed some photographs apart to reveal a close up of the stomach of one of the victims, where strange runic symbols had been carved into the flesh.

Jamie had caught a glimpse of these when she was

flipping through the files earlier, but hadn't lingered long. 'I don't know,' she answered truthfully. 'They look Nordic, but I can't say more than that.' She folded her arms, the frustration already setting in. 'I'm Swedish, so the link is obvious, but what they say ... who knows.' She shook her head. 'A clue? A message? A wild goose chase?'

'Hey,' Hassan said, looking right at her. 'Take a breath. I know this is weird, but—'

'Weird? It's fucking nuts,' she said sharply.

He took stock of that. Of Jamie being rattled by it. Which was the strangest thing of all. 'We'll figure it out. We'll find this guy. I promise.' Hassan turned to Elliot. 'And what about you? Any savant-esque observations? Any lightbulbs to help us out here?'

Elliot looked up at him slowly. 'No.' And then he turned and walked away from the table. 'I have to go,' he said.

'What? Where?' Jamie called, following him to the door.

He strode down onto the gravel driveway and towards his car. 'I need to think,' he said.

'Think about what?'

He paused at the door to the car and looked back at her with an expression more unsettled than her own. 'I'll call you.'

And then he got in and drove away.

Hassan appeared behind Jamie in the doorway. 'What was that about?'

'I don't know.' She shivered in the cold air. 'Let's go inside,' she said, scanning the quickly darkening tree-line. 'And make sure all the doors are locked.'

Hassan's eyes followed her around the farm and then he gave a firm nod. 'Yeah. Let's do that.'

THE MORNING CAME SLOWLY AND FITFULLY. Jamie slept in brief intervals but spent most of the night rolling around in her sheets.

When she finally ventured out into the hallway at just after five in the morning, she could hear Hassan snoring from the room at the end of the hall.

She paused briefly by Alina's door and pressed her ear to the wood, listening to the soft breath sounds filter through – along with Hati's huffing and puffing. The mutt refused to sleep anywhere except at the foot of her bed. That warmed her. She was glad all the others could sleep, even if she couldn't.

She knew what she needed to do: fix a big pot of coffee and then settle in and make a plan. She needed to get into this guy's head, figure out what his message was, what his endgame was. Did he have an axe to grind, and if so, why?

A list of all her previous arrests, killers and everyone else she'd brought down. Anyone who had a reason to come after her. Then it would be known killers, those uncaught. Those capable of this kind of thing. See if maybe she'd somehow caught any of their attention.

She could find their patterns easy enough, cross-reference them with the kills they had here.

She let out a tired sigh thinking about it. And the coffee wasn't even brewing yet.

She'd need to see the bodies too, in person. Get a look at them. Which was scary. Photos were one thing, but staring these women in the face? She didn't know how that would make her feel. But she supposed that was the point.

This was terrorism. The killer was trying to scare her, show her that she wasn't safe, that he was coming. This was a game for him, fun for him. But why? What had she done to this person? This wasn't a spur of the moment thing. No, this took planning, time, resources, dedication. Hopping around the country, finding and following these women, abducting and killing them, staging their bodies. It took skill and it took precision. This was no first timer. They were dealing with a pro. And that meant that this person had been operating for a while – with impunity. And there was only one killer Jamie knew who was good enough, connected enough, and creative enough to think of something like this. And he was standing in her kitchen just last night.

But no, this wasn't Elliot. It couldn't be. Could it?

She caught herself thinking that as her first spoonful of coffee grounds were halfway to the filter machine.

No, no, she told herself, setting it to run.

She stood there, listening to the water burble to steam, the first aroma of brewing coffee drifting from the top of the machine. Elliot stopped all that. And anyway, what would be the point?

But then again ... he had run out last night without a word. And Elliot *always* had something to say. He knew something, Jamie thought. But what?

Too early for questions that difficult to answer. And without coffee, she didn't have a hope in hell of coming close to thinking of a reasonable explanation.

She hung her head forward and groaned. So much for a quiet winter in the hills. That's all she'd wanted.

But it was clearly too much to ask.

'Hey.'

The voice startled her, and she turned to see Hassan lingering in the doorway in an oversized T-shirt and shorts. He had his eyes screwed closed against the light in the kitchen and his hair was ruffled from sleep.

'Guess I don't need to ask what you're doing up,' he yawned, shielding his mouth with his hand.

'Sorry,' Jamie said, 'I woke you.'

'Smell of coffee woke me,' he replied, grinning. 'Stronger than any alarm clock. I'd sleep through fireworks. But the first whiff of coffee ...' He made a rocket motion with his hand.

Jamie smiled at that. 'You want a cup then?'

'A jug if you've got it.'

She laughed. 'Coming right up.'

. . .

THEY SPENT THE HOURS BEFORE DAWN LAYING out a chronology of Jamie's cases, and her life since her first murder investigation. They found nothing of note except clear evidence that Jamie couldn't keep still for more than five minutes. That, and her partners had a nasty habit of getting maimed and injured. Hassan could attest to that, and did, reminding Jamie how many times he'd been shot on her account. And *she* reminded *him* that the last time was his own fault and he should have been more aware of his surroundings.

Other than their playful jabs at each other though, the mood was sour, and the case grim.

They'd gone over the forensic reports and the detectives' notes on each of the murders, but in none of the three was there any evidence to suggest motive or culprit. No DNA, no security footage, no witnesses, nothing.

Each followed the same pattern. All three women had been abducted while they were alone. They'd all had their phones removed from their persons and left in their cars, along with their keys, purses, and anything else they had on them.

From there, they were taken, and then within twenty-four hours, their bodies were discovered, all within a few miles of their abduction sites.

This told Jamie a few things. While it was a myth that you had to wait twenty-four hours before reporting someone missing, it certainly was much harder to get a full-blown investigation going in that short of a time.

There'd be no clear evidence of foul play, and even if the police did find the car before the body – which they did in the second victim's case – by the time they traced their movements beforehand, interviewed family members and work colleagues, cracked the phone, and then pulled nearby security footage, the body was already found. In a place that it would obviously be discovered. And yet, there were no witnesses to the placing of the bodies, either.

This meant that it was all meticulously planned. That the killer was finding these women based on their names, looks, and proximities to where one of Jamie's cases could be recreated. Then he was watching them, following them, stalking them, making sure he knew their routines and habits well enough that he could take them with ease and without risk.

None of the bodies had signs of defensive wounds, which meant they didn't fight back. None of them had any sort of drugs in their system, either. Which means they weren't dosed. Light bruising – barely visible – around the neck, suggested that the assailant came up behind the victims and put them in a sleeper hold, or a choke hold. When applied correctly and with enough force, the victim would experience syncope in seconds. Jamie had read up on it a few times before when she was training seriously in Tae-Kwon-Do, but a quick refresh that morning confirmed her theory. The restriction of blood flow to the brain by compressing the carotid artery causes a rapid loss of consciousness. It cuts off the blood flow and stimulates the baroreceptors in the tissue around the arteries which monitor the blood flow, and all but trips a fuse in the brain, much like one goes in a light circuit.

The killer was skilled then, knew enough about the body, or martial arts, to do this correctly – and by correctly, Jamie meant that he wasn't actually *harming* the women by doing this. He was just putting them to sleep, and then carefully binding and gagging them by the looks of it, not to leave heavy marks – though the discolouration around the corners of the mouth told Jamie a soft gag was used.

What was his end goal then? Drugging the women would be easier, but he wanted to preserve their health until the kill. Make the kills untainted, pure even. He'd have to be a sizeable guy to take the women with such ease and have the confidence not to *ensure* their compliance with some sort of narcotic.

Jamie slumped back in the chair, the sun now up behind her through the kitchen window, and tried to process all of that.

He had the victims, the modality, the methodology of the kills all planned out. He had a dump site, and no doubt he used a prep site too in order to get them from the abduction location to where he was staging them.

A house or a building would leave a paper trail, physical clues ... And he was taking them at their cars. Coming home from work, coming home from a friend's house. In the case of the third victim, it was on the street outside her house. She was thirty feet from her front door and her children when he took her.

'A van,' Jamie said, the thought coming on its own.

Hassan looked up from the report he was reading. 'Hmm?'

'A van. That's how he's taking them.'

Hassan pondered that for a moment and nodded. 'More than likely. They're always on a road or in a car park.'

'He stops next to them, goes through the back, opens the side or back doors, grabs and drags them inside, gags them and then drives away. Finds somewhere quiet … kills them. And then dumps them and drives away.'

'Clean,' Hassan said. 'Alright. So, we get in touch with the local police and let them know?'

Jamie shook her head. 'No, we have to go there.'

'That's a long way, Jamie. First one's in Yorkshire, second in Manchester …'

'Right,' Jamie said. 'And?'

'And … Don't you think our time would be better spent—'

'These women are dead because of me,' she said, finally saying it aloud. 'I don't know why, and I don't know who's doing it, but it's pretty fucking clear that they're being killed because of me. We've been through the original killers I caught, and they're either dead or still in prison. All of them.'

'Except one,' Hassan muttered under his breath.

Jamie ignored that. 'So, this is someone else.

Someone new. Someone who hates me and wants to make me squirm. Who wants me to fester in dread and fear, and I refuse to do that. And considering the list of people who might want me dead - who I've caused harm, cost money, or just generally ruined their lives - I don't really fancy sitting here trying to figure out who that is while the net closes on top of us. I need to see these women, I need to ... I need to understand.'

Hassan laid down the report and folded his arms, watching her. 'Okay,' he said after a few seconds. 'We'll go. But I can't help but feel like they chose Yorkshire and Manchester *because* they were so far away. Is leaving the house, leaving Alina, really the right call?'

'Leaving her?' Jamie shook her head. 'No, she's coming with us.'

Hassan chuckled. 'Of course she is. I assume Elliot's coming too?'

'He's part of this team, whether you like that or not. Radcliffe's orders.'

Hassan tutted. 'It's not *Elliot* I've got a problem with.'

Jamie leaned on her elbows and sipped some of her lukewarm coffee. She didn't think she could do another fresh cup, she was shaking already.

'I know you don't like this, working for Radcliffe, but we don't really have any other offers here.' Jamie gestured to the table in front of her. 'And this isn't exactly something we can just walk away from.'

Hassan looked back at her, the pain in his face visible. 'You know what they did.'

'I know. I do. I know that Radcliffe gave the order, and Mallory carried it out, and Ash died. I know that, and—'

'If you say it's a shame or it's just bad luck, Jamie ...'

'I was going to say it's unforgivable. But we can make a difference doing *this*' — another gesture to the table — 'and if we tell him where to stick it ...'

He just got up then.

'Where are you going?'

'Bathroom,' he said flatly, leaving the room.

But he wasn't. Jamie knew that. He was just finding it more than difficult to accept they were working for the man who'd already signed the death warrant for one of his co-workers. No, that wasn't right. Ash was his partner. His friend.

And Jamie had to admit, it didn't instil her with confidence in Radcliffe. Well, that wasn't true. She had confidence in the fact that he'd screw them over if it benefitted him.

She just hoped they were smart enough to see it coming when the time came.

CHAPTER
SIX

There really was no time to waste, and they had a long drive ahead.

It was mid-morning by the time they were loading up the car. Jamie's old habits died hard, and she still kept a go-bag in the bottom of her wardrobe, packed and ready to leave at a moment's notice. A clean pair of jeans, three long-sleeve Henley shirts, three pairs of socks, three pairs of underwear, a travel toiletries bag, her travel wallet with a passport, credit card, and a few hundred pounds. She also had a few thousand Swedish Kroner in there, which she supposed would be pretty useless now. But the last time she'd stocked this was before coming here to the UK from Stockholm. She wondered, as she picked it up and carried it downstairs, whether there'd ever be a time she *didn't* have one of these packed and ready to go.

Was it bad that the thought of that scared her? Probably the sort of question you should ask a therapist she surmised before shutting that thought down. No chance. Not going there. Nope. Get your head straight, you've got a case to work. You can shrink your own head when a murderer isn't killing your doppelgangers.

As Jamie arranged the luggage in the boot of Hassan's Audi estate - his bag, Alina's, hers, and their gun cases - a car came trundling down the drive.

She hoped it was Elliot. She'd called him three times that morning but he'd not picked up or even bothered to text. That wasn't like him, and though she was reluctant to be worried about him – seriously, of all the people to worry about ... him? – she couldn't help but feel a little uneasy. It was very out of character for him not to call her back. But she was sure he had a good reason.

It wasn't Elliot, though, but Hallberg instead. She had once again agreed to babysit the dog, and despite what happened last time she was happy enough to do it. She liked the farm much better than her apartment in the city. Jamie wondered why she wasn't making a home closer to the Interpol office, but her years of detective work hadn't completely failed her – she liked being here. She liked being around Jamie and working with this team. She'd bounced from job to job and moved through the ranks at Interpol, but moving was hard on you. Socially, physically, emotionally. And once you find a little bit of stability, something that felt like a

... home, it was hard to walk away from that. Jamie thought Hallberg had always viewed her as a look into her own future. But that meant no husband or wife, no kids, no family, no friends. Just the job, and a body littered with scars. A past littered with the broken and the dead. So now, with Jamie here, Alina, Hati, Hassan, and even Elliot ... they were a family of misfits that had come together. The lonely, the orphaned, the lost, the divorced, and the *murderous*. And though no one could have predicted it, they were making it work. Jamie didn't want it to fall apart, and she thought Hallberg probably didn't either. And hell, it wasn't a chore having her around. She was great. Jamie's closest friend. And Jamie – though it felt risky to think it – thought that she was Hallberg's best friend, too.

She walked around the car to greet her and she stepped into the farmyard with a smile, hugging Jamie warmly.

Alina came out of the house, Hati in tow, and gave her a hug too. The dog paused short, steady on his three legs, and eyed Hallberg cautiously. Alina released her hug then, and Hati padded forward slowly, letting out a low, rumbling growl.

Hallberg stared right back at him and then dug in the pocket of her coat.

Hati's one good ear pricked up as she withdrew her hand, keeping it in a tight fist, and crouched down.

He got a whiff of what she was holding, and came

forward close enough to confirm she was indeed attempting to bribe him.

A gentle tail wag was all the encouragement that she needed to show him the treat she had. He darted forward and all but put her entire hand in his mouth, sucking the treat right from it before bounding back into the house, leaving long shoelaces of drool hanging from her fingers.

'Yuck,' Alina said, laughing hard.

Jamie couldn't help but join in.

'What's so funny?' Hassan asked, stepping from the house with a grin. He spotted Hallberg and headed towards her, arms wide.

Alina looked at Jamie, holding in an expectant giggle, and Jamie shushed her silently.

Hallberg, as though they'd all prearranged it, stood and opened her arms too, embracing Hassan and promptly wiping off her hand on his back.

He rubbed her back in turn, believing it to be a show of affection. Alina promptly burst into a howl of laughter.

Hassan pulled back and narrowed his eyes at Alina. 'What?'

'Nothing,' she squeezed out, barely able to breathe.

'I told a joke,' Jamie offered.

Hassan looked at her, then back Alina, and then at Hallberg, who's slobbered hand was still on his shoul-der. 'Now I know you're lying.'

Hallberg smiled up at him. 'Don't be so paranoid, Nasir.'

He scowled at her for a moment. 'It's a good thing you're cute. Or I'd have to force it out of you.'

She blushed. Almost violently, and then promptly removed her hands from his shoulders.

Alina's laugh stopped and she looked at Jamie with wide eyes, an expression that screamed *did you see that*!? Jamie did, and she was surprised too.

'Right then,' Hallberg said, not looking at Hassan at all as she moved past him and towards the house. 'It's freezing out here, so I'm going to get the kettle on.'

Hassan watched her go, keeping his grin, but trying to hide the mild embarrassment Jamie thought he was feeling. She was hardly well versed when it came to romantic entanglement, but that was pretty clear. Hassan liked Hallberg.

But did she like *him*?

Jamie looked at the house, where Hallberg was now in the kitchen, peeking out of the window. They locked eyes and Hallberg looked down at the sink, still blushing.

Oh yeah. She did.

'Shall we get on the road?' Hassan asked loudly, heading around the car. 'We're burning daylight.' He climbed in promptly and started the engine.

Alina skipped towards Jamie and grabbed her hands. 'Eeee!' she squealed, smiling wider than Jamie had ever seen her do.

This was exciting, Jamie supposed, but what was clearer was that it was exciting to Alina. This was a time, an age, where she should be with friends, thinking about, talking about boys. Doing all the things a teenager should. Jamie never really had – or wanted – that experience, but she was odder than most, and her teenage years weren't exactly filled with joy or solid parental support. When she was Alina's age, she'd been taken from her home and her father, brought to the UK by her mum, and forced to watch her go through a phase Jamie now referred to in her mind as her slutty forties - a parade of men who swept into her mother's life and left her heartbroken. Though that was romanticising it. Her mother slept with these men, and then one would toss the other aside depending on who lost interest first. It seemed to be a race to do so in most cases.

Jamie was almost the exact age now that her mother was when she brought her to the UK. And Alina was now almost the same age as Jamie was when *she'd* been brought to the UK.

Jamie had no friends, nothing of a social circle when she'd arrived. She was dumped into school here and left to flounder. Her mother hadn't cared, and it had been awful for her. Then again, the whole reason she brought Jamie to the UK was to hurt Jamie's father. Which she succeeded in doing.

And Jamie had promised herself that she'd never have kids because of her mother. But now here she was

... so she supposed the only thing she could promise was not to do the same thing her mother did. Not the slutty forties bit. Not being a neglectful parent who didn't see or tend to the needs of her daughter.

Jamie had decided then. Alina needed school. She needed friends. And she needed a life outside of this place if she ever hoped to lead something like a normal life ... and not end up exactly like Jamie. As much as that scared her.

'Go on,' Jamie said, motioning Alina towards the car. 'Go torture him, I know you're dying to.'

Alina opened the back door and jumped in, hounding Hassan immediately for more details on his undying love for Julia Hallberg.

Jamie thought two-on-one was unfair, and she wanted to say goodbye anyway, so she went back into the house to make sure Hallberg was alright.

She leaned in the kitchen doorway, Hati sitting on the floor behind Hallberg who was just standing by the sink staring out of the window.

'So ...' Jamie said.

Hallberg laughed, turning to Jamie. 'Please, just don't.'

Jamie held her hands up. 'I didn't say anything.'

'You didn't have to.'

'You and Hassan, then?'

She shook her head. 'No, no. We're friends, sure. But ... I mean, I don't think he ...'

'I think it's pretty obvious what he ...'

Hallberg waved her arms. 'I'm too busy anyway, and we work together so, you know. Even if I wanted to, it's just ... It can't, alright?'

Jamie watched her friend. 'Okay,' she said. She wouldn't pry. Wouldn't push it. Playing the supportive gal pal was not something she was well versed at. And she didn't want to put a foot wrong. 'If you want to talk, I'm here.' The words felt awkward and ungainly. But that's the kind of thing friends said, right?

Hallberg just nodded, but said nothing else.

Jamie hooked a thumb towards the door. 'We're gonna hit the road. You got everything you need here?'

'Uh-huh.' She lifted the hem of her jacket to show off her pistol in its holster. 'Fool me once.'

Jamie smirked. 'Yeah, we feel the same way.' She reached for the coat rack next to the door and peeled aside a waxed parka to reveal a Beretta 1301 Tactical semi-automatic shotgun hanging from the same hook. 'It's loaded if you need it. But it kicks like a mule, so hold on tight.'

Hallberg laughed. 'Jesus. You keep that thing loaded with Alina here?'

'It's got the safety on,' Jamie said, shrugging. 'And after the last few months, can you blame us?'

Hallberg sighed. 'I suppose not.'

Jamie released the parka, hiding the shotgun once more.

'Oh, before I forget,' Hallberg said, digging in her

pocket and pulling out a folded brown envelope. 'These arrived this morning.'

Jamie took the envelope, feeling the shape of a billfold inside. She reached in and pulled out two leather wallets, unfurling one with her thumb as she'd done a thousand times before.

'Your warrant cards,' Hallberg said as Jamie looked down at them, the metal NCA crest shining from the middle.

'Special Investigator,' Jamie read. 'Got a ring to it, for sure.' She felt a little relief as she slotted her and Hassan's badges back into the envelope.

'That's pretty much a skeleton key, but if you run into any problems, give them my number. Radcliffe would rather stay out of it, naturally.'

'Naturally,' Jamie said, chuckling.

'York Police are expecting you. You shouldn't have any trouble.'

Jamie thought on that. 'Hope not. Well, actually ...'

'Don't pray for things to go wrong.'

'I'm not, but maybe we'll get lucky, find this guy before any more bodies turn up.'

Hallberg smiled sadly. 'There's always hope.' She held out an arm and gave Jamie another hug. 'Give them hell.'

'Will do,' Jamie said, hugging her tightly.

She left the house promptly, jogging through the cold morning air towards the car.

The momentary diversion was nice. A little bit of

gossip, a little bit of fun and laughter before the reality of things set in.

She climbed into the car, hoping the feeling would persist for a while.

But as they pulled out of the farm and got on the road, it didn't. It promptly disappeared.

And the feeling that they were hurtling towards something dark and dangerous set in.

And then, predictably … it never left.

CHAPTER
SEVEN

I took them a bit over four hours to reach York.

Jamie booked them a little house not far from the police station, and though she feared Alina would be bored, the last thing she wanted was to be four hours away from her if something went wrong at the farm. She had no way of knowing yet whether this whole thing was a way to lure her away from Alina again. The Petrosyans were finished, their criminal empire shattered, their business empire in the hands of Aram Petrosyan's son. They had an accord, and he'd promised not to come after Jamie, but she'd trusted and been burned before, so she wasn't taking any chances.

Alina was excited at the prospect of seeing the city, and Jamie made her a deal: that they'd make time to see the sights once Jamie had what she needed. She thought the idea of just turning it all off and walking the city like everything was normal seemed alien and wrong, but she suspected that's what parenthood was all about. She couldn't expect to exclude Alina from her work and then have her be okay with her being affected by it. No, Jamie needed to be both warrior and mother. She just didn't know how yet.

They were all hungry by the time they got into the city, and seeing as Alina was about to be cooped up for a few hours, Jamie relented and they ate at Nando's, her favourite restaurant. Thankfully it had supplanted McDonalds, and though Jamie wasn't quite as militant as she once was with her diet, chicken was good protein, and who could really turn their nose up at a double wrap?

They ate quickly and left quickly. All the while, Jamie had the distinct feeling that they should have been working while they were eating. Alina knew the stakes though, and was seemingly much better at reading Jamie than vice versa, so she was the one to suggest that they go to their rental.

They pulled up outside, and Alina retrieved her bag from the boot before telling Jamie she'd go in by herself. It was a code to enter, after all, and self check-in.

Jamie gave her a relieved nod. 'Thanks,' she said. 'We'd come in with you, but—'

'Yeah, I know,' Alina said, smiling softly. 'Go catch some bad guys.' She glanced over her shoulder at the house then, a mid-terrace town home on a quiet street. 'Unless you feel the need to do a walk-through to make sure there's not a killer hiding under the bed?'

Jamie's smile dropped and she couldn't help but look at Hassan, who also didn't seem plussed by the joke.

She reached for the handle and got out, grabbing her satchel off the back seat as she did. 'Maybe just to be safe, hey?'

Alina shook her head as they walked up together. 'I wasn't serious.'

'I know, but ...'

'Yeah, yeah, fool me nine times, shame on you.'

'It does feel like that, doesn't it?' Jamie sighed as she punched in the code and walked into the house.

It was a beautiful period home with a small enclosed garden, three decent-sized bedrooms, a bright kitchen, and a sizeable living room with the original fireplace, wooden floors, and big bay window.

Jamie took one look at it and immediately went over and dropped the blind and drew the curtains.

She heard Alina tut and chuckle behind her, but the girl had been right the first time. They'd had too many incidents not to be paranoid.

Jamie did a walk-through, as Alina had suggested, checked the closets and under the beds, and then made sure the back door and ground floor windows were locked.

When she was satisfied, she returned to the living room where Alina was standing, her bag over her shoulder.

'You want me put the TV on mute and keep the lights off too?' she asked, bordering on glib.

'I don't think we need to go that far,' Jamie said, reaching into the satchel under her arm, 'but keep the curtains drawn and the door locked. And ... here.' She handed Alina the P229 Compact pistol she'd brought back from Sweden, the smaller of the two weapons.

Alina took it wordlessly and held it in her hands before looking at Jamie. 'Seriously?'

'Yeah, seriously.' Jamie looked at her carefully. 'Phone first though.'

Alina's brow crumpled.

'It's just in case. If you're worried about something, call and we'll come running. This is a last resort. A *last* resort, alright? And I'm sure you won't need it. But it'll make me feel better.'

Alina nodded. 'Okay.' There was nothing glib about her voice now.

Jamie opened her arms and hugged the girl, kissing her gently on the head. 'And do me a favour?'

'What is it?' Alina whispered into her shoulder.

'Don't tell Hallberg, alright? She already thinks I'm a gun-toting nutcase.'

Alina laughed. 'Sorry to burst your bubble, Jamie ... you kind of are.'

HASSAN HAD KEPT THE CAR RUNNING, AND AS Jamie walked down the front steps towards it, she

realised why. This much further north, it was blister-
ingly cold. Radcliffe had been right in his assessment: it
was going to be a hard winter.

She climbed into the passenger seat and Hassan
wasted no time in setting off, weaving through the
streets, following the satnav towards York Police
Station.

He drove almost in silence, neither of them wanting
to offer anything before they knew what they were
looking at. And even after they arrived at the station,
they didn't know if they'd have any idea of that.

Hassan guided them in, parking in front of the huge
brick building. The Fulford Road station was substantial, but Jamie wasn't intimidated walking in. She'd
gone into what felt like hundreds of stations, and
though each was different, they all had the same buzz,
the same smell. She used to think it was the smell of
justice. But now she knew it was the smell of bureau-
cracy. As much as she missed the formality of it, the
rigor, she had to admit that the freedom that came with
her new role suited her. Even if it did come with a
higher price tag. One that usually needed to be paid in
blood. She was just glad it was usually other people's. At
least in larger volumes than her own.

They approached the front desk and the woman
behind it looked up.

'Jamie Johansson and Nasir Hassan,' she said,
holding up her new NCA warrant card. 'We're expected.
It's about the ...' She didn't feel like she needed to

finish. The woman behind the desk had paled. Like she'd seen a ghost.

She sort of was seeing one.

A murder was always news, and no doubt the face and name of the victim had been playing on repeat. Julie Johns sounds an awful lot like Jamie Johansson, and Julie was as good as Jamie's double.

The woman just lifted a hand towards the magnetically locked door to her left and then buzzed them through, unable to find words, seemingly.

Jamie didn't know if she'd have words either, if a murder victim up and walked into her station.

She pursed her lips, trying for a smile and failing, and then headed on down the corridor with Hassan in tow, just catching a snatch of what the woman said as she picked up the phone to alert the detectives before the door closed.

'The NCA are here, and you won't believe—'

Jamie knew exactly what they wouldn't believe.

Ahead of them, bodies began stepping from doorways to goggle at the spectacle. Each of them came out with expectant eyes, and then they all blinked in astonishment, watching Jamie unabashedly as she walked by, trying not to look at any of them. She did everything except shield her face with her hand.

She lowered her head and pressed on, moving faster, unsure where she was really going, but desperate to get there.

When she almost bumped into the chest of a man

standing right in the middle of the corridor she paused and looked up.

He was in his fifties, with close-cropped hair and deep-set eyes. His skin looked a size too big for his face.

He had his arms folded across his broad chest, rumpling his already unironed shirt.

'You must be the NCA detectives,' he said gruffly, with the kind of tone that all detectives had when they were told another 'senior-ranking' agency would be swooping in to stomp all over your investigation.

Jamie drew a deep breath and stood straight, looking at him. She extended a hand. 'Jamie Johansson,' she said. 'This my partner, Nasir Hassan.'

'JJ,' he muttered, inspecting her face with a kind of morbid curiosity, like she was a waxwork. She sort of felt like it, an imitation of something he'd already studied. He extended a large, calloused hand. 'David Brandt, DCI.'

'A pleasure,' Jamie said courteously, shaking firmly.

He withdrew his hand almost too quickly and nodded Jamie sideways into his waiting office.

They stepped into the tired room, the walls lined with shelves stacked high with files and paperwork. His tenure as a DCI had been a long one, preceding the necessity for everything to be digital. It was as much a museum as a work space now.

He walked around his desk but didn't sit in his chair, just stood with his hands on his hips. 'Suppose it's no coincidence you're here,' he announced, bristling. 'Julie

Johns, Jamie Johansson ... And I'd guess your next stop will be Manchester? Judith James?'

There was nothing to hide and no point lying about it, but Jamie didn't like the insinuation in his voice that she was somehow the cause of these murders, though she sort of felt like she was.

'That's right,' she said, clearing her throat. 'And the third victim, Jana Jelinek. We'll see about her after.'

His expression told Jamie he didn't know there was a third, but it didn't surprise him all that much. He sighed a little. 'You got anything that might help us? Don't suppose so judging by your round shoulders.'

Jamie smiled politely. 'We just arrived. Only heard about it all yesterday.'

'So, no creepy letters written in blood or magazine cutouts arriving on your doorstep indicating what the hell all this is for?'

'Not that easy, I'm afraid.'

'But it's clearly something to do with you, right?' Brandt narrowed his eyes slightly.

Jamie didn't feel like she needed to answer that. 'There are several suspects we're considering for this, but the list is short. We expect to have this solved quickly, without further bloodshed.'

He harrumphed a little. 'The list is short, is it? And why's that?'

Jamie understood his stance. Someone had turned up dead in his city, and the closest thing he had to a person responsible was standing in front of him. But that didn't mean she was going to stand there and take it. 'Because most of the killers I've hunted are in prison, or dead.'

Brandt lifted his eyebrows a little, but said nothing.

'What this has to do with me,' Jamie said, 'I'm not sure. We're considering all options. It's pretty clear that it's not something obvious, otherwise we wouldn't need to be here at all. You've got nothing to show for your investigation because the killer wasn't doing it for themselves, or for you. They were doing it for me. And that's not conceit. Look at my face, say my name. You were right, it wasn't coincidence. Isn't coincidence. The killer is sending me a message, and I'm here to read it. Because I think I'm probably the only one who can. So, if you're done posturing I'd like to see what you've got so far. And I'd like to see the body.' She stared right at Brandt. 'Please.'

He considered it for a moment and then let out a long sigh. 'Fine. Quicker we get this solved, the better. It goes on too long and he might be liable to send you another message, and I don't think any of us want that.'

Jamie ignored the barb in his tone. 'No, we don't.' She liked it when detectives could swallow their 'pride' and just focus on the work. It made *everything* so much easier.

They ducked back out of his office and headed for the operations room. The watchers in the corridor shrank back inside their rooms as Brandt led Jamie and Hassan back towards the front of the building and then cut left without warning into a large room filled with desks and detectives.

Along the far wall were several offices of more senior detectives, and a couple of rooms with numbers on them that Jamie expected to be where the ubiquitous whiteboard and conference tables would be. Where the magic happened.

All eyes turned to Brandt, Jamie, and Hassan as they walked in, and he didn't need to even hold his hands up for everyone to fall quiet.

'This is Jamie Johansson and Nasir Hassan,' he said, with the sort of unease that suggested he knew what kind of reaction it would garner.

Mumbles rippled through the room.

Brandt held his hands up. 'Yes, yes, we can all very clearly see the resemblance. It's why they're here. If you have any questions or thoughts or observations, please direct them to Johansson and Hassan – much better than saying them behind their backs. Who knows, they might well be helpful.' He glanced around. 'They're here at the behest of the NCA, who have linked two other murders with the same MO to this one, which means this is no longer just us and Manchester. We have a serial killer. So, if you were holding anything back up to now, it's time to pop the cork and get moving, alright?'

Jamie looked around at the faces in front of them, listening to Brandt's northern twang fill the room.

'They'll be in three,' he continued, gesturing to the

numbered doors. If you have anything on your desks, take it in there and give it to them. If they need anything, you give it. If either of them speak, pretend the words are coming from my mouth, alright? We're doing everything we can to accommodate, help, and ultimately solve this case.' He clapped loudly. 'Good. Now let's catch us a killer.'

He smiled for all of half a second, then stepped back, clapped Jamie on the shoulder hard enough that she moved a step, and then promptly disappeared back into the corridor, heading for his office.

Silence reigned in the room, all eyes on Jamie.

She held her head high, not sure what to say, or if there was anything to say.

So she just lifted a hand towards room three, gave them a nod, and went towards it, feeling the weight of their collective gaze, and the weight of the investigation which now, unceremoniously and suddenly, had been dropped onto her shoulders.

It was all she could do not to collapse under it.

CHAPTER
EIGHT

There seemed to be a fleet of DIs and DSs working the case, as well as a lone DC who looked to have drawn the short straw by being forced to call all the women in Yorkshire whose names began with the initials J-J.

They came in on rotation, each with little to offer, mostly to gawk at the spectacle that was the living corpse before them. The case file that Jamie was given by Radcliffe seemed to contain the entire investigation. Which wasn't much. And nothing to go on reaffirmed her first thought: that the killer was a consummate professional.

They all seemed interested in the case and keen to contribute, suggesting things Jamie had already considered, asking questions she'd already asked, and ones she didn't have the answers to.

Why do they look like you? Is it someone targeting

you? Do you think you're in danger? Could this be a stalker, someone with a grudge? Maybe, probably, yes to all of the above.

She sighed and asked a particularly enthusiastic detective to go and get her and Hassan a coffee. Mostly to shut her up.

'Sure, how do you take it? White, black, you want a latte, cappuccino—'

'Surprise us,' Jamie said, forcing a grin.

The second she was out of the room, Jamie stood and motioned Hassan to come with her.

'Where are we going?' he asked.

'You learning anything new here?'

He stared at the files in front of him, carbon copies of what was in Jamie's satchel in the car.

'No,' he said after a second. 'Though it's kind of hard to think with the parade going on.'

'Exactly. So let's get out while we have a chance.'

Hassan lingered, looking at the door. 'I do actually quite fancy a coffee, though ...'

'I'll buy you a Starbucks.'

'I prefer Costa.'

'Now you're just messing with me.'

He grinned and got up. 'Yeah, I am. Where are we going?'

'We'll let Brandt know about the van angle, and then we can get out of here. There's a couple of stops to make and we're not going to catch this guy sitting on our arses here.'

Hassan got out of his chair and grabbed his coat off the back. 'You want to go speak to Johns' family?'

She tried not to scoff. 'Show up on her husband's doorstep looking like his dead wife? Scare the living hell out of her kids? No thanks,' Jamie said, more tiredly than she meant to. 'I want to see where she was taken. And then I want to see her.'

'You think that's a good idea?'

'I do. Whoever did this wants to get at me, wants to show me something. So let's let him show me. He recreated my first murder case for me, let's see how close he got. I'll ask Brandt to let the coroner know we'll be coming.'

Hassan was usually a little stronger than he was being now. He'd usually offer something, protest, try to convince her of his own theory. But instead he just proffered her the door and followed her out without a word.

Luckily, the coffee machine seemed to be dragging its heels so they slipped into the corridor before they got harangued.

Jamie made a beeline for Brandt's office and stuck her head through the open door. 'We're all done here.'

'Already?' Brandt looked up from his computer.

'There's nothing to learn that your team hasn't already gone over.' Jamie felt bad noting the particularly empty whiteboard and a lack of any suspects or theories so far. 'So we're going to hit the streets. I want to see where she was taken, where she was found. And I want to see the body.'

Brandt looked at her for a moment. 'I'll arrange it with the coroner's office. They're holding the body in cold storage at the hospital, but I'll have the examiner meet you there. Just let me know what time.'

Jamie just gave a nod, ready to pull back out and hit the road. But then she realised that she didn't have to do all this alone. She had the entire police department here at her disposal, and she should use it. 'We had a thought,' she said, still hovering at the doorway. 'There didn't seem to be much in the file about where the victim was held before she was dumped. The report said your detectives were looking into vacant properties and that sort of thing ...'

Brandt just stared at her.

'It's a van,' Jamie said, honestly surprised that it hadn't occurred to anyone. 'Sliding side door I'd bet.'

'To take the victims?'

'And hold them. The victim was bound before she was dumped, and drugged too, the coroner's report said. Right?'

'That's right.'

'He pulled up alongside her while she was walking, or maybe he was waiting for her to walk past, and then opened the door, dragged her inside, drugged her, and then drove off. He kept her in the van until he was ready, drove to the dump site, and dropped the body into the river. Then just drove away. It'll be a rental van, I suspect. I'd likely think a high-top, just so there's more room to move around, but that's just a guess.'

Brant's brow creased. 'A rental, really? Why do the paperwork? Stealing a van or buying something in cash and leaving it in someone else's name would be much easier, wouldn't leave a trail.'

'I think that's the point,' Jamie said. 'The bodies, the runic symbols ... he's *trying* to leave a trail. He's cocky, he's self-assured, this killer. The more he can give us, the more exciting it is. You might be right, he might well have stolen a van or bought one in cash. But my guess is that he rented one on the day he abducted her, and returned the next day. He was that sure he'd get it done first time around.'

Brandt didn't look sold.

Jamie shrugged. 'It's worth looking into. And you've got the manpower. All of whom are sitting on their hands right now. But it's your call.'

Brandt scowled a little. 'I'll get them on it.'

Jamie knocked on the frame. 'Let me know. I'll leave my number at the front desk. And thanks, for the reception. We'll catch this guy.'

Brandt gave a slow nod, and Jamie didn't stick around for more chit-chat.

They had ground to cover, another two cities to visit on this trip, and she knew that they were counting down to the next body. And she knew what came next.

The killer's pattern was tracking with her cases: the homeless kid in the Lea, the sex worker in the bedsit, the violin prodigy in the tunnel ... And next, the girl in the woods, the birch branches in her back like wings.

As Jamie walked, she shivered a little, the frigid cold of a Stockholm winter ringing in her bones, her mind casting back to the Angel Maker once more. She hoped she wouldn't have to see that again.

But she knew, deep in her gut, where a feeling of growing dread had taken root, that she would do.

And soon.

THEY MANAGED TO REACH THE CAR AND SET OFF without crossing paths with any of the other detectives. They knew where Julie Johns worked, which was where she was taken - in the car park a short distance from the building. It seemed strange that the killer would choose here, but once Jamie dug into it, she realised why. Johns usually parked her car here. Two kids in the morning meant she was rarely on time, or so said the statement taken from her boss. So the 'good' parking right next to her office was never available.

She worked in compliance for a big insurance firm, a decent job. She had responsibilities, things she couldn't shirk. So staying after hours was not rare at all. And on the night she was taken, that was just the story. A big case needed scrutiny and she didn't get out of the building until seven. Which meant the car park was all but deserted. The interview with her husband said that food often hit the table by seven, so she was late for dinner. Rushing. She didn't see the van parked near her car. Didn't think twice as it started up and drove towards her.

By the time it'd stopped and the door opened, it was too late.

As Hassan pulled into the open-air car park, Jamie looked around. A few old streetlamps meant it was poorly lit. It had been raining on the night in question, visibility reduced further.

This wasn't a public car park, but nor was it gated or monitored otherwise, too far from the centre of town to be of use to commuters. You needed a badge to park here, but the security was leased out to an outside company and they patrolled at ten in the morning and ten at night. Jamie hoped that the detectives would turn up some useful CCTV from nearby sources, but she wasn't holding her breath it'd be of use. Even if they clocked the van, it'd come back as a rental, so it was futile.

'Here,' Jamie said, waving Hassan in.

He pulled up opposite the spot where Julie's car had been. It was gone now, as was the police cordon set up around it.

Jamie sighed, knowing she'd learn nothing, know nothing more than when they'd left the station after seeing it. But she still hoped. For something. For anything.

She walked into the middle of the space and looked around. It backed up to the fence, on the other side of which was a tall hedge. She wasn't far from the corner, a straight shot to the exit too. The nearest lamp was thirty yards away or more. Jesus, it couldn't have been more perfect for the killer.

She put her hands in the pockets of her coat, the wind cold on her face. Not Sweden cold, but still chilly.

'Fuck,' she muttered, staring around, waiting for a lightning bolt idea that wasn't coming.

With an exhale, she pulled her phone from her jeans and looked at it. No missed calls or texts. She sent a quick message to Alina. 'Everything okay?'

She looked at the screen, waiting for a response.

At home, Alina was never further than twelve inches from her phone, so Jamie's expectance wasn't unfair.

Characteristically, the teenage Alina just texted a thumbs up emoji and nothing else.

Jamie was about to stow her phone when an idea struck. Or at least a thought. Where the hell was Elliot?

She called him, but it went straight to answerphone. Again.

'Who you ringing?' Hassan asked, standing at the open door to the car, his thoughts on coming here apparent from his position.

'Elliot.'

'Still not picking up?'

She shook her head, her phone buzzing next to her ear. She lowered it to see that Alina had texted something else. 'Getting hungry ...'

'You could call his wife,' Hassan offered.

'Yeah, I'd love to,' Jamie said sarcastically, 'and then maybe I'll stick pins in my eyes for afters.'

He chuckled. 'Come on, let's go. I wouldn't mind a bite.'

It was getting late. 'Alright,' she said, though she wasn't hungry. 'Let's head back. Alina's asking about food too. You can drop me off, and then take her for some dinner.'

Hassan's brow creased as Jamie approached. 'You're not coming?'

'I want to see the body, remember?'

'Alone?' The tone provided all the disapproval needed.

Jamie climbed in, sighed. 'I need some time to think, and seeing the bodies ... It always helps. Reminds me of the stakes.'

Hassan got in and circled the car park. 'You manage to somehow forget them?'

'You don't think it's a good idea?'

'You got that from my face, or the incredulity of the question?'

'Both,' she retorted.

'Yeah, historically going anywhere alone is a bad idea, especially when it comes to murderers out for your blood.'

'I'm armed,' Jamie said flatly, 'and I'm expecting it. Hoping, even.'

Hassan laughed, the incredulity building. 'God, you say the stupidest shit.'

Jamie just shrugged. She was getting pretty tired of this jaunt down memory lane already, being reminded of her greatest hits.

'Why is that stupid?' she asked absently, staring out of the window as they headed for the house they'd rented.

'Because a dangerous killer specialising in abducting blonde-haired women is roaming freely like a fucking ghost, and you want to willingly put yourself in harm's way.'

She just shook her head. 'The morgue is in the hospital, there'll be cameras, locked doors, coroners, staff. All sorts there. You don't have to worry.'

'Let's just get dinner all together, and then I can come with you—'

'Will you just take the hint? I want to do this on my own. I'm going to be staring down at a fucking clone on a slab, and I don't want you breathing down my neck as I do.' Jamie shifted uncomfortably in her seat, knowing the words came out much sharper than she'd meant. But she didn't apologise.

Hassan just quietened, pulling out his phone and typing in *hospital* on his maps app.

When the route popped up he hung a right, all in silence, and drove them there.

He pulled up outside and when Jamie climbed out, he took her wrist, stopping her.

She looked back, seeing genuine concern in his eyes.

'You don't have to. We can go later. Tomorrow. There's time. We can take it slow. Do it right.'

'I appreciate what you're saying,' she said, 'but there's never enough time. Not for whoever's next on his list. And he will keep killing. You know that. I know that. So I need to see … I feel like … I feel like he *wants* me to see. To look at her. At them. I don't know why, but it's just what I feel. Okay? You need to trust me on this.'

He closed his eyes, a slow blink, and then stared up at her, releasing her wrist. 'You've definitely got your pistol?'

'I never leave home without it now.'

'Make sure the safety's off. Just in case.'

She cracked a small smile. 'Red is dead.'

'Hopefully him, and not you.'

She nodded firmly. 'I'll see you after dinner, alright?'

'What should I tell Alina?'

'Tell her the truth,' Jamie said, stepping from the car and resting her hand on the roof. 'I had to go to work.'

CHAPTER
NINE

amie went to the front desk and was directed to the basement level. There was something about storing the dead underground which felt right, she thought.

She took the stairs, this whole thing reminding her starkly of the person she used to be. A person who always took the stairs, who ran every day, religiously. Who always played by the rules and minded her office. She didn't know where she'd lost that person along the way, but she had. And now she barely even thought of those things.

She sighed, pushing through the door and into the basement corridor where the pathology lab, the morgue, and some of the radiology equipment were located.

As Brandt had called ahead, the lab was expecting her, but it wasn't like they'd rolled out the red carpet or anything. The coroner herself was out, so the only person to greet her was a young assistant.

He had the kind of pale complexion that told Jamie he'd been working underground a little too long, and his excitement to see another living person confirmed that.

Jamie knocked on the lab door and he sprang from his seat behind his desk in the office. It was separated from the lab itself which was complete with steel slabs, refrigerated drawers, and a tiled and sloped floor so all the blood could be hosed right down into the drain.

The man came over quickly. He was wearing a rumpled grey shirt, his thin and hairy arms poking from the rolled-up sleeves. He had quaffed-over hair and round glasses for that deliberately nerdy look. Pulling a fob on a retractable string from his belt, he flashed it against the reader, unlocking the substantial magnetic door.

It clicked and opened slowly, and Jamie couldn't help but feel a little better about being there on her own. Even the window in the door was wired glass. No one was getting in that lab without authorised access.

She stepped inside and he closed the door behind her.

'Hi, are you the police officer?' he asked, grinning a little. Jamie supposed this must be rather exciting for him.

She didn't have the heart or the energy to correct him properly, so she just nodded. 'That's me.'

He stared at her with fascination.

'See something interesting?' she asked dryly.

He looked down bashfully. 'It's just ...'

'I look like the dead woman, yeah. I know.' She lifted her chin towards the drawers in the next room. 'Can we ...?'

'Right, of course.' He wasted no time heading through into the morgue, which was appropriately cold and smelled exactly like all the others she'd been in. Like bleach and rubbing alcohol.

He walked towards the drawers and found the one he wanted without hesitation. He unlocked it and pulled it outwards, the whole thing sliding into the middle of the room at waist height.

'Ready?' he asked, reaching for the sheet covering the body in the drawer.

Jamie just motioned for him to get on with it. She couldn't speak just then. She was holding her breath, teeth clamped together. She wasn't sure how she was supposed to be feeling, but she guessed *sick to her stomach* was probably appropriate.

He pulled back the sheet and Jamie all but fell over. A deep wave of nausea rose up through her stomach and vomit almost burst between her teeth. She closed her eyes, gritted her teeth harder and breathed through it, the smell of bleach acrid in her nose.

'Uncanny,' the assistant breathed.

Jamie forced her eyes open, seeing him goggling at her.

'You don't interact with people much, huh?' she growled.

'Hmm?' His brow crumpled.

'You got any bright insights?'

'Into what?'

She looked down at the body between them.

'Oh! Ah, um ... no.' He cleared his throat. 'I mean, we conducted our assessment and everything we discovered is in the report.'

'Right, so would you mind?' Jamie tilted her head backwards, towards the door to the office.

'Leaving you with ...'

'The body, yes. Is that a problem?'

'I don't think so. I mean, no, it's just—'

'This is an investigation,' she said sharply. 'Privileged information, and I intend to record some observations, so it wasn't really a polite request.'

'Understood.' But he didn't move.

Jamie raised her eyebrows.

'Now?' he said.

'Now.'

He gave her a quick smile, a little disappointed that he wouldn't get to catch any more of the freak show, and then slinked off.

Jamie had all but memorised the case file and the pathologist's report along with it, and she did her best to dredge up that memory, to separate herself from the reality of what was in front of her. Something that was ultimately a type of psychological warfare. The killer wanted her on this investigation, but he wanted her off balance. Either that, or he wanted her to see something only she could see. He wanted her to understand something no one else could. To hear a message everyone else would be deaf to.

'So, what is it?' she found herself muttering as she looked down at the body. That's all this was. Just another victim.

She swallowed the bile at the back of her throat and got to work.

There was a box of vinyl gloves on the shelf next to the drawers and she drew a pair from it, tugging them on and pushing them down into the webbings of her fingers. Despite the coolness in the air, her hands were still sweating, so she was glad they were powdered.

She cracked her knuckles and returned to the body, gingerly reaching out and pulling the sheet from the collarbones down to the hips so that everything above the pubic bone was exposed.

She studied the woman's body, her skin, noting the faded stretchmarks on her stomach from her pregnancies, the white band on the third finger of her left hand. The lack of bullet and knife scars. Signs of a life well-lived. Of a life that could have been Jamie's if she'd just made a few different choices.

And yet despite the good life this woman had lived, the clean criminal record, and the quiet existence - here she was, dead. And here Jamie was, alive. And responsible, somehow, for this death. And though she didn't know why yet, she felt every ounce of the weight of that guilt crushing her.

But she supposed that was the point.

'Julie Johns,' she said aloud. It didn't feel okay not to say her name.

She reached, with care, and lifted each of her hands in turn. The abduction of Oliver Hammond ... No, *Elliot's* abduction of Oliver Hammond – Jamie's first murder case – had been characterised by his being kept in a wooden box. Jamie turned Julie's right hand over, exposing her forearm and the crease of her elbow where a needle mark was present. A barbiturate had been administered via an IV, in the same way that it had been with Oliver Hammond. She knew that Oliver was never supposed to regain consciousness in that box, scratch at the inside until his fingernails peeled off, and then break free. Elliot had simply miscalculated the dose. Or at least underestimated Oliver Hammond's drug tolerance. Julie Johns was supposed to come to, however. It had been designed that way. With her box just weak enough for her to scratch her way out.

Jamie looked at the nails, raw, broken, two missing. She'd fought hard to free herself, to get back home, to her husband, her children. And even with her hands bound, her wrists damaged from the zip tie that had been used, just like the one Elliot had used, she'd managed to get free from her box and make a run for it.

Though that was the point.

She'd made a run for it, straight into the river. And it

was cold, and she was still coming down off the drugs. So she sank, like Oliver Hammond did. And drowned. Like Oliver Hammond did.

Jamie laid the hand down carefully.

She already knew all this. It was familiar. But what wasn't, were the runes carved into her body. Jamie guessed they must have been done while she was unconscious, but what tool had the killer used to make them, and why?

She homed in, stooping to inspect them more closely. The coroner's report said that they were made with a very sharp implement, smooth-bladed and small. It suggested the cuts were congruent with a scalpel. Which wasn't wholly surprising given that this was trying to imitate a crime committed by Elliot Day, and he was a doctor, his weapon of choice a scalpel.

But what they said was another thing. Though Jamie was Swedish herself, she had no experience with runes, which is what these clearly were. They were a message, perhaps a code to be cracked that would lead her to where she needed to be next. But despite the obvious mystery there, she didn't like the idea of being on someone else's strings, and doing what someone else wanted her to, especially not a killer like this.

And yet she couldn't ignore them.

The back of her neck lit up in gooseflesh and she stood straight, the feeling of being watched unmistakable.

She met the eyes of a tall man in scrubs watching

her through the glass. He had a surgical cap on, a surgical mask covering his features.

He stood in the corridor, towering to almost the top of the window frame, and just stared at her.

Jamie stared back, taking him in. A doctor. Or not?

The longer she stared, the less sure she was that he really worked here.

The thought came quickly, naturally.

Was this the killer? Was this the man she was chasing?

She dashed around the body and headed across the lab towards the door.

The second she began moving the big surgeon disappeared.

She reached the door, half jogging, her hand reaching under her coat and unfastening the safety clasp on her pistol.

She pulled at the handle and the door didn't budge.

'Fuck,' she muttered, looking for a way to open it.

After a second, she found the release button and hit it. The door clicked open and she pulled it towards her, stepping into the corridor and unholstering her pistol. It hung at her side, her grip steady as she stared down the hallway.

But there was no one there.

The sound of a closing door echoed back to her, the sign for the stairwell that she'd come down hanging from the wall about thirty feet away.

She narrowed her eyes slightly, breathing slow. 'Fuck.'

The door to the lab was about to close at her elbow when the assistant caught it and pulled it open again. 'Is everything okay?' he asked, his eyes falling to the gun in her hand.

Jamie saw what he was looking at and holstered it quickly, forcing a smile. 'Sure, everything's fine.'

'Then why did you—'

She cut him off with a question of her own, not wanting to answer that. 'Did you see that man?'

'What man?'

'Big guy outside the window, surgical scrubs and cap?'

'No,' he said. 'I was working. Why, was something wrong?'

'It's nothing,' she said, keeping the forced smile. 'Are there any tall surgeons here?'

'At the hospital? I don't know, we don't get many visitors down here. But there's over three hundred people on staff.'

'Is there a good reason for a surgeon to be down here?'

'There's a nuclear lab,' he said. 'They do some procedures that require a surgeon.'

So it's plausible that it was nothing, Jamie thought but didn't say. 'Alright.' She walked past him and back into the morgue. 'You've had no one particularly interested in the body other than the police?' she asked lightly.

'This body?' he questioned, looking at the woman on the slab.

Jamie resisted the urge to be glib. 'This body.'

'No, no one.' He watched Jamie carefully as she circled the drawer and stood behind Julie Johns.

The assistant was clearly smart, and though he didn't seem to grasp the idea that perhaps the killer had been just feet from them, he knew something was up.

It was highly unlikely a killer like this would return to the scene of the crime, let alone the morgue. And it was even more unlikely he'd don surgical scrubs just to peer through the glass for a few seconds. But unlikely wasn't impossible, and Jamie found that unlikely was more likely than it seemed in a murder investigation such as this.

But there was no point fretting over what might or might not have been. She had the real mystery lying in front of her. 'I'm going to take some photographs of these markings,' she said, just so he knew what she was doing when she pulled her phone out.

She didn't know Norse runes, but she was sure someone would, and that whatever they said would be the next piece of the puzzle.

As she snapped, she thought about the other two women awaiting her. Judith James and Jana Jelinek, and whether the experiences with them would be the same as this.

She thought they would be, that all this was a grand design to get under her skin. To unsettle her, to rattle her.

One thing at a time, Jamie, she told herself as she catalogued the marks on the woman's body.

When she was done, she couldn't really muster words. It had been a long, long day, and though she was exhausted, she knew she wouldn't sleep. But that didn't mean she didn't want to get home, or at least get back to Alina. She still didn't feel like anywhere was home, but being with that girl ... it was the closest Jamie had.

So, as she bid the assistant goodbye and left the lab, she pulled her phone out, told Hassan to pick her up, and as she took the lift back up to the ground floor, she couldn't help but feel a little better about things. Though as she stepped from the hospital, the darkening sky overhead bringing with it a chilling wind, the feeling quickly faded.

And as she watched the second hand on her watch tick around as she waited at the curb, she knew that it was counting down to something bad. To more death. To more bloodshed.

And the thought that she couldn't do anything about it just about drove her mad.

Though, she guessed, unfortunately, that was the point.

CHAPTER
TEN

Jamie didn't know if they were expecting the call or not, but Hassan arrived quickly with Alina in the passenger seat. She lowered the window, grinning.

'Need a lift?' she called as they pulled up.

Hassan smirked from behind the wheel.

'Aha,' Jamie said, struggling to find the will to laugh. 'In the back, go on.' She hooked a thumb towards the back seats.

'Uh-uh,' Hassan said, leaning across so she could see him. 'She called shotgun, fair and square. If you wanted the front seat, you should have come with me earlier.'

Jamie grumbled and climbed into the back.

As Hassan pulled off, he eyed her in the rear-view mirror. 'Learn anything interesting?'

'No,' Jamie said tiredly. It was the truth. 'I got a better look at those markings, but otherwise—'

'What markings?' Alina asked, piqued.

Jamie met Hassan's eyes. Alina didn't need to, and shouldn't, know. This was an active investigation.

'You can tell me,' she repeated, cutting the silence. 'Maybe I can help?'

How could she? And anyway, Jamie had no intention of exposing her to a world she'd only just escaped.

'I'm going to keep asking. Come on, it'll be good practice.'

'Practice?' Jamie asked, doing a double take. 'Practice for what?'

'For when I'm a detective,' Alina said, with the sort of plainness only a teenager could summon. As though it were the most obvious thing in the damned world.

'What?!'

Hassan stamped on the brake violently and the car ground to a halt, almost hurling Jamie into the front.

'Sorry, red light,' he said quickly, looking up through the windscreen. 'Got distracted.'

Jamie, hands on the sides of the front seats, fingers curled into the leather, still couldn't believe what she'd just heard. 'Did you say you're going to be a detective?'

'Well, a police officer first, but you work your way up, right? DC, DS, DI ... then to whatever you guys are now.' She grinned again, looking at them in turn.

Hassan's mouth had puckered and bunched up like Alina had just shoved a lemon down his throat.

Jamie tasted something sour too. 'No,' she said,

bordering on emphatic. 'You are absolutely not going to be a detective.'

Alina scoffed. Loudly. 'Pshhah. Yes, I am.'

Jamie shook her head, dumbfounded. 'Why would you want to?'

'Why do you do it?'

Jamie was hoping that question wasn't coming. 'Because ...' She sighed, trailing off. Alina had her dead to rights.

'Because you want to help people, right? To save them, from people like the one you're hunting. From people like the ones who ...' She turned her head to look at Jamie, the words not coming easily.

The people who took you, Jamie knew she wanted to say. 'I've given up everything,' she said quietly. 'It's not a life you want. It comes at a price.'

'Would you pay it again?'

Jamie didn't answer.

Alina gazed out of the window, unflinching. 'You've seen what people do', she said. 'What evil people do. And that's enough to want to stop it. I've lived it, experienced it. And if I can stop it from happening to just even one person, I'd give anything. Pay any price.'

Hassan watched Jamie in the mirror. She prayed he wouldn't speak, but if he did, she knew what he'd say. *She sounds like you. A lot like you.*

'And anyway, if you didn't want me to do what you do, then why did you give me this?' Without hesitation,

Alina lifted the pistol Jamie had given her earlier into the air.

'Jesus!' Jamie said, pulling it down out of view of the other cars around them, and snatching it from her.

Hassan shifted in his seat, scanning their surroundings to check if anyone saw.

'Chill out,' Alina said, rolling her eyes. 'The safety is on.'

'That's not the point,' Jamie said, as she ejected the magazine. She pulled the slide back to check the chamber for a round and found it empty – thankfully. 'You shouldn't be carrying this around. It's for *emergencies.*'

'You give a fifteen-year-old a credit card for emergencies. You give them a P229 Compact for a whole other reason,' Alina said flatly. 'And anyway, one of the primary reasons that guns go off when they shouldn't is because the user isn't familiar with them.'

Jamie opened her mouth to retort, but Alina was right. 'That's—'

'Still not the point?' Alina sighed. 'Yeah, I know. But you gave it to me for a reason, and I'm getting comfortable with it. That's surely what you want, isn't it? And it's not like I'm not used to being around them with all the others stashed around the house.'

Jamie and Hassan exchanged another glance. 'You know about those?'

'Kind of hard to miss when you fancy a bowl of Cheerios and you find a Glock 17 in the box.'

Jamie cleared her throat, making a mental note to move that one. 'It's just with everything that happened …' she said sheepishly.

'I know. And there still might be more people coming. And if not them, then this killer. And the next one, and the next one after that …' Alina kept going as though reading Jamie's mind. 'But that's no reason to send me away, or move, or anything like that. If those people do come, then I'll want to help. I'm *going* to help. And I can help now, too.' She looked from Jamie to Hassan and back. 'So, if you're going to take my gun, the least you could do is tell me: what markings on that body? And if you're worried about me finding out that the women being killed all look like you and have names like yours … don't be. I was surprised for, like, all of five minutes.'

'How did you find that out?'

'Uh, this thing called *the news*. Her name and face are public record. Wasn't hard to find. I got over it pretty quick. I just thought, what would Jamie do?'

'And what did you come up with?' Jamie asked, almost afraid to hear the answer.

'I thought you'd get on with it. Shit's weird. Serial killers are fucked up people. But they aren't going to catch themselves.'

Jamie let out a long, slow breath. 'I wish you wouldn't swear like that. You're not grown up just yet.' She pinched the bridge of her nose. 'Wouldn't you rather be doing something more appropriate for your age instead?'

'Like surfing Tinder, meeting boys for sex in the back of their cars, getting into clubs with someone else's driver's licence, getting shit-faced drunk on glitter bombs, and dropping pills of ecstasy like Smarties?'

Jamie shook her head in shock. 'That's not what teenagers do.'

Alina rolled her eyes again. 'Come on, you must have seen Euphoria. Wait, who am I talking to? Of course you haven't. But let's put it this way, that's *mild* compared to what some girls my age are doing.'

Jamie was quickly rethinking the whole sending her to public school thing.

'So, count yourself lucky that I'd rather be learning to service a 9mm than servicing a six inch—'

'Okay!' Jamie called out, laughing awkwardly. 'I think you've proved your point, and though I don't really like the emotional blackmail ... Shit.' She shook her head, disbelieving that she was bringing Alina into this. But, hell, was she right? She was whip smart, and if she was determined to go down this route, this path, this life ... the least Jamie could do was try to steer her away from the mistakes she made. And away from Tinder, too. For as long as she could, at least.

The sooner she accepted Alina was never going to be a normal teenager, the sooner they could move forward. But towards what?

'Here,' she said, reluctantly passing Alina her phone,

showing the photographs of the markings on the woman's body. 'They appear to be—'

'Runes,' Alina said, barely looking at them. 'I've seen them before.'

'You have? Where?'

'I looked into the history of Sweden when you told me we were going there, went down a bit of a Norse rabbit hole. I read up a good bit on runes.'

Jamie was shocked. 'And you recognise them?'

Alina snorted. 'No, I'm not that smart, God.'

Even when she was being self-deprecating, she still had that unshakeable teenage cockiness. 'Right, of course.'

Alina's brow crumpled. 'Hey, didn't your first case in Kurrajak have something similar?' She tapped the phone on her leg in thought and Jamie got a flash of déjà vu. She did that. 'Wasn't the boy who was killed there marked like this with a knife?'

'He was marked, but they weren't runes though. Wait, how did you know about—'

'I may have checked out some of the case files when we were clearing your house there.' She waved it off. 'Doesn't matter, anyway. I overheard you saying that this killer is recreating your old cases, do you think this could be linked? Seems weird that it wouldn't be?'

Alina was going a mile a minute, and though Jamie was impressed – despite herself – this wasn't her methodology. She needed time to think, to process all this. 'Yeah, but look, hold on here—'

'We should get these translated, don't you think? The marks on Julie John's body.'

'Yeah, when I got back tonight, I was going to see if I could find someone who—'

'Like this guy?' Alina's thumbs worked like lightning and she held Jamie's phone up in the gap between the seats for her to see. It displayed a photograph of a university professor holding up a rusted Viking sword and grinning. He was slim, with long white hair hanging around his ears, and thick-framed glasses. 'Professor … Rundle,' Alina said, craning her neck to read the screen. 'Expert in Norse mythology and chief authority on Viking-age runes and language. Seems like if anyone would be able to help, he would, right?'

Jamie grumbled a little. She would have found him, but she couldn't be angry at Alina for doing it faster. Though she didn't particularly like how happy Alina seemed about being involved. 'Yeah, seems like,' she said. 'Where is—'

'Manchester University.'

'Manchester?' Hassan turned his head now, looking at Jamie out of the corner of his eye while he drove. 'Isn't that—'

Jamie finished the question for him. 'Where the second body was found? Yes, it was. Judith James.'

He lifted his eyebrows. 'Seems like a coincidence, doesn't it?'

'No such thing in a murder investigation,' she replied.

Alina's eyes twitched as she watched Jamie say it, and Jamie could see Alina filing it away for future use. She wondered how long it would be before she parroted those words back to her.

'So, we're off to Manchester, then?' Alina asked.

'A little sooner than intended,' Jamie replied, 'but it seems like.'

'We still have time for dinner though, don't we?'

'Yeah, Of course.'

'Great,' Alina beamed, slumping back into the front seat and reaching for the stereo.

She flicked through the stations until some dancey-pop-music came over the airwaves and she cranked it up, singing along with nothing short of glee at all this. Jamie sat back, closing her eyes and repeating words to herself she hoped she never would ...

It could be Tinder and drugs. It could be Tinder and drugs. It could be Tinder and drugs.

This is better, right?

The question echoed in the darkness.

And no answer came.

CHAPTER
ELEVEN

Jamie didn't sleep well.

She never did, but last night was particularly bad.

Habit still dictated that she brought her running shoes everywhere, even if she rarely put them on anymore. Though when the sun cracked the night, and dawn started to roll around, and with sleep not coming, she decided that perhaps doing something from her past would elicit some memory that might help. Some way into her old self. And maybe that would aid her in figuring some of this – or any of this – out.

Jamie dressed and slipped from her bedroom, Hassan's snoring echoing down the hall.

She was down the stairs and halfway to the door before she froze, seeing Alina sitting on the couch, her headphones in, scrolling on her phone.

Jamie looked at her bagged eyes, her ruffled hair. She'd not slept either, but Jamie hadn't heard her get up.

'Hey,' she whispered, though she needn't have. Hassan damn well needed a bell to be rung above his bed to wake him.

Alina looked up, taking her headphones from her ears. 'Hi.'

'Can't sleep?'

She shrugged.

Yeah, stupid question. For all the reasons Jamie didn't sleep, for all the shit bouncing round her head, it must be tenfold for Alina.

'What're you doing?'

She laid her phone on her chest, her baggy hoody drowning her. 'Just watching some videos.'

'What kind of videos?'

She didn't answer, just slowly turned her phone towards Jamie. She moved a little closer, seeing that it was a documentary on how the mind of a serial killer works.

Jamie had to smile. It wasn't like she wasn't doing the exact same thing at her age. She so looked up to her father. He'd taught her to shoot, to hunt, to never stop fighting. And she knew Alina wouldn't stop fighting either, whether Jamie was there to guide her or not.

'You bring your trainers?' Jamie asked.

Alina nodded slowly, cautiously.

'Great. Go get them on.'

'Why?'

'Because you're coming for a run with me.'

'You're not serious?' she asked, craning her head backwards to look through the window blinds behind her. 'The sun's not even up.'

'You want to be a detective? That takes discipline. Running does too. So come on.' Jamie beckoned her off the couch. 'We're out of the door in two minutes.'

Alina grumbled but got to her feet. She scowled as she walked towards Jamie, but as she passed, Jamie saw her face break into a smile, though she did her best to hide it.

Sometimes you just had to stop fighting the current, Jamie thought.

She remembered her father's teachings, to never give up. But now she just thought she was wise enough to pick her battles, instead of trying to fight them all.

BY THE TIME THEY GOT BACK, THE SUN WAS UP. IT was a little after seven, which meant they'd been out almost an hour. It wasn't continuous running – Alina was fit, but her cardio left a little to be desired. Though Jamie wasn't against the idea of a running partner. It might be quite nice, actually. Especially if today was anything to go by. They rarely got a chance to just spend time together and talk. Jamie let Alina guide the conversation, but she mostly just asked about Jamie's life, her father and mother, her childhood, uni, her early days in the Met. And in turn, Jamie asked about her childhood and upbringing, what it was like living in Georgia, whether she missed it – she did not – and what she hoped for in the future.

She'd purposely left her phone behind so that Alina would do the same. Which was nice, honestly, to just have the break, the disconnection. Or at least it was nice for *them*. When they arrived back at the house, Hassan was up, and frantic.

They came in and he immediately burst into the hallway, eyes wide. 'Where the hell have you two been?!' he demanded.

'For a run,' Jamie said. 'What's wrong? What happened?'

'What's wrong? What happened?' he all but scoffed. 'What happened is I woke up and found both of you gone, your phones on the kitchen table! I thought you'd been abducted, or … or, I don't even know!'

Alina cocked an eyebrow. 'And our missing running gear didn't clue you in on where we might be?'

He opened his mouth to reply, but no sound came out.

'Is there breakfast?' Alina asked, 'I'm starving.' She breezed past him, leaving Jamie to receive his glare alone.

'Shit,' she said, dropping her voice. 'I'm sorry, I didn't think.'

He grumbled disapprovingly. 'A note next time, at least.'

'I thought you'd still be asleep by the time we got back. It went on longer than anticipated.'

He shook his head. 'It's fine, I was just worried that's all. Here.' He handed Jamie her phone. 'Brandt called – they found our van.'

'Oh?' Jamie perked up immediately despite the lack of caffeine in her system. The smell from the kitchen was beckoning her. 'Returned to a rental agency?'

Hassan could see her twitching for a fix, so he led the way into the kitchen and served her a cup.

She cradled it while he spoke, languishing in the smell.

He shook his head. 'No, found parked on the street about a hundred metres from the police station.'

Jamie almost spat out the coffee she had in her mouth.

'We drove past it. Twice.'

'For God's sake,' she muttered.

'They're still working on it. SOCOs are going through the thing with a fine-tooth comb. As you can imagine, Brandt's not exactly thrilled. Not great for optics. Means the killer was within spitting distance of his office and he never even knew about it.' He leaned on the kitchen table while Alina slugged down honey Cheerios. They were her favourite.

'We'll head there on the way to Manchester.'

'Call Professor Rundle's office on the way,' Hassan said. 'Sooner we go, the better.'

Jamie closed her eyes. 'Let me drink my coffee first. I've got a feeling it's going to be another long day.'

'Yeah,' Hassan said, melting away towards the stairs. 'I do too.'

CHAPTER
TWELVE

When they got close to the police station, they slowed to a halt. Up ahead was a sea of blue flashing lights, and temporary 'Road Closed' signs had been put up, causing people to bottleneck as they tried to turn back or funnel down side streets to get where they needed to be.

'Mayhem,' Hassan said from behind the wheel.

Jamie had managed to reclaim the front seat, thankfully, and from her position she could see that there was no way they were getting close.

'Find somewhere to park, we're walking.'

'Where?' Hassan asked, looking around.

'Side street there,' she said, pointing. 'There's spaces.'

He leaned forward and squinted at the sign in the distance. 'It's residents only. I'll get us a ticket.'

'Seriously? You do know what we're doing today, don't you? Radcliffe will cover it, I'm sure.'

'I can't get there anyway,' he said defensively. 'There are cars in front.'

'Mount the curb.'

'Mount the curb?' he parroted back, incredulous. 'You know how expensive these alloys are?'

Jamie all but growled in frustration. 'Radcliffe will cover it. Just go, or I'm getting out.' She reached for the door handle.

'Jeez, okay, okay, God.'

Alina snickered from the back seat.

'Shush, you,' Hassan warned her, glancing in the rear-view. With a look of physical pain, he slowly eased up onto the curb with a whimper. The bumper scraped the concrete, and they trundled forward, two wheels on the pavement towards the side street. People beeped, but Jamie just flashed her badge through the passenger window as they passed, until Hassan jostled down into the residents only parking and squared up.

'See, that wasn't so bad, was it?' she asked, unbuckling.

'If you don't understand why it *was* so bad, then there's no point explaining it,' he said haughtily.

Alina snickered again, unbuckling too.

Jamie and Hassan turned to look at her.

'Where do you think you're going?' Jamie asked.

Alina pointed towards the scene. 'I just thought ...'

'Thought what?'

'You said—'

Hassan jumped in, sensing Jamie's inability to be sensitive when it was required. 'Look, helping us out when we're working through stuff, that's one thing. But we can't take you into an active crime scene. You get that, right? Smart as you are, kiddo, you're still just fifteen.'

Jamie thought the *kiddo* was a little much, but Alina seemed to understand. 'So, I just sit here and wait?'

'Yes,' both Jamie and Hassan answered in unison.

She harrumphed and folded her arms, looking sullenly out of the window.

Even if she *could* come, Jamie didn't want her to. They had no idea what they'd be walking into, and though Alina might have set herself down this path, Jamie still needed to be careful with what she exposed her to. She'd seen so much already, but Jamie was determined not to normalise it, not to trivialise it. And certainly not to turn it into some game, or something other than what it was: evil manifested. It was people hurting each other, and you had to let it affect you. If you didn't, nothing ever would. You'd just empty out inside and become a shell of a person.

And she wasn't going to let that happen to Alina. Not ever.

Jamie and Hassan climbed from the car and headed back to the traffic jam, making their way to the scene.

Hell, it was right outside the police station.

And they'd all but stopped next to it when they pulled in there themselves, waiting to cross the lanes.

A hundred police personnel probably had. Brandt included.

So it was no wonder that a swarm of officers, detectives, and SOCOs were crawling all over it like they were.

Jamie and Hassan flipped open their badge wallets as they approached the police cordon and they were let through. Thankfully it wasn't a repeat of what happened on their last case where they were all but turned away at the line.

The uniformed officer lifted the tape and they stepped into the melee, navigating past the marked cars blocking the road until they reached the van. It was a Transit. White, a newer model. Nondescript. As nondescript as vans came. No wonder everyone missed it.

Jamie paused to take a look at it, noting the side door as she'd predicted.

Brandt appeared from behind it, hand extended. 'Thanks for coming,' he said, shaking both of their hands.

'Of course,' Jamie said.

He looked tired and frustrated. To have this on his doorstep for weeks and not even notice it? It was a media shitstorm waiting to land at his feet.

Jamie noticed now that even the windshield was

plastered with half a dozen parking tickets. How had no one noticed this thing?

'Your idea paid off,' he said, 'though the thing is clean. Surgically so. Well, except for the box.'

'The box?'

'Yeah, it's got the works. Blood, hair, fingernails. All Julie Johns', we're guessing. But outside of that it's like he bleached and pressure washed it.'

'Probably did,' Jamie said, already gravitating towards the open back doors to get a better look at this *box.*

Brandt trailed off and watched her go.

She stepped around the open door, careful not to touch it, and stood staring into the van. She had to give it to this guy – he was a pro.

Two SOCOs sat in the back, either side of the 'box', showing how centred it was, and that there was space to move around it.

It was about three feet wide, and a little taller. It looked to be made by hand, constructed of three-quarter inch plywood. It didn't sound like much, but to a human hand it was nigh unbreakable. Unless you designed it to be.

Jamie inspected the thing. It was a solid cuboid, with the only open side facing the back doors of the van.

On one of the long sides, a pair of runners was installed, along with a clever hinging system, so that the 'lid' for the open end could be pulled into place quickly and securely, locking via a snap latch on the other long side.

Jamie closed her eyes and envisioned it. The box was open and waiting for Julie Johns. The killer pulled up next to her and jumped into the back – possible because he'd rented a van without a bulkhead. He threw the back doors open, grabbed Johns, held her, dosed her with a sedative and shoved her into the box head first. In seconds, he would have slid the lid into place, locked it, closed the doors, and driven away, trapping her inside.

Once she was in there, Jamie thought there would have been enough room for her to wriggle around onto her back. And from there, she would have started clawing, kicking, screaming. And she would have got out.

The end closest to Jamie, closest to the door, was broken. The top section of the box was bent upwards, the wood cracked and warped. Jamie leaned in, inspecting it further. The far end of the box, the 'top', was fastened together with screws, corner brackets. Steel. It was unbreakable.

The bottom, the end she was closest to, that Julie Johns had broken free from … That was held together by trim nails, tiny, thin nails that were designed to hold skirting boards onto walls. She reached out, inspecting the wood where it was bent and broken. It looked like it had been partially sawed through, weakened intentionally.

He wanted her to break free, there was no doubt about that.

How long had it taken her?

Had he pulled up somewhere quiet, next to the river, maybe? Climbed out, waited until she got free, jumped from the back doors, only to find him waiting. She would have turned every which way, but found there was only one option: the water.

He'd watched her jump, not thrown her. No, if he did that, it wouldn't be a recreation. Not a perfect one.

Julie Johns had gone willingly to the water. Willingly to her death.

'Sick bastard even wrote her a message,' Brandt said, appearing at Jamie's elbow. 'Gave her something to read while she was inside.'

Jamie stooped a little to look in, shuddering at the sight of the inside of the box, the thought of it.

She could see something written on the wood but couldn't read it from here.

'SOCOs have been through it,' he said. 'If you want to …'

'Get inside?' Jamie asked, grimacing. She let out a long breath, knowing she'd have to. That she was supposed to. Hassan offered a hand and she took it, turning and leaning backwards so she could feed herself into the box.

Hassan took hold of her boot and slid her in there.

The light faded and Jamie steadied her breathing, squinting up in the darkness at the words above her, clear, even through the blood smears and fingernail scratches.

It took a moment for her eyes to adjust.

'What do you think?' Brandt called, leaning down and peering inside. 'More mind games? Is our guy just that sick he wanted to torture this poor woman even more?'

Jamie read the words:

RIGHT WHERE I WANT YOU

Her blood ran cold.

'Looks like black paint?' Brandt called. 'That's what they said.'

Jamie squinted at it, fishing her phone from her pocket and flicking the torch on. The interior of the box flooded with light. 'Doesn't look like paint,' she said, reaching up and touching it. Her fingers came away black. She rubbed the substance between her forefinger and thumb, lifting it to her nose. It smelled acidic. Burned. 'Charcoal,' she thought aloud.

'Charcoal?' Brandt said back. 'Bit weird, isn't it?'

'This is all a bit weird,' Hassan snorted from his position on the street.

Jamie laid back, looking at the words. 'They were written after,' she said. 'After Julie Johns got free.'

'After she got free?' Brandt asked doubtfully.

'They're written on top of the scratches, the blood.'

'In charcoal? Why? What good would a message to

Julie Johns be *after* she got out. Do you think something went wrong? Was he going to put her back in there?'

'No,' Jamie said, reading the words again and again. 'And it wouldn't be any good to Julie Johns. But it wasn't meant for her. It never was.'

'So, who was it meant for then?'

Jamie was almost reluctant to say it. 'Me. This message is meant for me. Right where I want you. Right here. Right now.'

'Jesus Christ,' Brandt said. 'The press is going to have a fucking field day with this.'

Jamie pulled herself out of the box and stood tall, squinting in the daylight.

'But why charcoal of all things?'

Jamie hesitated.

'If you've got any ideas, now's the time to spit them out.'

'I don't know if it'll help, but I think I know what wood was used to make the box, and why ...' Jamie said, the words coming out a little strained.

'And what would that be?'

'Birch. Silver birch.' It made her sick to say.

'And how could you possibly know that?'

'Because it was the wood that the Angel Maker used to make his wings. The wood he drove through the backs of the girls he murdered.'

Brandt paled a little. 'Do you think that means ...?'

'If he hasn't already, he's about to. This is him

taunting us, playing with us. He's ten steps ahead, and we're just following the trail of bodies.'

'So how do we stop him?'

But Jamie didn't have an answer for that. So she said nothing.

And the three of them just stood there, a sea of flashing lights around them, and a distinct chill in the air.

CHAPTER
THIRTEEN

They headed back to the car at pace. Jamie was keen to be away, heading south, hopefully towards brighter skies. Though she knew the path ahead wasn't going to be an easy one. This was just the first of three bodies to see, and she knew that the fourth was coming quickly - if it wasn't out there already, waiting to be found.

She couldn't help but notice that the crimes were travelling southwards, too. Towards London, her beginning. Her genesis. But also, towards home.

The charcoal was still dark on her fingers as she closed in on the car. Birch charcoal. No doubt from the branches the killer would use for his next kill. Jamie was aware of the tactic of sharpening stakes using fire; lighting the end of a branch and then scraping it on a flat rock to rub it into a point. It had been used for millennia. Is that what the killer had done? Sharpened the branches he'd use to kill his fourth victim even before he'd claimed his first? How far ahead had he planned? How long had he been—

Jamie froze ten feet short of the car.

'What is it?' Hassan asked, stopping and looking at her.

'Alina,' Jamie said, looking into the empty back seat. 'Where the fuck is Alina?'

Hassan turned to face the car. There was a moment of stillness and then he surged forward, tearing open the back door and sticking his head inside as though she might be crouched in the footwell.

He pulled himself back out and looked at Jamie. 'Where could she be?'

Jamie didn't want to think about it, but the words written on the inside of that box rang in her ears. Right where I want you.

Was this why? So Alina would be alone? So he could take her while Jamie and Hassan were a hundred yards away?

God. God! How could she be so fucking stupid? So reckless! Idiot. Fucking idiot!

'Jamie?' Hassan asked. 'Jamie? What do we do?'

But she was rooted to the spot. Frozen. She could have screamed. Could have collapsed. Her blood was ice in her veins but her head was on fire. Among all this, the killer now had Alina. And there was nothing she could do about it. The most hideous slideshow played in her head. Was this what the stakes were for?

Was she going to discover Alina posed like an angel, impaled like those poor girls in Stockholm? Or would Jamie discover her on an altar, death by a thousand cuts? Would she be eyeless and tongueless, sent wandering until she collapsed? Or would she be sent out to be hunted like an animal? Every one of Jamie's cases flashed in her mind and her stomach churned in time.

Hassan was in front of her then, hands on her shoulders. He shook her. 'Jamie? Talk to me. What are we doing here? Do we call this in, do we—'

'I don't know,' she whispered, the words not feeling they were coming from her mouth.

'What did you say?'

'I said I don't know.' She met his eyes and he flinched. 'I don't ... know what to do.' Her lip began to quiver, her knees began to shake. Just that morning she and Alina had gone for a run, had talked, connected, shared something real.

And now this.

Now she was gone.

And Jamie knew, deep down, that the next time she saw her, she'd be dead.

Hassan's grip tightened on her shoulders and then, perhaps sensing she was about to fall, he pulled her into his arms and held her tightly, resting his chin on her shoulder. She buried her face in his chest, clutching at the back of his jacket, nails digging into the fabric so hard that they hurt.

'Jeez, you two,' came a voice from behind them, 'there something you want to tell me?'

They blew apart from each other like a grenade had gone off between them, both turning, bleary eyed, to see Alina standing in the middle of the road. She was holding a big takeout cup of bubble tea, slurping on the oversized straw with a derisive teenage look on her face.

Jamie surged towards her, the momentary anger she felt transforming into pure relief. She swept her up in her arms so fast that Alina had to lift the cup straight up not to have it crushed between them. 'My bubble tea!' she cried, the words all but strangled as Jamie hugged her so hard she squeezed the breath out of her.

'Don't ever do that again!' she hissed.

'Get bubble tea?' Alina said, the words strained.

'Disappear like that.' She released Alina and held her at arm's length.

'Sorry,' she said, turning her head. 'I just went to get a drink. I thought you'd be longer.'

'Well, we weren't,' Jamie said, still holding her. 'You should have let us know.'

'Uh,' she replied, leaning out of Jamie's arms and looking at Hassan. 'I did. Neither of you thought to check your texts?'

Hassan got his phone out and frowned, turning it towards Jamie. 'She's right. She did text,' he said sheepishly.

'Well ...' Jamie replied, searching for some other way to justify the overreaction.

'I should have called?' Alina scoffed, sucking down more tea. 'Now you're showing your age,' she said playfully, offering the straw to Jamie for a taste. 'Want some?'

'I'm good,' Jamie said, finally releasing her. 'We should get on the road.' She turned back to the car, with only Hassan noting her grin of relief that it was just a false alarm.

'Did you find anything out?' Alina asked, jogging back to the car and climbing in.

What to tell her? 'Yeah,' Jamie sighed. 'Sort of.'

'Good sort of?'

As Hassan pulled out and began their journey south, Jamie rested her cheek on her hand and watched the city drift by. 'No,' she said. 'Not good at all.'

AS THEY CLOSED IN ON MANCHESTER THEY SET A course for the university. Jamie called ahead and got Rundle's office. He was teaching when she called but told her he had office hours twelve until two, which suited their timing perfectly.

They parked up at a little after one, and once more Alina reached for the door handle.

Jamie and Hassan rounded on her again, but this time her argument was a little more solid. Before they even got a word out, she was speaking.

'It's not an active crime scene, we're not here officially

as part of the investigation, he's not a person of interest in the case – at least not yet – and I promise not to say a word when we're in there, or afterwards. No one will know I was with you. But if you leave me here, I'll get bored and go and explore this university campus, and probably smoke cigarettes and drink alcohol and try heroin.'

Jamie and Hassan's shock was apparent.

'Okay, so I won't do any of that last stuff, but I'm not sitting in the car again.'

Hassan and Jamie glanced at each other. At least they'd know where she was if she was with them.

'Fine,' Jamie said, lifting a finger. 'But not a word when we're in there. You listen, but say nothing.'

Alina dragged her fingers across her lips, as though zipping them. Yeah, Jamie thought, we'll see how long that lasts.

They all got out, and Alina did her best to stifle a grin of triumph as they approached the building where Rundle's office was.

'Did you like uni?' she asked Jamie as they walked.

'No. I didn't really have a very good time.'

Alina pondered that and turned to Hassan. 'What about you?'

He laughed. 'I had a ball, but then again, Jamie and I had distinctly different experiences.'

'Why's that?'

Jamie sighed. 'Because I didn't drink, and everyone else did. And when you're the only one who doesn't drink, people don't want to be around you and, honestly, you don't really want to be around them.'

They went inside, and Hassan pushed the call button for the lift in front of them and folded his arms. 'Translation: boring.'

Alina snickered.

'Yeah, well I saved myself a few brain cells along the way,' Jamie said, then murmured out of the side of her mouth and nodded towards Hassan. 'Can't say the same for present company.'

They all laughed as the lift arrived. Jamie gave the stairs a final look before stepping inside, wondering if she preferred the person she used to be to the one she was now, and thinking about that lost, sullen kid she was when she was Alina's age.

At the second floor they got out and headed to Rundle's office. The building was a little tired, but then again, Jamie didn't think that the modules Rundle taught – Anthropology and Nordic Studies – were ones that had a throughput to gainful employment, and as such didn't really demand the big bucks.

Strangely, there wasn't a line at his door either.

Jamie knocked and waited for an answer.

'Come in,' was the reply, and they obliged.

He was smiling at first, as though inflated by the idea that one of his students was keen enough to come by to talk or ask more about his classes. It faded quickly as the three of them funnelled into the small office over-flowing with books and papers stacked high on book-shelves. They crowded his desk, which backed up to a small window around which multiple pieces of paper were tacked, displaying various photographs of Nordic sites, newspaper clippings and online articles, including the one of him that Alina had pulled up.

'Professor Rundle?' Jamie asked to confirm.

'Yes,' he answered diligently, clasping his hands on his desk, his long white hair shining in the sunlight. 'How can I help?'

Hassan and Jamie showed their badges, and Rundle looked from one to the other.

'My name's Jamie Johansson, this is Nasir Hassan. We're special investigators with the NCA, and we were hoping for a few moments of your time.'

His face lit up. 'Oh, Jamie Johansson from the NCA.' He rubbed his hands together as though he'd been dreaming of this his whole life. 'And you need my help with something.'

'That's right.'

He leaned forward, resting his elbows on his desk, savouring it. Revelling in it. 'I'm at your command. Just tell me what you need.'

'Thank you, we appreciate that. We've run across some symbols throughout the course of an active investigation and we believe them to be Nordic runes of some kind. We hoped you might be able to translate them.'

He pulled a pair of reading glasses from the side of his desk and fastened them on the bridge of his nose.

'If anyone can, I can,' he said proudly. 'Let's have a look.'

Jamie nodded another thanks and pulled her phone out, opening the photograph of Julie John's midriff, and handed it to Rundle.

He took it gladly, inspecting the screen. Then he did something Jamie wasn't expecting, and put the phone down. 'Oh,' he said with audible disappointment, taking the glasses from his nose with a sour expression. 'Is that it?'

'I'm sorry?' Jamie said, 'I don't think I understand.'

'I thought you'd have something interesting for me. Something *new*.'

Jamie glanced at Hassan. 'New? Now I really don't understand.'

'Hold on one second,' he said, spinning on his chair to grab something from behind him. He picked up a brown envelope and handed it to Jamie.

'What's this?'

He flicked a hand at the thing. 'You should know, you sent it to me.'

'I'm sorry ...' she began, still not following. But as she opened the envelope, she saw exactly what was going on.

Inside was a letter on headed paper. Across the top it read 'From the desk of SI Jamie Johansson, NCA'. Jamie froze with the thing halfway out, steeling herself for what she was about to read.

She pulled it free and scanned the page. 'Dear

Professor Rundle, we were hoping you might be able to help us,' she read under her breath, 'we have found these markings during the course of an investigation and we'd appreciate your assistance. I hope we can count on your discretion as this is a highly confidential matter. Please await our arrival in the coming weeks. Sincerely, Jamie Johansson.' She looked up at Rundle, who was staring back at her. 'When did you receive this?' she asked.

'Two, no, three weeks ago?'

'Before Julie Johns was murdered,' Hassan muttered, leaning in to Jamie's shoulder.

Jamie leafed over the page to see another piece of paper, the runes that were cut into Julie Johns drawn on the page. Or at least, it was a grainy photocopy of a page on which they were drawn. It was cleaner, impossible to trace, to analyse in any meaningful way.

She looked up at Rundle. 'And you already translated them?'

'On the first day. I had no idea how long it would take you to get here. I'd hoped it would be sooner. And that there'd be more ...'

'If there were more, then other women would be dead,' she said bitingly.

Rundle shrank a little.

'I'm sorry, it's been a long day. Long *few* days, actually.'

'Ahem, yes, well, here are your translations.' He opened a desk drawer and pulled out a folded piece of paper, handing it to Jamie. It had miniaturised versions of the runes with their translations beside them. 'They're a series of inversions – opposites. Quite odd, really. But I suspect you'll have a better chance understanding the *why* than me.'

She looked at Rundle's notes, reading aloud. 'Choice and duty ... good and evil ... light and dark ... life and death... attack and defence ... and save or sacrifice ...'

She turned to Hassan, who looked as perplexed as she did.

This wasn't a conversation to have in front of Rundle. Their shared silence confirmed they both thought that.

'Thank you for your help, Professor.' She held the envelope up. 'I'm going to take this, alright?'

'Well,' he said, rising from his chair, 'I had hoped, actually, I might keep it.' He gestured to the wall next to the article he appeared in. 'Hang it here, to ...'

'That won't be possible,' she said. 'I hope you understand.'

He snatched his phone from the desk. 'A photo at least?' he asked hopefully.

Jamie just offered a brief smile and then pushed the envelope inside the hem of her jacket. 'I'll mail it to you when we're done with the investigation.'

'You promise?'

'Sure.' And with that, she turned on her heel and walked out of the room.

This time, she didn't bother with the lift, and took the stairs two at a time.

Alina ran to catch up with her. 'Are you really going to mail that back to him?'

'Not a chance,' Jamie said gruffly, rounding the switchback in the stairs and heading towards the ground floor.

'Yeah, thought it was odd you said you would. Guessing that's from the killer?'

'Mm,' Jamie growled, her jaw locked, temple vein pulsing heavily.

'And he mailed it before he even killed the first victim, knowing that we'd eventually find our way to Rundle, and—' Alina was cut off as Jamie's hand hit her chest, stopping her on the bottom step. 'Oof, what was that ...' She trailed off, following Jamie's eyes to the back of the door leading into the lobby.

It bore the words:

GETTING WARMER ...

Alina gulped. 'You don't think that's from ...?'

'I do,' Jamie said, trying to steady her breathing.

'How did he know you'd take the stairs?'

'Because ...' she said slowly, coming to accept the stark and chilling truth of this case. 'Because he knows me. And he knows me *very* well.'

CHAPTER
FOURTEEN

They got back to the car and sat in silence.

Hassan massaged his mouth, staring out across the car park at the streams of university students moving across the campus, blissfully unaware of what was going on, of what he and Jamie were doing.

'Guess we can add forgery and impersonating a government official to the list of crimes this guy's committed,' he said after a while. It wasn't particularly funny, but Jamie suspected it was as much to break the silence as anything else.

It was Alina who spoke next. 'So now we know *what* the runes mean ... what do we think they *mean*? What were they again?'

Jamie didn't even need to look at the envelope. 'Choice and duty, good and evil, light and dark, life and death, attack and defence, save or sacrifice.'

'They're opposites,' Alina said. 'That's what Rundle said, wasn't it?'

'I don't know if we're the ones who are supposed to understand,' Hassan said, turning to face Alina. 'Everything so far has been for Jamie. For Jamie to know and understand. So trying to work it out might not even be possible.' He turned his attention to Jamie. 'What are you thinking?'

'I don't know,' she said. 'I need to think.'

'So where do we go from here? To the police station? See the next body?' Hassan reached for the ignition, ready to slot the key and set off.

Jamie's arm shot out. 'No,' she said, her fingers tight around his wrist. 'I can't. I—'

'Jamie,' he said, resting his other hand on hers. 'It's okay, it's okay. We don't have to.'

She hunched forward, drawing a shaky breath. The runes, the opposites, they did mean something to her. They were all decisions. Decisions she'd made, and dichotomies she'd wrestled with. Duty and choice – what she was supposed to do, and what she did instead. Good and evil – what did that even mean? It was arbitrary, and Elliot had never tired of telling her that. That it doesn't matter. It never did. Light and dark, life and death, to attack or defend, to save or to sacrifice … The people she'd left behind, those alive and those dead. The people she'd cast off, the ones she'd killed. She'd hunted people like the killers she'd told herself she was so much better than. How many times had she pulled the trigger, when putting them in handcuffs was the right call? Was all this just punishment? What she deserved coming back around?

She couldn't say that it wasn't, that this didn't seem like a fitting end, a good reminder of why she was supposed to be as dead as the *evil* people she'd killed.

Of why she was just like them.

There was nothing that either Hassan or Alina could say. Nothing she wanted to hear. Jesus, the only person she wanted to hear from was Elliot. He was the only one who could make any sense of this shit. He was the only one who could say the words she needed to hear to get her straight, to focus her mind. To make it all better. To give her a fighting chance here. And how fucking stupid was that? She'd spent the last half a decade pushing him away, and he'd always come back like a bad smell. And now ... now that she needed him? The one time she *actually* needed him, he was nowhere to be found and not picking up his phone.

'Take me home,' Jamie said, eyes screwed shut.

Hassan started the car wordlessly.

'Wait, we're going home?' Alina questioned, shocked by it.

'Have you heard from Elliot?' Jamie asked her, ignoring her question.

'Elliot? No, I haven't, why?'

'Text him. Call him. Now, please,' she said, eyes still shut.

Alina did as she was asked, putting her phone on speaker.

It rang through to voicemail.

'That's weird. He always picks up when I call. Always.'

Jamie opened her eyes and sat bolt upright.

'What is it?' Alina asked.

'I'm worried,' she said, a coldness spreading through her.

'It's okay, you'll be okay, and we'll figure this case out, and—'

'Not about me. Not about the case,' Jamie said, looking at both Hassan and Alina in turn. And then she said the words she thought would never come from her mouth. 'I'm worried about Elliot.'

CHAPTER
FIFTEEN

They drove south at speed, each of them trying Elliot several times. Each time it went to voicemail, and by the time they crossed the border back into Wales, Jamie was more than a little nervous.

She tried to think back to their final exchange before she'd left for Yorkshire. How they'd been standing around the table and he'd been silent, deep in thought. Rarely did he pass up an opportunity to flex his grey matter in front of them. But that night he'd been reluctant to. And then he'd practically run for the door. And when Jamie had asked where he was going, he told her he needed to think, that he'd call her.

What did he need to think about? And why hadn't he called? He never said things he didn't mean, and he never went back on his word.

If he wasn't picking up it was because he *couldn't*.

Which could only mean that he knew more about any of this than he'd let on. And that very possibly he'd gone out on his own to hunt this killer.

And that he may well have found him.

Jamie turned her head, thinking about this, about how none of them could get hold of him, and how there was only one other person who might have heard from him, and who may know where he was. And how that person was the one person Jamie *really* didn't want to reach out to.

Elliot's wife.

But she didn't have a choice. None of them did. First thing in the morning, she would—

'What's that?' Alina asked, pointing out of the window.

Jamie squinted into the gathering darkness at the side of the road, the open landscape north of the Beacons stretching out around them as they wound south.

She could see dim lights burning in the distance. A town? A house? No, there was nothing out here.

The lights flickered, yellow and small.

Fires.

Campfires, maybe. No, they were too small and there were half a dozen of them. All in a circle. She squinted harder, cupping her eyes against the glass to get a better look.

The fires blinked, blotted out by trees. A copse of

trees. Her eyes adjusted to the darkness, the meagre light catching the colour of the trunks.

White and black, like tiger stripes.

'Stop,' she whispered, her voice catching in her throat.

'What?' Hassan asked.

'Stop the fucking car!' she all but shrieked.

Hassan swore, stamping on the brake and wrestling the car off the tarmac and into the grassy verge. The bumper crunched into the bank, the car jolting and gouging itself to a stop. But Jamie didn't even feel it. She was already out of the door, hurdling the long grass and sprinting towards the silver birch trees.

The same trees the Angel Maker used to create their angels.

It was too dark for her to see anything, but she knew exactly what awaited her, and as she sprinted across the uneven ground, tears began streaming from her eyes.

'No, no, no,' she gasped as she reached the treeline, ducking and weaving between the trunks. The low branches whipped and pulled at her hair as she fought her way forward towards the flickering lights ahead.

Her chest heaved, knees pumping as she stomped through the long grass towards the clearing she knew was ahead.

And then she broke through, clawing her way into the open with such force she collapsed forward onto her hands and knees.

She could feel something wet under her hands, and

prayed it was groundwater and not something else. And yet she couldn't open her eyes, couldn't face what was in front of her.

Damn it! Jamie, grow a fucking spine!

She lifted her head and forced herself to look.

And for a moment, she thought she was looking in the mirror.

Staring back at her was a blonde-haired woman with piercing blue eyes.

She was looking right at Jamie.

'Oh my god,' Jamie breathed. She was alive! She scrambled forward, unable to tell whether the dark liquid on her hands and knees was mud or blood.

Her hands reached out, her eyes not seeing anything except the woman's face. Her pale complexion, her angular face, the subtle lines and wrinkles around her eyes and mouth, carved in the glow of the fires around them.

Jamie cupped the woman's face, felt her skin warm, smeared black across her cheeks as she cradled her head.

'It's okay, it's okay,' Jamie whispered, 'I'm here, I'm here. You're going to be okay, you're—' But the words died in her mouth as the woman's eyes stared vacantly into the space between them. Her lips parted, a thin strand of saliva running from between them and dripping to the ground.

Jamie took it in then, her hair tied back, fastened to the branches of wood that were holding her up, that were ... Oh God ... That were staked through her. Pushed through her back, between her ribs, through her body and out through her chest and stomach. They were driven into the ground, like they had been with the girls in Stockholm.

The woman was held in place on her knees by them, her body doubled over, her head held up, and above her, spreading into the gathering night were great wings. The branches split and extended further and further, until the ends, rustling with the last leaves of the year, stretched their tendril-like fingers skywards, reaching for heaven.

Jamie recoiled, realising now that the woman was dead. She hunched over, retching and vomiting, emptying the contents of her stomach into the bloody earth.

She stared at it through tears, seeing that the woman's blood had filled the spaces between the grass like oil. It lay there, thick and warm around Jamie's legs, catching the light from the torches.

Still warm, Jamie thought, vomit hot on her lips and chin. Still warm. She shoved herself to her feet, covered in blood, and ripped her pistol from its holster, dragging the sleeve of her coat across her mouth before she threw her head back and loosed a vicious scream.

Her eyes refocused, scanning the treeline, looking for him. This had just happened. He was here. He was just here!

'Where are you?!' she roared, pointing her pistol into the darkness. 'I know you're here!'

Her voiced echoed and faded.

'Come out! You fucking coward! How can you do this!?' Jamie's words were choked, interspliced with sobs. 'Show yourself! You want me? I'm right here! I'm right fucking here—'

A branch snapped behind her and she whirled around, finger already squeezing the trigger, ready to blow a big fucking hole right through him.

But before she even turned halfway, big hands closed around her wrists and drove them upwards.

The trigger hit the grip and the slide kicked back, fire spitting from the muzzle, sending a bullet into the air.

She was forced forwards, the man dragging her towards him, twisting her around like she weighed nothing. Her body slammed into his, and his arms crushed hers against her chest, pinning her back to him.

'No!' she wailed, crying uncontrollably. 'Let go of me!'

'Shh, shh, Jamie, it's me, it's me,' Hassan said, holding her fast, one arm keeping her in place, the other pulling the weapon from her grasp. 'It's okay, it's okay, I'm here,' he whispered.

She whimpered, her legs shaking and then giving out.

They both went backwards, sinking into the long grass in front of the angel.

Jamie turned her head, closing her eyes once more. 'I couldn't ... I couldn't save her,' she mewled.

'It's okay, it's okay,' Hassan told her. 'There's nothing you could have done.'

She let go of the gun, and a second later she heard the ringer on Hassan's phone as he dialled someone.

'Hello?' Radcliffe picked up. 'Hassan. What is it?'

'It's another body,' he said hurriedly. 'You have to send them. Now, send them now.'

'Who? Send who?'

'Everyone.'

CHAPTER
SIXTEEN

Hassan stayed there with Jamie until the first wail of sirens echoed across the open landscape.

The torches were still burning around them, the victim growing colder as the sky darkened.

Jamie didn't remember much of what happened as it seemed to go by in a blur. She was lifted, and two SOCOs in white overalls held her hands up and slipped evidence bags over them before leading her carefully back to the road.

She caught a glimpse of Alina in the back seat of the Audi, her face pressed to the glass, wide-eyed at the woman covered in blood in front of her.

The officers sat Jamie in the back of a van and took photos of her clothes and samples of the blood, and then did the same with her hands, taking photos, picking blood from under her nails with forceps.

One of them said, 'Wait here,' and then they both left.

She kept her hands aloft, not really thinking about it until Radcliffe appeared and told her to lower them.

She looked up at him and blinked a few times.

He pocketed his hands, his dark hair reflecting the flashing blue lights around them, and rocked on his heels. 'Suppose it's a stupid question to ask how you're doing.'

'Was that a question?' she asked slowly.

'Only if the answer isn't *like shit.*'

She just huffed a little.

'I'm more concerned whether or not you're losing your mind. This is ...' he turned to look at the scene, the fleet of uniforms and overalls scouring the area, the dogs, the drones, the camera flashes and torches sweeping around, '... it's a lot. And forgive me for speaking plainly here, you're at the receiving end of it. These victims look like you. This whole thing is *for* you. That much is pretty clear isn't it? It's supposed to be messing with your head, but is it too much?'

'No,' she said firmly, feeling the case suddenly slipping through her fingers.

'It was rhetorical.' He sighed. 'I think, based on what we know, and what Hassan told me, that if you *don't* work it we'll never solve it, or at least it'll take much longer. So, what do I do? Do I keep you on this knowing that it's breaking you, hoping you catch this guy before he kills too many people and you go *completely* insane?

Or do I pull you off it and hope that we find him before he kills even more people?'

His questions hung in the air, and Jamie thought any answer she gave wouldn't sway him either way.

'You'll go home, tonight. The crime scene will be swept thoroughly, we'll have roadblocks up at five, ten, and twenty miles on every road we can spare a man for, and we'll be implementing full stop and search procedures to try and catch this guy.'

'You won't catch him.'

'I know,' Radcliffe said plainly, 'but that's no reason not to do it anyway.' He eyed Jamie carefully. 'Tomorrow, first thing, you'll go to see Dr Dumont—'

'I really don't think—'

'Don't interrupt me, Johansson. You almost shot and killed your partner tonight, and he reported you screaming *"Come and get me you coward"* into the trees.'

'That's not what I said,' Jamie muttered. She felt a pang of anger towards Hassan, but she knew his intentions would only be pure. He was worried about her, and he was right to be.

'You'll go and see Dr Dumont first thing. And you'll talk to her. About this, about how you're feeling, about what you're thinking. She'll likely advise me not to put you in the field, but I don't know that I have any other choice. Still, I'm taking your service weapon from you—'

'You can't do that.'

'You'll have it back when I think you're safe to use it.'

'I am safe.'

'Did you or did you not discharge your weapon and fire a bullet into the air tonight?'

Jamie didn't answer. Mainly because her only answer was *yes, but only because Hassan stopped me from blowing his head off by aiming my gun there.*

'And speaking of your weapon. Where is it?'

Jamie's hand leapt to her empty holster. 'It's ...'

'It's right here,' Radcliffe said, holding it up. He ejected the magazine and then the round in the chamber, 'and that's where it'll stay until I hear that you're okay from Dumont. Do I make myself clear?'

Jamie just nodded.

'Good. Now go home. You and Hassan are both dismissed. Dumont is expecting you at nine. Don't be late.' And with that, he turned and walked away.

Hassan appeared and knelt in front of her. 'Let's get out of here, huh?'

There were so many things she wanted to say, so many things she wanted to scream. But Radcliffe was right. She wasn't right. She needed time, space, and, as much as she hated to admit it. She needed help.

The last thing she wanted was someone poking around in her head, but maybe seeing someone would be the best thing for her.

'Alina doesn't need to be here,' Hassan urged her, 'and we could all do with a decent night's sleep.'

Jamie nodded slowly and let herself be lifted to her feet.

They headed back to the car and Hassan went around to the driver's side.

'Hey,' Jamie called across the roof. 'Thank you. For tonight. For everything.'

He nodded. 'Of course.'

'I mean it,' she said. 'I'm glad you're here. I don't know what I'd do if you weren't. This is all …'

'I know it is,' he said, offering a warm smile. 'Now let's get you home, hey? You look like shit.'

Jamie glanced down at herself, caked in mud and blood, her hair rife with twigs and her face scratched up from the errant branches. 'Yeah, guess I do,' she laughed, albeit sardonically.

When she climbed into the front seat, the world outside died away. The clamour and noise of the officers, the barking of the dogs, the calls of SOCOs and hum of generators powering floodlights taken down to the scene. She welcomed the peace, the silence.

Alina's hand snaked over the seat and squeezed at her shoulder. She reached up and put her hand on it, expecting Alina to recoil from the blood. But she didn't. She kept it there, holding on to Jamie as Hassan started the car and pulled away.

Jamie watched the scene fade into the distance in the rear-view, glad that they were away from it, if only for tonight.

Because tomorrow she knew it would all come

crashing back, and that it was going to get worse before it got any better.

She just hoped she was strong enough to make it through.

And for the first time in her life, she wasn't sure if she was.

CHAPTER
SEVENTEEN

J amie didn't sleep well.

She took a long shower, and though she managed to get the blood off, her mind refused to shut down. So many questions swirled. How did the killer know exactly where she was, when and where to stage that kill? Was he tracking them? Was he watching them? Had he been watching them every step of the way? Jamie's mind went to the big surgeon at the morgue. Was that him, or just some curious onlooker?

And where the hell was Elliot? She had her day mapped out, and was almost glad she was able to push the investigation aside for just a moment to look at other things. The details of these kills were so intimate, so precise, that it wasn't someone recreating news stories. No, this killer had access to police files. And that meant Jamie had to make some calls, had to catch up with some old colleagues to make sure there'd been no breaches, or at least none she was aware of.

She'd go and see Elliot's wife then. She'd get an answer as to where he was, and she'd find him, and get the truth of what the hell was going on here and how exactly he was wrapped up in it. Because she was convinced of one thing – that he definitely was.

But first she had to go and see Dumont.

She'd thought about it a lot since their first interaction. She'd always abhorred the idea of seeing a therapist or, more truthfully, *feared* it, but having someone to talk to right now didn't seem like that bad of a deal. She thought that person was Elliot, someone who'd never judge her, never look down on her for what she said, thought, did. But now, Jamie didn't know. Elliot had abandoned her when she needed him the most, and she was struggling. More so than ever before.

She was in the kitchen, already finished with her second cup of coffee, when Hassan came downstairs.

Hallberg stayed an extra night after Hassan explained the situation, and agreed to hang around for Alina and the dog. Alina was still asleep, or at least still in her room, as was Hallberg, along with Hati the dog, who'd taken a shine to her. Which confirmed Jamie's suspicions that he liked pretty much everyone except her. She didn't mind though. Hallberg had been here, holding down the fort, when Seda Petrosyan's men burst in and took Alina, so she thought maybe having

Hati sleeping by her bed made her feel a little better. And who was Jamie to take that away?

She rose from the table to greet him and get him a cup of coffee, but he hugged her instead. A long, warm squeeze. The touch of someone who genuinely gave a shit.

'How are you doing?' he asked, releasing her and giving her the kind of intense stare there was no hiding from.

She didn't much feel like lying. Though she suspected that was sort of progress. She just shrugged.

H nodded and let her be, fixing himself a coffee from the pot. 'You want to head out soon?'

'Yeah, better had. I can drive myself though. No need for you to take four hours out of your day just to ferry me back and forth.'

He held a hand up, dismissing that. 'It's fine. Radcliffe said to drive you, and it's no trouble. What else am I going to do today otherwise?'

She laughed a little. 'I don't know. Attend to the gristly crime scene five miles from our front door, hunt down a vicious serial killer ... The list goes on.'

'When I could just sit in traffic instead?' He made a *pshhh* sound, sipping his coffee. 'No thank you.'

She knew he was trying to be nice, trying to play it off as a joke, but the short answer was that Radcliffe had taken all of two seconds to see that she was coming apart at the seams and she had no doubt that he'd instructed Hassan to keep an eye on her. Stay on top of her, manage her if, and when, she came back to work.

Because the killer wasn't just killing, he was waging psychological warfare.

Jamie didn't feel much like speaking to him, despite his best intentions, so she just sort of gestured to the door and then headed outside.

Hassan put down his coffee after a long slurp and followed.

The drive in was pleasant, the sky clear and bright despite what was going on out there. Jamie thought about all the people just going about their normal lives as they drove, without a care in the world.

They passed two of Radcliffe's police checkpoints and Hassan flashed his badge at both as they sailed on through.

Jamie kept her elbow on the sill of the window and her eyes on the passing scenery. She was dog tired, and though she was desperate to get back to work, to the investigation, she also wanted to just wake up and find it had all been some sort of bad dream.

The stack of things she had to do only seemed to be growing, and with each item that piled on, she felt like she was getting further and further from this being over.

By the time they reached Dumont's office, Jamie was in desperate need of another coffee. Luckily, Dumont had a coffee machine.

Jamie climbed out thinking of it, but stopped when Hassan called her.

She turned back to the car and found him leaning across the centre console. 'Everything okay?' she asked.

He seemed to take a second to choose his words. 'I know this is tough,' he said.

Jamie almost rolled her eyes, but she could see how sincere he was being, so she just stood there.

'But it's what Radcliffe needs before he lets us back on this. And honestly, I think it might be good for you. You hate psychologists, I know, but ... try, okay? For Alina, for me, for you. Try opening up. I think it'll help.'

She gritted her teeth, biting her tongue. She surprised herself that she was able to stay quiet instead of saying something snide. Maybe she was getting better. Or maybe she was just that tired.

She gave a slow nod. 'I'll see you in a few hours.'

He reciprocated and then gave her a wave as she closed the door. He pulled back into traffic and Jamie stepped through the nondescript glass door and into the tiled foyer of a private office building. She climbed the stairs slowly and moved through the empty corridor. There were maybe six offices in the entire building, but only Dumont's was occupied. Jamie knew that she wasn't from Cardiff, and gleaned that she worked primarily, if not entirely, for the NCA, or at least for the government. She thought it must have been quite interesting, dealing with the likes of special investigators, counter-terrorism officers, intelligence officers ... probably spies too, elite military operatives, the list went on.

She found herself in front of Dumont's door, her

hand raised to knock. But she couldn't bring herself to do it.

A voice echoed through the wood. 'Are you going to come in, or just stand out there all morning?'

Jamie's fist tightened a little and she lowered it, pressing down on the handle with her other hand and entering.

Dumont smiled up at her, already in position in her chair, legs crossed, her tablet lying on her lap. She was wearing her usual brow-line glasses, her dark hair up in a bun, her thick fringe just touching her eyebrows. She was a smart woman, tall, with keen, dark eyes that Jamie could feel on her skin as she entered.

Dumont was older than Jamie, and oozed the confidence that all highly intelligent people do. That palpable aura that made you feel a little stupid, even before you said anything.

'Please,' Dumont said, offering the chair before her.

Jamie sat, and then there was just a coffee table between them.

Her hiking boots squeaked slightly as she adjusted herself.

'You can take your coat off,' Dumont said, not phrasing it like a question.

We'll be here a while, Jamie thought, as though finishing Dumont's sentence.

'How have you been doing?' she asked, as Jamie took off her jacket.

'Uh ...' Jamie said, blinking a few times. This was a test, she thought.

'It's not a test,' Dumont said.

God, she did remind Jamie of Elliot. Able to read her mind at every turn.

Dumont sighed. 'Look, I'll just be straight with you here, because time really isn't something we have a lot of. Radcliffe wants you stable and focused. He's gone past wanting to know if you're up to this job, he just needs you not to kill someone while you're doing it – or at least the *wrong* person. It's not my place to say whether I think that's a good idea or not – and for the record, I think it's a *horrible* idea and you're way too close to this case.'

'You don't know anything about this case,' Jamie retorted.

'You're my patient, I know *everything* about this case. It's my business to know the business of my patients. It's what I'm paid to do.'

'I'm not your patient,' Jamie said, almost reflexively.

'Look around, Jamie. You're my patient, whether you like it or not. So talk to me, because we don't leave here until we do. You have complete client confidentiality inside these walls, so all the things you've got bottled up inside you ... this is the place to let them out. I know you want to, you just don't know how. But if you let me, I can show you.'

'Is this where you ask me to lay back and listen to

the sound of your voice, maybe swing a pocket watch in front of my face?'

'That's a neat defence mechanism you've got there. I'm guessing it works a lot. Deflecting like that, maybe even throwing in a hint of condescension so people don't want to dig deeper. Thing is, you think it doesn't tell me anything, but it does. And we can keep going round and round and round if you want, but ultimately there's a much simpler way that requires no trickery, no hoodoo. Nothing except a little bit of honesty, and a little bit of courage.'

'And what's that?'

'I ask a question, you give me an honest answer.'

Jamie tutted. 'Doesn't seem fair, you get to open my life up but I know nothing about you.'

'I'm an open book, and if I genuinely thought that you'd actually be more forthcoming if I shared something personal, I'd do it. But you're just fishing for a way out of this.'

'I'm not,' Jamie lied. 'I'd genuinely feel more comfortable if you shared something.'

'Fine. When I was eighteen, I hit someone with my car and they died. I was charged with manslaughter, but the case was dismissed because it was dark, the guy was riding a bicycle, wearing black, and a CCTV camera caught him suddenly veering into the road without warning. But despite all that, not a day goes by where I don't think about it and it still keeps me up at night thirty years later.' Dumont had spoken plainly, her throat tightening a little at the end.

'Is that true?'

'Completely. Now you.'

Jamie swallowed, stiffening in the chair.

'I can play your part if you'd like? What about your blossoming relationship with Elliot Day during your first murder case? You were supposed to have dinner with him the night you discovered he was the killer you were looking for. How does that sit with you, that your first romantic entanglement in several years was with a serial killer?'

Jamie felt her cheeks flush violently.

'Or what about shooting and killing Mimi Paganelli in the line of duty? The first person you killed. Do you still think about her? I bet you do, every time you get out of the shower and see that scar on your shoulder.' Dumont was as cold as ice. 'Or what about when you returned to Stockholm and found your mother hadn't sold your family home? Or when you found out your father never stopped trying to contact you before he died?'

'Stop,' Jamie muttered, her voice strained and weak.

'Or what about the two men you killed on that oil platform? The one you left under the ice in Sweden to drown? What about Gotland? You killed Victor Hellström – shot him while he was in the sea, didn't you? When you could have arrested him instead.'

Jamie closed her eyes. 'Stop,' she said again, a little harsher now. 'Stop.' The blood began roaring in her ears.

'Or what about your partners? You've been through a few of them. Paul Roper – he was stabbed because of you, wasn't he? Or your current partner, Nasir Hassan. I'm surprised that he came around so quickly after he took a shotgun blast to the torso for you. Or Anders Wiik. He's still taking prescription painkillers for his hand. Sixteen pins putting it back together. Does that sound right? Or perhaps it's Kjell Thorsen who's eating you up. You're not in touch anymore, are you? I hear his rehab is coming along after you—'

'Stop!' Jamie screamed, suddenly finding herself on her feet. She opened her eyes and saw that she was standing over Dumont, shoulders heaving, tears streaming down her face. Her left hand was balled into a fist, her other tight at her hip, where her holster usually was.

She stared down at Dumont who looked back up at her, expression cool. 'I guess it's a good thing Radcliffe took your service weapon from you isn't it?'

Jamie swallowed the bile rising in her throat. 'I'm leaving,' she growled, turning and heading for the door.

'You walk out of that door and you're walking out on everything. This case, your career, everything. They'll take it all away, and you'll be alone.'

Jamie froze.

'And as much as you try to convince the world that's the way you prefer it, you and I both know that's total bullshit. I pushed you a moment ago because I needed to. Because it was the only way to get the ocean that's built up behind your wall to spill over it. And now you can't deny that it's there. So why don't you grow a spine and come back to this chair. Do the real work, and stop playing games. You can't hide from yourself, Jamie, your past – this case has proved it. And you can't hide from me either.'

Jamie let out a long, shaking breath.

'You want to cry? Then do it. You want to scream? Punch pillows? This is the place. You've got all this anger, all this guilt, all this sadness inside you and it can't be denied anymore. You're going to explode, and you're going to kill someone if you continue to try. So turn around. Look at me.'

Jamie did so, slowly, still hovering by the door.

'You don't have to tell me everything, just one thing. Just tell me one thing, Jamie.'

'And what's that?' she whispered, her words drowned out by the ticking of the clock on the wall.

'What are you so afraid of? If you let down your walls?' She took off her glasses so she could look at Jamie with nothing between them. 'What do you really think is going to happen?'

'I ... I don't know,' Jamie mustered.

'None of us do,' Dumont said, offering a brief, flickering, genuine smile. 'But, God ... don't you want to know? Even just a little? After all this time?'

Jamie just stared back at her. She wanted so desperately, so very desperately, to just say yes.

But she was just too scared to do it.

CHAPTER
EIGHTEEN

t took all morning, but Dumont was relentless, and eventually prised Jamie open like a clam. And now she was exhausted, standing at the curb, waiting for Hassan.

She still couldn't believe she'd said the things she had, talked about the things she had. Things she'd never spoken about. She'd been ... vulnerable. Spoken about her father, her mother, her work, her partners, her childhood. She'd talked about her relationships, romantic and otherwise. And despite herself, despite hating psychologists and their need to scratch and scratch ... she felt better. Clearer. About herself, and about the case. About what she needed to do now.

She had to recognise that Dumont was good at what she did. And now, it seemed to her that it was more of a performance coaching role than one of a psychologist. That her mandate wasn't to help, to treat, to fix. But to focus and distil her patients, get them working again, and get them working well.

She'd said everything Jamie had needed to hear, got her to say everything that she was holding inside, let out all the emotions and fears she'd bottled up, and that freed her mind to think about the investigation. To see it in new ways, in a new clarity.

She was excited to share her new-found motivation with Hassan. And upon seeing it, along with her new-found stability, she hoped he'd pass that along to Radcliffe and they could get back to doing what they did best.

But where the hell was he?

She'd texted him to say what time they'd be done, given him plenty of notice. But he was now going on thirty minutes late. Which was not like him. At all.

As if to answer her thought, a marked police car came around the corner and trundled to a stop in front of her.

The window lowered and a young officer with tousled hair leaned out. 'You Jamie Johansson?'

Jamie's brow furrowed. 'Yeah,' she said. 'Where's Nasir Hassan?'

'I'm here to pick you up,' he said, not answering the question.

'Where's Hassan?'

The officer sighed, seemingly not thrilled with this mandate. 'He's, uh, he's at the hospital, getting checked out.' He lifted a hand quickly to quell Jamie's reaction.

'He's alright, he was just involved in a minor traffic collision.'

'Minor traffic collision?' Jamie repeated. 'And he needed the hospital for that. What happened?'

The officer looked at Jamie, assessing whether he had any hope of getting her in the car without telling her everything. His assessment proved correct.

'He was rear-ended while driving across the Beacons and went off the road. He was then mugged and struck before the assailant drove off.' He said the words plainly, but it didn't detract from their weight.

Jamie felt like repeating it all back to him to confirm it's what he said, but she didn't have the desire to waste any more time. She circled the car and climbed in the front. 'Take me to him.'

The officer sighed again and pulled away quickly.

He navigated the city at speed until they reached the hospital, and then dropped Jamie at the front door.

'Is that all, or—'

'No, wait here,' she ordered him.

He rolled his eyes and then sodded off to find a nearby space.

Inside, Jamie got directions from the desk and was sent through to A and E where she found Hassan sitting on a gurney in an examination room. A nurse was taking his blood pressure and he looked suitably pissed off.

His left eye was swollen shut, a gash on his forehead closed with butterfly stitches. There was another cut at the corner of his eyebrow running around his eye socket. His nose was swollen, and dried blood was congealed around his nostrils and through his stubbled upper lip.

'Holy hell,' she said, stepping into the room.

Hassan batted the nurse away as she tried to shine a pen light in his eyes, and grumbled, eyeing Jamie with his one good eye.

'What happened?' she asked, approaching as close as she dared.

'I got run off the road and robbed,' he said gruffly.

Up close, Jamie got a better sense of the damage. His nose and forehead wounds were from an airbag blast, the eye from the blow.

'By who?'

'Who do you think?' he practically snapped. 'Took my gun, my badge, my wallet, everything.'

Jamie swallowed. 'The killer?' she said, keeping her voice a little hushed.

The nurse took a quick look at each of them and then scurried from the room, pulling the door shut behind her.

Hassan just shrugged, his lips twisted into an angry grimace.

'Jesus,' Jamie breathed. 'You think he followed you?'

'How the fuck should I know? I'm just driving along, minding my own fucking business, next thing I'm in a fucking ditch!'

Jamie kept herself even, all the tiredness she'd felt

just minutes ago now gone. She felt wired. 'Did you get a good look at him?' she asked, the hope in her voice apparent.

Hassan laid back on the gurney with a pained grunt, and gingerly rested the back of his left hand on his forehead. Jamie could see cuts across his skin, his knuckles. She wondered if the driver's window had shattered in the crash or the killer had put it through.

'No,' he answered, 'I didn't even think ... I mean, I thought it was an accident. By the time I pulled my head out of the airbag he was there. Just a flash, a shadow. Then nothing, I was slumped forward again. He pulled me from the car onto my stomach, stripped my weapon, my pockets ... left me there and drove off. Not a word. Nothing. Honestly, it could have been anyone.'

'No, it was him. It had to be.'

'Fat lot of good that information does us.'

'Not true. We know where he was, and at what time. There'll be witnesses, CCTV footage. This is good.'

Hassan eyed her fiercely. 'Good?'

'Not *good*, I don't mean ... It's not good, you're in the fucking hospital. I'm sorry. I just mean—'

'I know what you mean,' he said, cutting her off. 'Fuck ...'

'Can I get you anything?'

'I just want to go home,' he said after a few seconds, his voice thin. 'I just want this whole thing be over.'

. . .

HASSAN NEEDED TO BE KEPT IN FOR observation, and was booked in for a head scan. The doctor was pretty sure there was no lasting damage, but he and Radcliffe were intent on making sure. Jamie couldn't say she wasn't glad of that.

She left the hospital and was relieved to see the officer still waiting for her. On the way back to the farm, they slowed for the tow truck and police cordon that was pulling Hassan's Audi out of the ditch.

Jamie stared at it as they passed, and then it was gone and they were hurtling along once more.

The officer wasn't impressed by the farm track, so Jamie told him he could drop her off at the turning from the road and bugger off to wherever else he was supposed to be. Hopefully somewhere he'd be of more use.

She tried to get her mind straight as she headed down towards the farm, and though she was exhausted, she was almost excited to get back to work. The killer was recreating the cases with such accuracy that she doubted it could be from the news coverage alone. So, her first calls needed to be to the people who had the files; former bosses and colleagues.

When she got down to the house, Hallberg was standing on the front step waiting for her.

'Hey,' Jamie said, lifting a hand. 'Everything alright?' She noticed Hallberg's expression – stressed was the word that came to mind – as she got close.

'Yeah,' Hallberg sighed, 'but I've got to go.'

Jamie stopped in front of her. 'Right now?' Jamie was actually sort of keen to get her thoughts on this whole thing. She'd been an excellent investigator when they'd worked together, and with no Elliot and no Hassan, Jamie was thinking she might have bounced some ideas off her.

'Yeah, like three hours ago actually,' she said with a short, sharp laugh. 'I've had a few too many annual leave days to do this and it's biting me now.' She gestured vaguely to the house behind her. 'Stuff's stacking up, cases are stalling, I've got a mountain of calls to make, and the French office want to coordinate a joint op for ... I don't even know what, because I missed the meeting.' The frustration in her voice was palpable.

'I'm sorry,' Jamie said. 'I didn't think ...'

'It's not your fault. You asked for help, I gave it. I should have said something.' She nodded, then touched Jamie's shoulder. 'But now I really have to go.'

'I understand. I just don't know what else to do, who else to call.' She watched as Hallberg stepped down from the doorway and headed for her car.

She paused and looked back. 'I don't know,' she said, 'but you'll figure it out. You always do. If you need someone to watch Alina or the house, doesn't your mother live—'

'No,' Jamie said, almost barking it.

'Alright, alright,' Hallberg replied, holding her hands up. 'Just a suggestion. This is, unfortunately, what being a mother is all about. You've got responsibilities now.'

'I'm not a mother,' Jamie said, almost too quickly.

Hallberg laughed. 'You've got a house, a dog, a teenager, and you need help managing it all. You're a mother, whether you like that word or not.' She opened the car door, taking a second to think before she spoke again. 'If it's proving too much, ask Radcliffe to give you some time away from it all until you can figure it out.'

'That's not an option,' Jamie said sharply.

Hallberg smiled. 'It's just a suggestion. Something's got to give, Jamie. And if it's not work, it's probably going to be you.' She gave a wave and climbed in, lowering the window as she pulled away. 'Give me a call, let me know how you're doing. Maybe we can grab dinner some time.'

Jamie almost laughed with incredulity. 'When?'

'Whenever you have the time. Be safe, and don't do anything stupid!' she called, trundling through the gates and up towards the road.

Silence fell across the farm, and Jamie took it all in. She was getting used to having people around, so much so that it now felt strange to be missing them all. Elliot was always buzzing around like a wasp that wouldn't take a hint, Hassan was forever brewing coffee and fussing with the dog … and now it was just Jamie and Alina. Which she should probably get used to, she thought.

Though seeing as it was a day of honest reflection, she didn't know if she was ready for it.

She let out a long breath, steadying herself, and then headed inside.

Music was playing softly from Alina's room, the door closed. Not much chance of a conversation then.

The clicking of Hati's nails on the flagstones reached her ears and she turned to see him pad into the doorway of the living room having just peeled himself off the couch.

She held her arms out. 'What about you? You happy to see me?'

He took a long look at her, and then turned away to resume his nap.

'Yeah,' Jamie said, 'that seems about right.' She turned in a slow circle in the kitchen, the only noise the ticking of the clock on the wall. 'Suppose you'd better get to work then,' she muttered to herself.

SHE FIGURED GOING CHRONOLOGICALLY WOULD HELP. FIRST up on the list was Henley Smith, her old DCI when she was working in the Met. It took about as long as she thought it would to get through to him, and when he answered he was more than surprised to hear from her.

'Jamie Johansson,' he laughed. It had been five years since she'd worked for him. 'This is a blast from the past. You still working in Stockholm? Can't say I wasn't surprised to get that call from their HR department. With you and Paul Roper leaving in such quick succession it did leave a good hole in my team.' He sounded like he'd got over it, but Jamie imagined he'd waited a few years to tell her that.

'Yeah,' she said, feeling just a little guilt. 'I'm actually back in the UK, contracting with the NCA.'

'How the heck did you ... You know what, I don't have the time to listen to what I imagine is a very long story.'

'A very long one.'

'But if you're passing through the capital, do stick your head in.'

'Will do.'

'What can I do for you in the meanwhile?'

It wasn't public knowledge yet that the JJ murders were linked, or that a serial killer was on the loose, but she didn't know whether he'd heard anything through the grapevine. 'There's a string of murders that are recreating old cases,' she said, without putting too fine a point on it. 'I'm calling around to see if there have been any security breaches, digital attacks, anything like that in the last year or so?'

There was quiet for a few seconds. 'No, nothing like that. No breaches that I'm aware of.'

'Can you double check for me? It's pretty important to this case.'

'Of course. I'll check with IT and let you know.'

'Great, I really appreciate it,' Jamie said, keen for

this not to turn into a trip down memory lane. She'd always liked Smith, but they hadn't seen eye to eye in her last year at the Met, and she'd got herself into a few scrapes. She often wondered what her life would have been like if she'd never had a call from Wiik, never returned to Sweden. Would she have gone back to London? Up there in Scotland, licking her wounds, she never had any intention of returning at all. The small, quiet life appealed to her more than she was willing to admit. Who knew, maybe it was out there waiting for her one day.

She ended the call quickly and moved on, calling Wiik.

Luckily, their relationship meant that he was slightly easier to get on the phone, but his characteristic abruptness and firm handle on everything going on at Stockholm Polis HQ reassured Jamie that no breaches had occurred. He would know.

She didn't think there was any point calling her former boss, Ohlin, in Kurrajak. She only worked one case there and the files weren't digitised. But then it occurred to her that it was that fact that made calling him completely necessary. If anyone wanted the details of that case, they would have had to go there and steal the file physically.

As such, she swallowed her pride and called. She connected pretty quickly, was promptly chewed out, laughed at, assured the files were safe in his filing cabinet, and then told to go fuck herself.

She never did like Ohlin.

And that call confirmed that he never liked her either.

Three out of three meant that the killer wasn't getting his information at the source. So how the hell he was getting the details of the cases, Jamie had no idea. Add it to the list of unanswered questions, she thought, putting her phone on the table and staring at it.

The next thing to do was work back through her former arrests to check whether everyone she'd put away was still where they were supposed to be. It would be a longer process, but not undoable. She already had most of the names in her head, and she could pass them along to Radcliffe to double check. But she had a feeling it wasn't going to be that simple, that they'd all be exactly where they were supposed to be.

And if she banked on that fact, then it meant she was still at square one.

She hung her head and laced her hands over the back of her skull, gently pulling forward to stretch her neck.

She could hear her heart throbbing gently in her ears.

She'd hoped that it would take longer to get to this point, because it meant she had just one thing left on her to do list: go to see Elliot's wife.

The last thing she wanted to do was go alone, but who knew how long it would be before Hassan was back?

Trying Elliot again seemed futile but she did it anyway. This time, it went straight to voicemail.

'Fuck,' she muttered, standing up and heading for the rack of keys next to the door. She grabbed the one for the old Toyota in the garage and hovered at the bottom of the stairs. 'Lina?' she called upstairs.

The music stopped and Jamie heard the door open. 'Yeah?'

'We're heading out, get ready.' She could leave Alina at home, but with what had happened to Hassan that morning, why take the chance?

'Where are we going?'

Jamie steeled herself to say it. 'Elliot's.'

Alina appeared at the top of the stairs in a second. 'He's home?' she asked, the seriousness in her voice striking.

'No, he's not. We're going to see his … wife.'

Alina's brow crumpled. 'Why?'

Jamie resisted the urge to shrug. 'I keep asking myself the same question.'

CHAPTER
NINETEEN

J amie didn't really think about the route, but she drove them right there. Alina was happy to throw her headphones in and zone out, which suited Jamie as she wasn't feeling especially talkative.

When they pulled onto the driveway, Elliot's car was gone, but Mila's sleek black Mercedes coupe was parked in front of the garage. Jamie had sort of hoped she'd be out. Guess there was no backing down now.

She kicked the car door open, feeling the sting of the cool afternoon air. Dusk was already closing in, and the temperature seemed to be dropping rapidly. It was a typical Welsh autumn by the looks of it - flat and grey, and desperate to be winter already.

Alina stowed her headphones and got out of the car, following Jamie up towards the front door. Jamie glanced back at the old Toyota behind her, the beaten-up exterior a stark contrast from the gleaming Mercedes in front of it.

'Why are we here again?' she asked, catching up to Jamie.

'We're asking about Elliot,' Jamie reiterated. She was certain that he had something to do with this, though she wasn't sure if it was a good thing or a bad thing. She was leaning towards the latter, as much as she hated that. Things had been good, he'd seemingly turned a corner, except for being married to some Russian—

She stopped five feet short of the door as it opened, revealing Mila. She was just as tall and beautiful as Jamie remembered her to be. Her long, silk-like hair was tied up and back, and though she had bags under her eyes and looked a little thinner than Jamie remembered, she still sideswiped her with her presence.

Mila's face dropped, as though she'd been expecting someone else.

'I thought you were ...' she said, confirming it.

Thought we were Elliot, Jamie guessed.

'I'm sorry,' she said, stepping back into the house and attempting to close the door. 'He's not here, so—'

'Wait,' Jamie said, 'that's *why* we're here.'

Mila's brow creased. 'I don't understand.' She was in a pair of jeans and a cardigan with long hems, and she wrapped them around herself to protect her from the cold, and from these unwanted visitors.

Jamie glanced around, not really wanting to do this on the driveway. 'Can we come in? We just want to talk.'

'About what?' Mila asked, standing firm in the doorway.

'About Elliot,' Jamie said, stepping closer. 'About where the hell he is.'

Mila lifted her chin, almost haughtily. 'I thought you might have a better idea than me.'

Jamie shrugged off the slight scorn she detected in her voice. 'I don't, but I want to know because he has something to do with this case.'

'What case?'

'You don't know?'

She narrowed her eyes. 'No, he doesn't talk to me about his work. He doesn't talk to me about much at all.' The scorn was definitely real now. 'He just stranded me here in this ...' she looked at the house around her, '... suburban nightmare, and then just fucking *disappeared.*' She shook her head, muttering something in Russian, and then looked back at Jamie. '*Voydite.*'

Jamie didn't know the Russian word, but judging by the fact that she made a beckoning motion with her hand and then disappeared inside, she guessed it meant come in.

She and Alina exchanged a quick glance and then stepped inside, closing the door behind them.

They followed Mila through to the kitchen, where a chair was pulled out and a cup of tea was still steaming. She must have heard the car pull up in the driveway and thought it was Elliot.

She took her place at the table, putting her hands around the tea to warm them.

The house, which had previously felt warm and full of character, a representation of the happy couple living here, now felt like someone else's entirely. Jamie stared down at Mila and realised how out of place she looked. How much like a foreign object. She'd described it like that: a suburban nightmare.

Jamie looked around briefly, saw that while everything was high quality, the furnishings were worn, well used. This wasn't a recently furnished place.

'How long have you been here?' she asked. She thought that dispensing with the formalities would be appreciated by both of them.

'Months,' Mila said with a shrug, 'Years. Who can say?' She laughed sardonically. One sharp note.

Months? Jamie arrived in Wales in August, and it was only November now. 'And Elliot bought it? Why here? Why this house?' Jamie was even more convinced now that Elliot had purchased this place fully furnished. That the life she'd mistakenly ascribed to him, to them, was all just an illusion.

She snorted, staring up at Jamie derisively. 'Isn't it obvious?'

Jamie looked down to hide her flushing cheeks. Me?

There was dissonance in her mind. 'But you two are *married*. I don't understand quite what's going on ...'

Mila took a sip of her tea and then put it down,

rotating it slightly until it pleased her. 'Well I'm glad to know it's not only me who he keeps in the dark.' She cleared her throat slightly. 'Our marriage is, what you might say, one of convenience. Didn't you ever wonder how Elliot moves freely in and out of a country where he's a wanted man? Didn't you ever wonder exactly *how* he accomplishes what he does, how he makes all of his money, how he's just ... untouchable?'

Jamie had wondered that. But so far, the most convincing thing she'd come up with was that he was a very talented magician of some kind, or was a real life wizard. 'I have,' she said instead. 'But I still don't get why you and he are—'

'It's my father. Or was, I should say. You understand, don't you? Daddy issues.'

Jamie prickled.

'He was, for lack of a better word; a real bastard. A high-ranking lieutenant in one of the major families in Russia.'

'The royal families?' Alina asked.

'No, darling,' Mila said. 'The *families*. Bratva.' The word rang with her Russian accent. 'The mafia. The bad guys.'

'That doesn't surprise me,' Jamie said, 'that he's wrapped up in that.'

'Wrapped up? That's putting it mildly. You know what he did, what his skillset was, yes? Surgery, transplants, specifically. Very sought after. He was highly valued by my father and the other families. He was neutral, not really tied to anyone specifically, but loyal to all. Very trustworthy, very highly regarded. Two years ago, he was in Russia with my father, readying himself to perform a transplant for the head of the Sokolov family, the *Old Man,* as they called him. Only they were waiting on a specific donor because the blood type was very rare. Very difficult to find.'

Jamie remembered the mother, the daughter they were looking for. That's why they'd taken them, because of their genetics. A match for this *Old Man.*

'But they found a match, a woman and her daughter were both viable donors. They couldn't risk being smuggled across the border, so the Old Man needed to go to them. In Sweden. Elliot was to go with them. Except right before it was all supposed to happen, we got word that a key member of one of the families' trafficking operations had suffered a near-fatal wound and needed to be tended to quickly.' Mila locked eyes with Jamie. 'He was stabbed in the chest. And then thrown out of a window.'

Jamie paled a little. 'Noah,' she said.

Alina looked up at her. 'Who's that?'

'A case Thorsen and I worked. We were looking for a missing family, and ended up finding a lot more.' She thought back to that place, that evil farm and the church on the island, and to what came afterwards. And to who appeared, as if from thin air.

'Yes,' Mila said, sighing, 'and you know what happened next, don't you?'

'Elliot heard who did that to Noah and came to find me, showed up in Kurrajak,' Jamie said, 'at my house.'

'And then went north with you to perform the surgery on the *Old Man* when he arrived,' Mila said, cycling her hand through the air. 'Blah blah blah, you got yourself into trouble … the families wanted you dead … Elliot promised to make that happen … but he lost his nerve, decided to cross the families instead. God knows why.'

Jamie didn't quite remember it that way, but she understood Mila's point. 'What happened then?'

'Then?' Mila took another sip. 'He fled back to Russia, with your deranged one-eyed dog. He was smart enough to kill all the witnesses to what he'd done, so no one knew what he'd done. He, of course, knew that once they found out they'd behead him, after feeding him his own testicles. So he did what any sane person would do. He cut a deal.'

'A deal?' Jamie said. 'With who?'

'Interpol, Europol, NCA … I don't quite know. But in one fell swoop he handed them the Old Man, my father, and about a hundred other members of the family.'

'Hallberg works with Interpol. She didn't say anything about that,' Jamie replied.

'I think it's probably a little above her pay grade, whoever she is,' Mila said quickly. 'You didn't think it was odd your boss Radcliffe was okay with Elliot joining your little *team*?' She chuckled to herself. 'How do you think that came about anyway? Oh, let me guess, you thought you were just that good, didn't you?' She laughed louder now. 'You don't get any of this, do you? Elliot set it all up, the whole thing. He bought his way back to the UK by handing over my father and the others, secured his freedom by selling out everyone he was supposedly loyal to. The only person he actually cared about, seemingly, was you.'

Jamie swallowed the lump in her throat. 'I don't think I quite understand. Elliot was already back in the UK eighteen months ago? More?'

'That's right.'

'So forgive me if I'm being dense—'

'You are.'

Jamie ignored that. 'But how the hell do you fit into all this?'

'Me? Well Elliot and I were … close. Friends. Lovers.' Her eyes flashed, the word dripping with disdain. For Jamie. She was hurt. Hurt by all this. Hurt by Jamie being there. 'He trusted me, told me the truth. What he wanted to do. What he needed to do. I would have been swept up in it all. During the arrests. Forced to turn evidence on my family or imprisoned, who knows? So Elliot gave me a choice. Help him put my father behind bars and go with him, or leave it up to fate.'

'And for you to go with him to the UK, to get amnesty.'

'We had to be married. Yes,' Mila curled a smile,

enjoying the discomfort that thought brought Jamie, 'and if you were wondering, we did consummate the union.'

'I wasn't,' Jamie said, hiding a grimace.

'What does ... consume ... consummate mean?' Alina asked. Her English was near fluent now, but she still didn't have a full vocabulary.

'It means that we—' Mila began before Jamie cut her off.

'Made it official,' Jamie finished for her.

'As you like,' Mila smirked. 'We didn't live here to begin with. No, we lived in the country, in Elliot's family home. A beautiful property. Just me, him, and your ... *dog.*'

Jamie didn't much like the mutt, but she didn't like Mila's dislike for him either.

'For a while we were happy. There was some animosity, as you can imagine. It's difficult to betray one's own and not harbour some guilt, some ill will to the man who forced you to do it.'

'Sounds like you had a choice,' Jamie said bitterly. 'You made it. Freedom over family. It's not the wrong choice, but don't put that on Elliot.'

'Even now you defend him.' She shook her head. 'Though it's not surprising. He's got you all twisted up.'

Jamie shifted her weight uncomfortably.

'I thought we might have finally seen the back of you and the cloud of death and chaos that follows you. You were gone. Far away. With your partner. Out of sight, out of mind. I had hope that it would stay that way. But like a bad smell, you just came back. Didn't you?'

Jamie tried to block out the burning in her throat. She was gone. Far away. She was in Greece. With Thorsen, her former partner. A man that she ... loved, in a way. That she could have stayed with. That she missed, even now. She thought they were happy. But he wasn't. He wanted to come back. And that led them to Gotland, to the Black Heart Killer case. And then to the NOD ...

As if reading her mind, Mila went on. 'And then, fate decided to fuck us once more, didn't it? And delivered you right to our doorstep. And you just had to reach out to him, didn't you? And then the next thing I know we're moving to ... wherever the fuck we are. And he's all wrapped up in you, and your drama, and this girl, and the NCA and the shit just starts all over again.'

Jamie was getting a real sense of why Mila didn't like her now. And honestly, she didn't blame her.

'He was out – for good. Done. Finished with it all. And you pulled him back in, got him all tangled up with the fucking Armenians, who are in bed with the Russian families. And now he's gone. And that's your fault.' She pointed at Jamie, her finger quivering with rage.

'You think this is recompense,' Jamie said. 'You think the Russians got to him? Know what he did?'

'You tell me,' Mila spat. 'You're the fucking detective.'

She got up, picking up her mug almost violently, and swung around to the sink, putting it in with such force that a loud crack of breaking porcelain cut the silence in the kitchen.

Jamie felt Alina's fingers lace through hers and squeeze as they watched her brace herself on the counter, visibly shaking. As much as Mila hated Elliot for what he'd done, and hated him for going back to Jamie, and hated Jamie for doing it to him, to them ... she cared. She loved him. And if he was gone ... she was alone here. In a strange land, with nothing, and no one.

But at least now Jamie had a lead. The Russians. They wanted Elliot dead, and they also wanted Jamie dead too. It made sense. Elliot had been rattled when he'd seen the photographs. When he'd witnessed what they were doing. They were announcing their intentions, maybe even to draw him out of hiding. To bring him to them.

Had he gone?

And was that what the kills meant? Were they working up to the kill that set all this in motion? The Ice Queen? Was that where Jamie would meet her end, and how?

She felt nauseous.

'Do you have any idea where he would have gone? He left so quickly, but didn't say where he was going ...'

'No.'

'Anything you remember at all ... Did he say something? Has he ever mentioned any contacts, or—'

'No!' Mila whirled around, fire in her eyes. 'No, he didn't say a fucking word! He came home a few days ago, was quiet. Quieter than I've ever known him. Like he was spooked. And he said he had to go away for a day or two, that he'd be back. And that was it. Out of the door and gone.' She snapped her fingers for effect. 'That's the last I saw of him. Not even a fucking goodbye. Just ... I have to go. Because of you.'

Jamie stared right at Mila, her cheeks red, her eyes shining.

'I'm sorry,' she said, feeling like it was the only true thing she could say.

'I think it's time you left.'

Was there anything to say? Anything she could say? Could she leave Mila here? Was she safe? 'What will you do now?'

'I don't know,' Mila said, holding back tears. 'I don't know.' She turned and walked towards the fridge slowly, pulling a business card from under a magnet and staring at it. She approached Jamie slowly, holding it in her hands.

Jamie looked down at it. It just said the word 'Plumber' and had a phone number on it.

'What's that?'

'He said if I was ever in trouble, to call this number. That she could help. Get me a passport, tickets, help me get away. Get me a new identity, a new life.'

Jamie stared at the number. 'Nyx,' she muttered. The mysterious Nyx, Elliot's computer-genius-hacker-extraordinaire. The one who'd helped with the last case. Jamie didn't have her number. Had no way to contact her. The thought had crossed her mind, but without Elliot there to reach out, she had no chance of finding her. But now … she could. She could reach out, ask where Elliot was. She must be tracking him, right? She'd know where he was. And if she could find Elliot, she could find whoever was behind this. And finish it before any more lives were claimed.

Jamie reached out for the paper but Mila pulled it away from her.

'I need that number,' Jamie said.

'No. He said I can only call it once.' She held it down at her side, out of Jamie's reach.

She could take it from her, Jamie thought. Just take the number. But then sense prevailed. She wasn't going to beat this woman to get what she wanted. She wasn't about to physically overpower a woman who'd just lost her husband, who'd been through so much to get here. Who'd given everything and now had nothing.

Alina was at Jamie's side, looking up at her, phone in her hands, waiting for whatever came next. She lowered it slowly, moving to the side, giving them space.

Mila and Jamie stared at each other.

'You can't have it,' Mila said. 'He gave it to me. And I might need it.'

Jamie settled herself. 'I understand.' She let out a

slow breath, the guilt of it all turning her sick. 'And I really am sorry.'

'You can keep your apology,' she said. 'What's done is done. Just leave my house and don't come back.'

Jamie opened her mouth to speak, but there was nothing else to say.

She nodded slowly, and then turned and headed for the front door.

Alina lingered for a second, and then followed her.

Whether Mila managed to hold back her tears, Jamie didn't know. But she had her own battle going on as she exited the house and stepped down onto the driveway, the autumn wind chilling her to the bone.

'Wait,' Alina called as the door snapped shut behind her.

'Come on,' Jamie said, already racking her brain for a way to contact Nyx, replaying every conversation they had, every interaction, every time they contacted her. She came up with nothing.

'Wait!' Alina called again, grabbing Jamie's hand.

'We don't have time to wait, we have to go and—' She stopped speaking and stared at what was on Alina's phone.

She was holding it up in front of Jamie's face, and though it was fuzzy and upside down, it was clear what was on there. A photograph of the paper in Mila's hand.

'I got it at the end,' Alina said, lowering her voice a little. 'It's blurry, but we can make it out, right?'

Jamie took the phone to steady it and zoomed in, feeling a grin spread across her face.

'You sneaky thing,' she muttered, looking at Alina.

'Was that bad?'

'Yes,' she said, pulling her into a tight hug, 'but I'm so glad you did it.' She rested her chin on Alina's head and closed her eyes. 'Because now we might have a chance.

CHAPTER
TWENTY

Jamie held on to the number until they got back to the farm.

She didn't expect Hassan to be there, but by the time they walked into the living room, he was lying on the sofa with an ice pack on his head. Jamie couldn't imagine how he must have been feeling.

He opened one eye as they walked in. 'Where did you two get off to? Anywhere nice?'

'Hardly,' Alina said, running over and kneeling down beside him. She pulled the ice pack away to inspect the damage.

Jamie figured that he'd reached out to Hallberg, or someone had, to tell her that he wouldn't be coming home right away. Or at least that's what she thought, judging by the way Alina wasn't surprised in the slightest that he was all banged up. Fascinated was the word Jamie would have used, the way she was poking and prodding at his face.

He hissed and batted her away. 'So where did you go?'

'To see Mila,' Jamie said, hovering by the door to the kitchen.

'Did she have any idea where Elliot was?' he asked, closing his eyes once more. Even with a concussion, he was still sharp.

'Yes and no,' Jamie said, hesitating a little bit.

'She does *not* like Jamie,' Alina said, laughing as she sank backwards onto her hip. 'She loves Elliot, but he loves Jamie. So she's a bit pissed off.'

Jamie turned her head to stop them from seeing her flush. Teenagers, they didn't half talk plainly.

Hassan chuckled. 'Well, that makes sense. But I'm guessing he didn't pack a bag to leave her?'

'No, it was the Russian mafia,' Alina said.

'The what?' Hassan sat up, groaning in pain.

'We don't know that,' Jamie reminded her. She tried to say it finitely, but she couldn't quite muster it. 'She said that Elliot double-crossed them and sold them out to buy his way back into the country.'

Hassan muttered, touching his stitched forehead. 'Why am I not surprised? Maybe they caught up to him so he did a runner.'

'I don't think so. But honestly, we have no idea if that's what has happened. Elliot ran out of here when he saw the case files, and Mila said that he told her that he'd be back in a day or two. And if they did catch up to him, they'd also come after her. So, if he was going to disappear, he'd have taken her with him. And me.'

'The three of you?' Hassan eyed Jamie. 'That sounds like fun.'

'Ha, ha,' she said sarcastically. 'He sold out the Russians to Interpol to save his own skin, and mine. It's a long story – you ever read *The Most Dangerous Game?*'

'Can't say I have.'

'Well, Google it.' Jamie folded her arms. 'If the Russians had caught on and come for Elliot, I doubt they'd go to all the trouble of murdering those women. They'd have come in the night and slit our throats while we slept.'

'Jamie,' Hassan warned her, glancing at Alina.

She sighed a little.

Alina looked at both of them. 'Don't stop on my account. That sounds pretty standard for the Russian mafia. Mila said that they'd castrate him, feed him his balls, and then chop his head off.'

'I can't say he doesn't deserve it,' Hassan said. 'Sounds like Karma.'

'Whether he does or not, we still need to find him and figure out who's behind all this – the Russians, or someone else.'

'And how exactly do we do that?' he asked, lying back and putting the ice pack on his forehead once more.

'Nyx,' she said.

'Nyx? Elliot's the only one who knows how to contact her.'

'Not quite. He gave Mila a number as a last resort. If something went wrong, if the Russians did show up, she was supposed to call and Nyx would set her up with a new identity, passport, the works. Help her get out of the country.'

'And she just *gave* you that number?'

'Well ...'

'You didn't kick her, did you?' he asked.

Jamie couldn't tell if he was joking or not. 'No, I didn't. Alina stole it.'

'I did not!' she protested. 'I took a photo while the two of them were arguing.'

'Well, that's better than what I was imagining. Just about.' With another groan he got to his feet, wobbling a little. 'Let me make some coffee first, and then we'll call her.'

'You think that's a good idea with a concussion?' Jamie asked.

Hassan gave her a weak grin as he headed for the kitchen. 'Probably not, but I need a cup after this morning.' He stopped and put his hand on her shoulder. 'And it's definitely better than drinking a beer with one, right?'

WHEN THE COFFEE WAS BREWED, THEY ALL SAT around the kitchen table. Once again Alina was under strict instructions not to say a word. And Hassan didn't seem much in the talkative mood. Night had fallen like it usually did in November in Wales: in the middle of the afternoon, seemingly.

There was no more time to waste, and nothing to be gained from waiting, so Jamie keyed in the number from Alina's picture, hit call, put her phone on speaker, and then laid it on the table.

It crackled for a few seconds, and then made one short beep.

Jamie glanced at Hassan and Alina, checking to see if they had any clearer idea of whether they were connected or not.

Alina seemed to think so, and shooed Jamie onwards with her hands.

'Hello?' Jamie asked into the ether.

There was silence for a moment. And then a familiar voice said, 'Jamie, why do you have this number?'

Reading from the tone, Jamie jumped in quickly. 'Don't hang up, please, Nyx,' she said. 'We need your help.'

She made a frustrated hum. 'I didn't give you a way to contact me last time because I don't work for you. And I *certainly* don't work for the government. I'm going now—'

'It's Elliot!' Jamie almost shouted. 'He's in trouble. He needs your help.'

'If there's anyone I've ever met who's not in trouble

and doesn't need anyone's help, it's Elliot.' She practically scoffed it. 'Goodbye, Jamie.'

'You're wrong,' Jamie said, a coldness in her voice now. 'Something's wrong. And if you hang up, I don't think we'll ever find him.'

There was another pause, then a sigh. 'For fuck's sake,' she muttered under her breath. 'Okay, what happened?'

'You know this case we're working?'

'No …' she said tiredly, as though it were obvious she wasn't keeping tabs on Jamie.

She supposed that Nyx wasn't, now that Elliot was in direct contact with her.

'Should I?' she asked.

'There's a serial killer murdering women with the initials J-J, women who are blonde, blue-eyed, and they are being killed in ways mimicking my old cases.'

'Sounds like you've got an admirer.'

Jamie bristled a little. 'Well, once Elliot got a look at the files, he said he had to go somewhere, and then just disappeared. Mila said he packed a bag, said he'd be back in a day or two, and then just left. She hasn't heard from him, he's not picking up, not answering texts.'

'You know you work for the NCA, don't you? You have *resources* at your disposal. Phone tracking, NPR and car tracking, all that sort of thing?'

'And I'm sure you probably made it so that Elliot's phone *can't* be tracked.'

She hummed again. 'Yeah, I might have done that.'

'And you know as well as I do that Elliot's slippery as hell. If he didn't want us knowing where he went, then we wouldn't have a hope in hell of finding him. Which means that you're our only chance. And I wouldn't be asking unless I was genuinely worried something was wrong.'

'I actually believe that,' Nyx said. She let out another long sigh. 'Alright, I'll look into it and if I find anything amiss, I'll get back to you.'

'How do I contact you?' Jamie asked.

She laughed now. 'You don't.'

And then she hung up.

CHAPTER
TWENTY-ONE

'We can't just sit on our hands.'

Hassan was right. Even after a blow to the head he seemed to be thinking more clearly than Jamie. They needed to get back to the case. Needed to refocus. There was nothing they could do about, or for, Elliot until Nyx called them back.

Radcliffe would be checking in soon enough and they needed something to show for themselves. Or better yet, they needed to be the ones calling him with a lead before he called them.

'What's next?' Hassan said, as Jamie paced back and forth in the living room. He was on the couch with Alina and Hati next to him, like three judges on the world's worst talent show.

And Jamie didn't need to just pull a rabbit out of a hat, she felt like she needed to lay a damned golden egg here.

'What kill is next? In your history,' Hassan asked.

Jamie slowed, thinking back. After Stockholm it was the Norwegian Sea. 'Stabbed to death and then hanged from a crane,' she said. 'On an oil rig.'

'An oil rig?'

Jamie sighed. 'Yeah, not somewhere I want to revisit. Physically or mentally.'

'Right, okay, well that helps us.'

'I don't know any oil rigs around here,' she said, trying not to sound too glib.

'No, well the last kill was off the side of the A470, not in Sweden, so I don't think geography is really his biggest concern.'

'But he did use the right wood – silver birch. So, place no, but *how,* yes.' Jamie pinched the bridge of her nose. 'Either way, I think that message was clear, and the one he sent to you this morning. He knows where we are. *Exactly* where we are. And he wants us to know he can get at us, any time.'

'He's taunting us,' Hassan answered, 'which is why I'm sleeping with a gun on my bedside table.'

'Me too,' Alina said defiantly.

'No, you're not,' Jamie replied. 'I'm right next door. If anyone comes in here, *I'll* be the one to shoot them.' She put her hand on her chest.

'Because you need to, or you want to?' Hassan pressed her.

'Does it matter either way?'

He stuck out his bottom lip and shrugged. 'Maybe I want a piece.' He gestured to his bruised face.

'Why don't we all shoot him?' Alina suggested. 'Or maybe we could dig a spiked pit, or have an axe that swings down from the ceiling when he stands on a trick step. Thwack.' She mimicked an axe hitting her in the sternum.

'Don't joke about this,' Jamie warned her.

'Who's joking?'

'I think we're getting off track here,' Hassan mercifully suggested. 'Let's get back to offense, huh? Rather than waiting for him to come to us, why don't we try and get to him.'

'And how do you propose we do that exactly?'

'We know his MO. We know his victim type – and it's pretty specific. We have a fair chance of guessing that he's going to kill again soon, and nearby. We also know how he's going to do it, and we could make a guess as to the type of locale. There's probably not that many places that fit the description. Which I think puts us in a much better position than most investigations, don't you?'

Jamie drew a slow breath. 'I guess it does, yeah.'

'Okay, so let's get this mother ...' He trailed off, looking at Alina.

'Fucker,' she finished for him. 'God, how hard did he hit you?'

'I was trying not to swear in front of you.' He

glanced at Jamie. 'You're already picking up enough bad habits as it is.'

'What's that supposed to mean?' both Jamie and Alina asked in unison, brows creasing, arms folding at the same time like they'd rehearsed it.

Jamie unfolded hers promptly. 'I'll call Radcliffe, fill him in. Be nice to actually feel like we're *doing* something, and not just waiting for the other shoe to drop.'

WHEN JAMIE GOT OFF THE PHONE, SHE FELT A little better. 'It'll be local,' she'd told him. 'Within fifty miles, probably twenty-five. It's going to be a woman, middle-aged, blonde-haired, blue-eyed—'

'With the initials J-J?' Radcliffe asked, a little on edge himself it seemed.

'Near a body of water, we think. The original kill he'll be recreating was a body strung-up from a crane.'

'There's not many of those around,' Radcliffe muttered. 'I'll speak to Cardiff and Newport police, get foot patrol doubled around matching areas.'

'And have them keep an ear to the ground for any missing persons, especially for anyone with matching initials.'

'Alright, I'll relay it. I'll call you if I get something. How's Hassan doing?'

'Better. I think he's going to recover quickly, and the hospital said that his concussion is mild. Something about him having an unusually thick skull.'

He harrumphed, a small sign of amusement. 'And how are *you* doing?'

Jamie took a second before answering. 'Good. Better.'

'Mm, Dumont said as much. You think you're ready to get back out there if it comes to it?'

'I am.'

'Good. Hassan has your weapon. If he hasn't given it to you already—'

'He hasn't.'

'Of course he hasn't,' Radcliffe said, disbelieving her.

Jamie didn't feel like arguing. 'I'll wait for your call,' she said instead, though she hoped it wouldn't come for days. Maybe even weeks.

Unfortunately, she wasn't that lucky.

It wasn't even midnight when the phone rang.

CHAPTER
TWENTY-TWO

J amie sat bolt upright in bed when her phone rang.

She reached for it on reflex and picked it up without even opening her eyes. 'Johansson,' she said groggily, her voice more of a grunt than anything else.

'Hi,' a voice said, her tone apologetic, 'this is Sergeant Siobhan Evans from South Wales Police. Sorry to wake you, but I was told by my senior officer to call this number if we had a report of any missing—'

'Yeah, yeah,' Jamie said hurriedly, swinging her legs off the bed and squeezing her eyeballs with the heel of her hands. 'What do you have?'

'There was a Jillian Jones reported missing earlier this evening. Her husband said she never came home from work, and when he went over there he found her car parked outside her office with her phone inside it.'

Jamie was immediately awake. The exact same circumstances as Julie Johns, victim number one.

'We've just had a report of a potential sighting of her. Someone called it in, saying she was being led unwillingly along the front towards the Cardiff Docks by an unknown man wearing a mask. We're dispatching units now—'

'No!' Jamie yelled, springing to her feet. 'Don't. Tell them not to approach them. We're on the way.'

'But—'

'If this is who we think it is, he's extremely dangerous, and extremely effective. Don't risk the lives of your officers or anyone else. Can I get you back on this number?'

'Yes,' she said, almost hesitantly.

'Send me the location of the sighting, and I'll call you when we're close.'

'Understood ...' she said slowly. How much she'd been told about who she was calling, Jamie didn't know, but she didn't argue and Jamie was glad about that.

There was thudding in the next room, Hassan getting out of bed and lumbering about. Jamie hadn't made any attempt to quieten her voice.

She put the phone down and flicked on the bedside lamp, squinting in the sudden illumination. She reached for her jeans on the back of the chair in the corner of the room and hopped around trying to put them on.

She could hear Hassan through the wall, swearing and grunting trying to do the same.

Less than thirty seconds later, Jamie exited the bedroom and saw Hassan's door open almost immediately. He tugged the hem of his shirt down into place and locked eyes with her, ready to go, despite his face looking even worse than it had that afternoon.

'You good?' she asked.

He gave a solid nod.

'You got my gun? Radcliffe said you did.'

His face dropped. 'Shit, it's in the boot of the car. And that bastard took mine too when he ran me off. Fuck!'

Alina's door opened and she appeared in the gap groggily, halfway through a yawn. 'Glock 17 behind the Cheerios box,' she said, 'and here's your 229 Compact.' She held it out to Jamie by the grip.

'I thought I told you ...' Jamie trailed off, grabbing the gun. 'Never mind.'

'Is this a *you guys* thing, or an *all of us* thing?' she asked, making a circle in the air with her index finger.

Jamie looked at Hassan.

'Safer if she stays,' he admitted.

'On her own?'

He shrugged.

'S'kay,' Alina said, yawning again and walking past Jamie down the stairs. She reached around the doorway into the kitchen and pulled the shotgun off the hook there, trundling back up the stairs with it. 'I'll be safe.

Anyone comes close, Hati'll let me know, and then I'll put a big hole in them as they come through the door.'

Hati lifted his head off Alina's bed at the sound of it.

'You've never even fired one before,' Jamie protested.

She shrugged. 'Point, squeeze, hold on tight. Pretty self-explanatory, right?'

Hassan looked at his watch. 'We don't have time for this. Bring her or let her get back to bed, we have to go.'

Jamie huffed frustratedly and grabbed Alina's arm as she reached her door, leaning in and kissing her head. 'Anything happens, you call, right?'

'Right,' she said, waving her hand over her shoulder. 'Go catch some bad guys, I'm going back to bed.'

Without waiting for an answer, she closed the door behind her and Jamie and Hassan were alone.

She looked at him and he checked his watch again. 'Yeah, yeah,' she said, 'we're going.'

A minute later they were in the Toyota and ripping south. It was late, the roads empty, so they could at least pick up some speed. Jamie didn't trust Hassan's concussion, so she drove. As fast as the old vehicle would let them, its engine whining, the thick tyres more at home over loose mud and country fields than tearing along tarmac at ninety miles an hour.

Jamie called Sergeant Evans from the car and was updated on the situation. The suspect had entered the docks, and a pair of uniformed officers were hanging back and observing. Jamie and Hassan were in the city in just over forty minutes, and at the location that the sergeant had sent in less than fifty.

They headed down into the docks – no longer a working shipyard, but a bustling and busy social hub filled with bars and restaurants, shops ... Hell, the Senedd was here. Jamie followed the road, knowing something didn't feel right, looping around Roath Basin and skirting the Queen Alexandra Dock until they reached Alexandra Head, a sprawling outdoor events venue.

The suspect had entered on foot through Cardiff Bay and headed all the way down here. Why? There's no way he wouldn't have been seen. She didn't have much time to think about it before they came upon the marked police car waiting for them.

Jamie pulled in behind it, glad to see its lights weren't flashing, and killed the engine.

Her hands were vibrating, partially from the feedback through the steering wheel as they drove, but more so from the adrenaline coursing through her. They were within striking distance of their killer, and if they moved fast they might not just catch him in the act, but still save Jillian Jones, too.

The two uniformed officers exited their car and walked to meet Jamie and Hassan, the sloshing of water in the bay echoing through the darkness.

The unis gave nods of acknowledgement, knowing who they were expecting.

'Suspect crossed the Locks Road bridge towards the

energy park about fifteen minutes ago,' one of them said, holding on to his vest with both hands at the collar.

Fifteen minutes. Hopefully they weren't too late. It'd been a long walk for the killer and they'd made good time in the car.

Jamie stared into the night, towards the big, cylindrical structures lit up by yellow lamps, cutting them out against the darkness.

Steam drifted through the air, the low hum of electricity ringing over the water.

Her eyes combed the steelwork, the metal bars and trusses around the park. The pipework and the catwalks ... all places you could easily hang a body.

'We need to go,' she said aloud.

Hassan unholstered his pistol.

The two officers looked at each other. 'You want us to follow you?' the second officer said.

'Hang back, call an ambulance. If we're not fast enough, we'll need one,' Jamie said gravely.

The officers both let out a silent sigh of relief - the guns, the situation daunting to anyone. It was understandable. But right now, Jamie didn't have time to think about that, to be scared.

A woman's life hung in the balance, and a killer who'd already gone on too long, claimed too many, was theirs for the taking.

CHAPTER
TWENTY-THREE

Jamie and Hassan pushed onwards, weapons drawn.

They crossed the water and came face to face with the energy park, a tall chain-link fence running around its perimeter.

Right ahead of them, in the pool of light beneath a streetlight, a hole was cut in the fence. Gaping and obvious.

They both stared at it.

There was definitely nothing about this that felt right.

'What, no *enter here* sign?' Hassan muttered, squinting in the gloom and checking their flanks.

'It's as good as, right?' Jamie replied.

'I don't think it's really a good idea going in there, do you?'

Jamie sighed. 'I don't think we really have another choice. If the killer doesn't know we're this close, maybe we'll get the drop on him.'

'On you then,' Hassan said, touching her shoulder.

He usually led the way, the more experienced tactical officer by far, but Jamie knew he wasn't quite firing on all cylinders with his concussion, mild as it may be.

Jamie pressed forward, hands clasped around the grip of her pistol, and stepped through the opening in the fence.

The light seemed to fade all at once and they were in darkness as they crept between two huge steel tanks, heading deeper into the energy park.

Jamie slowed, scanning the open area ahead. Access roads looped around, criss-crossing the park, and in the distance she could see a few stacks of shipping containers, a crane hanging over them.

She looked down, surveying the floor. She was by no means a tracker, but it was clear someone had been through here, the stones on the ground scuffed and kicked, an obvious trail left for whoever was due to discover the body come first light, she suspected.

And it led straight towards the crane.

Jamie stepped down off a small curb and onto flat tarmac then paused, looking around, listening. There was no movement, no sound except for the gentle off-gassing of steam, and the hum and whirr of the machinery around them.

'This way,' she said, heading onwards. She was distinctly aware that each second wasted was one that Jillian Jones didn't have. But that each hasty step could put them further into what might just be a trap.

And yet they had no choice.

Jamie gave a little mental *fuck it* and picked up her pace, easing into a stealthy jog.

The shipping containers rushed out at her and she came to a halt, steadying her breathing.

Hassan formed up behind her, both of them sticking to the shadow afforded by the hulking steel box. This seemed to be some sort of storage area to the side of the energy park, likely where they took receipt of machinery, parts, that kind of thing. Yellow lines designating where containers should go criss-crossed the floor, and as if to mark the trail of breadcrumbs, a scarf was strewn on the ground, leading around this set of containers and into the small amphitheatre they formed.

What awaited Jamie and Hassan, she couldn't guess. Something brutal, something twisted. They couldn't hear crying or sobbing. Was it too late? Or had he simply given Jillian Jones something to make her a little more pliable?

Jamie lowered her head and Hassan leaned in.

'We head out fast, no warning. You have a shot, you take it. Don't give him a chance to run, or harm Jones. I want him put down.'

Hassan gave a firm nod.

'Good.' Jamie let out a long, steadying breath, and then broke from cover, sweeping into the glare of the floodlights overlooking the loading area.

She screwed up her eyes against the light, willing them to adjust, looking for something to home in on, *someone* to home in on.

But there was only one figure in the space.

Jillian Jones was alone, sitting down in the middle of the loading area, her legs splayed in front of her, doubled forward with her hands tied behind her back. Jamie could see the gag in her mouth, her shoulders rising and falling softly as she breathed.

She was alive. Jesus Christ, she was still alive! It wasn't too late.

She lowered her weapon, looking around. No sign of anyone else, of the killer. He must have heard them and got spooked, or maybe he'd gone off to prepare something else, the next steps in his diabolical plan.

'Jillian?' Jamie called out, keeping her voice soft. 'Jillian Jones?'

The woman stopped breathing for a second, and then lifted her head.

She had blonde hair, blue eyes. Her fringe was tousled, glued to her face through the tears, her make-up spread down her cheeks in dark lines.

'It's okay,' Jamie said, her voice catching in her throat. 'We're here to help you. We're the police.' She stretched out a hand to show she meant no harm.

Jillian Jones stared back at Jamie, like she was seeing a ghost. They could have been sisters, twins even.

Jillian began mumbling something through the gag.

'I can't understand,' Jamie said, edging forward, 'but it's okay, I'm just going to come over there and untie you, alright?'

Jillian started saying something else, her long coat pooled around her awkwardly.

'Don't try to talk,' Jamie said. 'You're safe now.'

Jillian began shaking her head, slowly at first, then more vigorously as Jamie began to approach with more speed. They couldn't waste more time here.

Her voice grew through the gag, stifled but urgent.

'Jamie,' Hassan said, looking around, his tone telling her he didn't like this.

She didn't either. But she couldn't wait. Screw it. She needed to get Jillian free now, before the killer came back.

She ran in.

Jillian screamed.

Hassan yelled. 'Jamie!'

But it was too late.

She was less than three feet from Jillian when the rope snapped taut.

It was laying behind her, trailing on the floor and snaking up into the darkness above her.

Jamie didn't even see it. Not until it was too late.

A shadow flashed above them, a big shape disappearing from atop the containers, just an afterimage in Jamie's peripheral vision as Jillian Jones was torn from the ground by her neck and hoisted violently into the air ten feet up.

Jamie's fingers grazed the toes of Jillian's boots and snapped shut a moment too late.

Jones flew upwards and swung away from Jamie, a blood-curdling crack ringing in the air.

Her hands and legs flailed and she swung by the neck in circles.

Jamie swore and stumbled under her, staring up, shielding her eyes from the floodlights.

Hassan was calling her name, but Jamie could only hear the roaring of blood in her ears and the squeak of the rope as Jillian Jones swung around.

She lifted her weapon and steadied it, aiming for the line.

She fired.

Once, twice, three times.

Every bullet missed, flying wild into the air, into the night, sailing out over the ocean.

'Fuck!' she yelled, backing up, looking for an answer, a way to get her down before she strangled to death.

The rope above her was attached to a steel cable, looped over the arm of the crane. Even if she could hit the stationary section of the cable from here, which was a hell of an ask, and in the dark too, the bullet would never cut the metal. No, she'd been strung up, and she could be let down the same way.

Jamie took off, running under Jones once more, looking at where the cable disappeared to – over the container and out of sight.

She hooked left, aiming for the gap between the containers at the back and side. Twelve inches wide, no more.

Her gun over her head, she leapt into the space, shimmying and forcing her way along, the metal edges digging into her stomach, her back. She ignored the pain, squeezing forward painfully, not thinking about anything except the sound Jones made when she left the ground. The gurgled grunt, the sharp inhale of air. A snapshot of her bulging eyes reared itself in Jamie's head, the moment where she grazed her boots with her fingers replaying over and over.

And then Jamie's fingers hit the corner and she gripped hard, ripping herself free of the metal and into open space.

Behind the containers the ground fell away, scrubby and open to the back fence.

But there, on the floor, a steel anchor loop mounted into a concrete plinth. And around it, fastened to a tow hook, was the line, shooting into the air and over the container.

How did it get like this? Jamie followed the line with her eyes. Had the killer been up there? Waiting for them, line in hand? As Jamie fell to her knees and tried to unhook Jillian Jones, the vision formed itself in her mind. How the killer had waited until Jamie had rushed in, and then jumped the top of the containers, his weight ripping Jones free of the earth.

That sick fuck!

Jamie's hands screamed with pain as she pulled at the hook as hard as she could. But it wouldn't budge, the weight of Jones on the other end too much.

She had to think fast, change tactic, create slack in the line.

She switched her position and crouched over the anchor instead, bracing her heels on the concrete. She took the line in one hand and pulled upwards as hard as she could. Her teeth threatened to crack she was gritting them so hard, her muscles straining and popping as she heaved at the line.

It moved an inch, then another.

She let out a low, guttural cry, her other hand moving to the hook, readying to release it. She'd only get one shot. She wasn't strong enough to do it again. The instant she released the slack in the line it would go tight again. She'd have a fraction of a second to pull the hook out before that happened.

She held her breath, put as much force on the line as she could, and then let go.

She exploded upwards, the hook flying free and throwing her off her feet.

It was torn from her grasp so fast it ripped across the skin on her hand before she landed square on her back.

The impact knocked all the wind from her lungs and she fought to find her breath, rolling onto her side, distinctly aware then that she might not be alone. That she'd been seconds behind the killer, and he could be right there.

She rolled to her knees, still raking in shallow, difficult breaths, and looked out into the darkness.

At first, she didn't see it, but then the figure of a man assembled itself from the shadows.

He was maybe twenty, thirty metres away, no more. Formless in the dark, just watching. Just watching Jamie try to undo what he'd done.

With curiosity? She couldn't say. But why didn't he come for her? Why didn't he just try and finish this.

He was just fucking standing there!

She looked down, looked for her gun. Where was it? She'd dropped it when she grabbed the cable, and now … there! She snatched it up, her bloodied hand slick on the metal. She couldn't even feel the gash in her skin.

But by the time she levelled it, the shape was gone, the killer gone. Melted away into the night once more.

She let out a vicious howl, cursing him, wishing him dead.

But it achieved nothing, just rang dully across the docks and washed away on the breeze.

Her mind came back to her. Jillian. Jillian Jones. Had she done it? Had she saved her?

She forced herself to her feet and loped back towards the corner of the containers, taking the long way round, too weak to squeeze through the gap once more.

She reached the corner, panting hard, still winded, and moved around it, resting her shoulder on the metal, practically staggering by the time she got to the loading bay, her heart still pounding.

Hassan was there, on his knees, Jillian Jones in his arms. Jamie got closer, saw he was cradling her head. But he wasn't saying anything. And neither was she. Was he supporting her spine? Was she injured? Was she ... alive?

The final question came too late.

Jamie came to a halt, her knees almost buckling under her. Jillian Jones' lifeless eyes stared right through Hassan. Her chest wasn't rising or falling.

'Her neck broke,' Hassan said, his voice quiet and devoid of emotion. 'The second she left the ground. We never had a chance.'

Jamie sank to the floor and keeled sideways, her bloodied hand staining the tarmac.

'It's what he wanted,' he said. 'He wanted us to come. To be here. To see this. To see her die. Like that.'

'I saw him ...' Jamie said, her eyes moving in and out of focus. 'I saw him, out there in the dark.'

Hassan just looked at her.

'He was watching. Watching us. Watching me. It's all just a big fucking game to him ...'

Hassan pulled Jillian Jones' limp body tighter to him. 'If it's a game, he's winning,' he said tiredly, 'and I

don't know how much longer I can keep losing, Jamie.'
He looked at her, waited for her to look at him. 'How do
we stop this? It has to stop.'

'I know.'

'But how?'

She just shook her head.

Sometimes there was just nothing to say.

CHAPTER
TWENTY-FOUR

The cavalry arrived quickly. A sea of flashing lights. Ambulances, marked cars, vans. Sniffer dogs patrolled once more, evidence markers were laid around, camera flashes lit up the energy park.

Jamie and Hassan were led away, their statements taken. Jamie's hand was bandaged and bound, and then before they knew it they were back on the road, driving numbly north towards home.

They drove in silence, the weight of another life weighing on their shoulders. Even going on the offensive like that, of trying to think one step ahead, they only seemed to prove they were capable of doing exactly what this killer thought.

Jamie was depleted. Utterly. She didn't know which way to turn or what to do next. And she felt like any direction she stepped in would only cost someone else their life. All she could do was wait. Wait and hope that

Nyx came back with something. Something tangible, something useful.

It all came down to Elliot.

Jamie felt that if she could find him, everything would just come into focus, that she'd finally understand what this was all about. Why her? Why was this killer targeting her? Was it the Russians? The Armenians? Some hired gun, or just some sadistic fuck who wanted her to suffer through all her trauma over and over again?

When her phone rang, she physically jolted in the seat.

Hassan reached down to the cupholder where it was sitting and lifted it without answering.

'Radcliffe,' he said.

Jamie swallowed.

'He'll keep calling.'

She nodded and Hassan answered the call.

There was silence on the line. Jamie didn't know what to say.

After a second, Radcliffe sighed. 'Fucking hell ...' he muttered. 'This has to stop.'

Neither of them said anything.

'There's a flood coming, a media explosion ... This is too many now. Five bodies. The dots are connected, and we're about to be in big trouble.' He paused to collect his thoughts, his voice tired. Hell, they were all tired. It was the early hours of the morning now, closer to dawn than midnight. 'Are you ready to be famous,

Jamie? I think when this story hits, your face is going to be everywhere. So if you don't want that, I think you'd better come up with a way to mop this up quickly.'

Jamie kept driving.

'No?' He sighed. 'Didn't think so. Get some rest, I'll touch base when the dust settles.'

He hung up without another word and they drove on in silence.

DAWN CAME AND WENT AND THE MORNING dragged on without Jamie getting out of bed. The sun climbed higher, streaming through the curtains and blinding her. She just rolled over and pulled the covers over her head.

She wasn't sleeping and wouldn't sleep all day, but she just didn't feel like getting up. You're tired, she told herself, you need to rest. But she knew that was bullshit. She just couldn't face what was outside her door. She could hear the others out there - Alina, Hati, Hassan, moving around, fixing their breakfast. And mercifully they left her to it.

But at a little after midday, her name echoed through the house.

'Jamie!' It was Alina calling. 'Jamie!' Her name increased in volume, the tone more desperate.

And despite the fatigue, she practically hurdled from the bed and tore the door open.

Alina was at the bottom of the stairs, staring up at her.

'What's wrong?' Jamie asked, reading her upset expression.

'It's Nasir,' she said, pointing out of the front door.

Jamie hammered down the stairs in her jogging bottoms and an oversized hoodie and dashed straight out of the front door without grabbing her shoes. The cold flagstones of the front step stung the soles of her bare feet, but she didn't care.

'What are you doing?' she called, watching as Hassan loaded a duffle bag into the boot of a taxi and closed it without even turning around.

'I have to go,' he said quickly, heading for the passenger door.

'Wait,' Jamie said, stepping down onto the chipped stones, ignoring the pain as they dug into her heels. 'Just wait, what's going on?'

He stopped at the open door and looked back. 'Another body showed up,' he said, bordering on frantic. 'Dumped on the street in broad daylight.'

'Another woman?' Jamie almost croaked. 'Another ...'

'No,' he said, shaking his head. 'A woman named Sadaf Hameed.'

Jamie blinked, not understanding. 'Who's that?'

He could only shrug. 'I don't know.'

'So why are you—'

'Because my wife's name is Sumrah. Sumrah

Hassan. S-H. And that body was dumped on the street in front of our first house. It's a threat. A threat against me, my family.'

Jamie's blood pulsed heavily in her temples.

'I have to go,' he said again.

'You can't,' Jamie said, her voice almost squeaking out of her throat. 'That's what he wants,' she added quickly. 'This is to split us up, to pull you away, to—'

'It's my family, Jamie. My wife, my kids—'

'But you're separated, and—'

'It's my family!' he shouted.

'We can get them into protective custody, we could—'

'I'm not having this conversation, Jamie,' he said, his voice hard. 'I'm going.'

'Don't leave,' she practically pleaded. 'He's doing this to pull us apart, he's—'

'I don't care.'

Jamie's words died in her mouth.

'I'm sorry,' he said, his eyes shining in the dwindling afternoon sun. 'It's my kids. If there's any chance … any chance at all they're in danger …' He shook his head, unable to look at her. 'I have to go.'

And then he climbed in and closed the door and the car drove out through the gate and up the driveway.

Jamie felt Alina at her shoulder.

She held Jamie's arm as the sound of the taxi died away. There was no birdsong, just the gentle rustling of wilting trees and crisped leaves.

'Is he coming back?' Alina asked, staring at the driveway.

'I ... I don't know.'

'What do we do now?'

Check the guns are loaded, Jamie felt like saying.

Instead, she turned and kissed Alina on the forehead, mostly so she wouldn't see the tears forming in Jamie's eyes. 'Why don't we put the kettle on, hmm?

CHAPTER
TWENTY-FIVE

amie worked through the accumulated washing up slowly, watching Alina and Hati playing outside in the fading sun.

They danced in circles and Jamie basked in Alina's laughter. For all the shit that girl had been through, she still didn't seem to struggle to enjoy the brighter moments in her day. Jamie wished she could do the same.

She pulled her hands from the soapy water and flexed them. Her palm was stinging, the cut oozing blood through the now sodden bandage.

She looked down at it, flexing her fingers stiffly before she moved her hand away from the sink and rested it on the pistol lying on the counter. The killer had been within her grasp just hours before. He'd been waiting there for them, knowing that they'd go in alone. If Jamie had just been smarter, if she'd told Radcliffe, got a fleet of police and dogs and guns there, they could have surrounded him, penned him in. Caught him. Killed him.

And this would have been over.

But now it seemed further than ever from that. It was clear to Jamie that they were further than ever from catching him. That they were now divided, scattered. No Elliot, no Hallberg, and now no Hassan either.

She was alone. Which was exactly how the killer wanted it.

That poor woman, Sadaf Hameed. Same initials and nationality as Hassan's wife. Dumped out of a vehicle in broad daylight, right in front of their first home in London. The message couldn't be clearer. But Jamie knew, deep down, that it was a ploy. One more tactic to drive her mad. To get her on her own, and twist the screws just a little more.

The killer already knew what he was doing. Hell, Sadaf was probably already dead and in his car or van already while they were chasing Jillian Jones. And then he went straight to London and dumped her on the street like a bag of fucking shit.

Jamie felt her blood pressure rising.

Her eyes lifted to the window once more, watching as Alina and Hati wheeled around, still laughing, still playing. And then stopped.

Jamie's grip on the gun tightened, eyes narrowing, sweeping the area outside for any sign of what had spooked them.

Hati turned then, facing the trees at the far end of the courtyard, and began barking.

Alina turned that way too, not moving an inch.

Jamie didn't move either.

She waited, holding her breath.

The clock ticked loudly behind her, splitting the quiet.

'No, no, no,' she muttered, watching them. 'Don't do it.'

But then Hati ran.

He sprang forward, bounding awkwardly on his three legs.

And before Jamie even saw Alina give chase, she was already moving, flinging suds across the kitchen as she bolted for the door. She was wearing shoes now, thankfully, and wasted no time leaping the step down onto the driveway.

What had Hati heard? Jamie knew the answer, she knew what he was chasing, but she prayed she was wrong.

That they hadn't once again walked right into a trap laid just for them.

Her heels dug into the loose stones and she raised her head, sprinting across the space towards the woods between the barn and the garage where the Toyota was sitting.

The long grass and branches were still swinging where they'd gone into the brush, and Jamie plunged in after them, listening to Hati's mad barks ringing ahead, to Alina's shouts for him to stop, to come back.

Jamie didn't have the breath to call out at this speed, she just needed to keep running to catch them up before they reached whatever it was that lay ahead.

She burst through a dense thicket of trees and reached a little clearing, looking around, her shoulders rising and falling rapidly as she tried to regulate her breathing. She was still a way off the property line, and had run maybe five hundred metres from the house. Despite there being another hour of daylight left, in the trees it was dark. Murky. They rose up around her like a wall, putting everything in shadow, making it difficult to know where she'd come from, which direction she was heading.

She could hear Hati barking, but the sound was splintered, difficult to place.

'Alina?' she called, cupping her hands around her mouth, the cold metal of the pistol pressing into her cheek as she did.

The noise rang and then died.

There was no answer.

'Alina!' she tried again, louder this time.

She strained her ears, listening for Hati's barks, trying to place the direction.

And then a sharp, shrill yelp reached her, making her skin erupt in goose pimples. Hati whined sharply in pain and then yowled, the noise distinct enough to place.

Her head snapped around to face it and she trusted her instincts, taking off once more.

The ground was uneven, threatening to break her ankles with each step. She tried not to think about it as she homed in on Hati's pained whines, growing louder and louder with each step.

And then suddenly, Jamie was there, bursting through a wall of foliage and onto a flattened game trail.

Alina was sitting on her knees, the dog sprawled across her lap, whining.

Jamie skidded to a halt and pulled her gun up, whipping it around, looking for him, for any sign of him.

But there was nothing. Just the forest rustling around them, the gentle wind whispering through the undergrowth.

Jamie lowered the gun, panting wildly, and looked down.

'You can't run off like that!' she snapped.

Alina looked up at her, eyes wide. 'He's hurt,' she said, not even registering the scold.

Jamie's anger dissipated instantly, the sight of Hati's wounds filling her with a cold dread instead. His chest and shoulder were cut, badly. A single, straight line carved into his flesh. Blood was running from the gash and over Alina's jeans.

'What happened?' Jamie asked, sinking down next to them.

Hati growled at the sudden movement and Jamie raised her hands to show she meant no harm.

Alina lifted a hand towards the trail in front and Jamie followed it, not seeing it at first. But then she did – a wire, strung across the path. Almost invisible. She wouldn't have seen it at all if Hati's blood wasn't beading and dripping from it.

She crawled forward on her knees and reached out, touching it.

It was sharp and Jamie hissed, a little surprised. It was a steel cable, sharp and fine. The kind you'd use to garrotte someone, she thought. Sharp enough to slice a leg clean off if you were sprinting. Hell, if Hati had all his legs and could run more than ten miles an hour, he'd probably look like he did right now.

But who the hell had put this here? Was it one of Elliot's? Had he put this up around the property to catch out those trying to get in from outside?

No, he wouldn't do that without telling her. Which meant …

'We need to go,' Jamie said, turning back to Alina, to the dog. 'We need to lift him up and carry him back. He's too heavy for me to do it alone. Can you do that?'

She spoke with the sort of certain tone that told Alina that it wasn't really a question. She needed her to do it.

Alina nodded diligently, then hunched forward, kissing the mutt on his cheek before she moved from under him, her legs soaked with blood, and took hold of his uninjured shoulder. 'I'll get his head,' she said.

'You sure? It's the heavier end.'

'It's also the end with the teeth,' Alina reminded her. 'You sure he's not going to bite you if you swap?'

'Good point. On three,' Jamie said, taking Hati's rear quarters. 'Ready?'

Alina nodded once more.

'Okay. One, two ... three.'

CHAPTER
TWENTY-SIX

t was very quickly becoming a long day.

Bloody and scraped to hell by twigs, they reached the farmyard. And despite Alina's demands to take him to a vet, Jamie refused. That's exactly what they *should* do, so it wasn't what they were *going* to do. No more playing this fucker's games.

No, a mobile vet and an emergency callout would be twice the cost, but it didn't matter. They weren't leaving the farm. Not when all the guns were right here.

They reached the doorway and laid Hati down. The door was open, and if Jamie was going to kill someone it'd be nice and easy to walk in the open front door and wait for them in their bedroom.

She swept the house, her finger firmly on the trigger, for any signs that anyone had been inside. And only once she was satisfied no one was there – after doing three sweeps – did she bring Alina and Hati inside.

It was after ten pm by the time the vet left, Hati was stitched, bandaged, and sedated, and they settled down for the night.

Alina, exhausted, fell asleep with her head on Hati's, the dog comatose and sprawled out on the sofa. Jamie was sitting in the armchair, its back pulled to the corner of the room, her pistol down the side of the cushion, and the Beretta 1301 shotgun laid across her lap.

She was determined to stay awake, alert, at least until dawn. But she failed, the darkness claiming her sometime during the night.

When her phone buzzed on the arm of the chair, she almost blew a hole in the living room door.

She woke suddenly, startled, and almost leapt to her feet. When she realised they were alone, she sank back into the chair and released the shotgun. She took a second to squeeze her eyes with her forefinger and thumb, cursing herself for having fallen asleep at all, and picked up the call. The time said it was after one in the morning and the number showed as blocked. She answered it, watching Alina and Hati snoring together on the sofa.

'Hello?' she whispered, knowing who it was.

'Jamie,' came Nyx's voice, 'I woke you.'

'It's one in the morning,' she said.

'I don't keep regular hours.'

Jamie sighed. 'That doesn't surprise me. What is it? You find Elliot?'

'No,' she said, 'but I think you might be right. I think he might be in trouble.'

Jamie sat up straighter, all her grogginess leaving her at once. 'What happened?'

'I'm sort of pissed that I set him up so well to cover his tracks,' she said. 'It's not been easy tracking his last movements. And I'll tell you now – I don't know where he is, and I have no way to find him. His phone's in a field somewhere off the side of the A40, but how much good that does you to find him I don't know.'

Not much, probably, Jamie thought. 'Why would he be on the A40?'

'I really don't know. I managed to track back to when he arrived at your place for the last time, when all your phones were pinging off the same tower at the same time. Then he left you, drove a little bit, and then made an outgoing phone call to a US number.'

'A US number ...' Jamie parroted it back, thinking about what Nyx had just said. He'd come to the house that morning, looked at the files, and then got in his car and disappeared. He'd returned to his house, told Mila he'd be gone for a day or two, but between here and there he'd made an outgoing call.

'I traced the number and found it connected to a Penhurst Wellness House. I looked it up; it's a privately-owned secure hospital a little outside Albany in New York. There's very little online about them, but I'm digging.'

Jamie didn't think she'd ever heard any unease in

Nyx's voice before. She didn't know the extent of her relationship with Elliot but she seemed on edge, and calling now at one in the morning instead of the morning? It wasn't sitting right with Jamie.

'Thanks,' Jamie said. 'This is good. Can you send me that number? I'll call them tomorrow.'

'Sure, and I'll look into Penhurst more, see what I can find out. I've known Elliot for a few years, but there's a *lot* I don't know about him. So ...'

'You're not making any promises, I understand,' Jamie said, 'but I appreciate you doing this. And wherever he is, he does too.'

She took a few seconds to answer, and then just said, 'Thanks. Their office opens at eight, so you can call from twelve with the time difference. I'll wait for you to get off the phone and then call you.'

Before Jamie could ask and then answer her own question as to how Nyx would know when she was on, and off, the phone, she hung up.

Jamie looked over at Alina, seeing her eyes glinting in the darkness. 'Anything?' she whispered.

'Not yet,' Jamie said, 'but we have a lead. We'll know more tomorrow. Just try and sleep, okay?'

She nodded, then rested her head on Hati's and closed her eyes once more.

Jamie just sat there thinking, glad she'd got a few hours' rest at least. Because now she knew she wouldn't sleep.

Penhurst Wellness House.

Why would Elliot be calling there?

She let out a slow breath, trying to steady her quickened heart, and grabbed her phone to Google it. She found their website quickly, and as she began reading, a coldness slithered down her spine.

"Penhurst Wellness House is a luxury facility offering premium security and comfort, catering to those deemed by the state to require special psychiatric care."

Special psychiatric care? It was a mental institution. And if it offered security required by the state it meant that it was a forensic unit. A locked one. A prison by any other name.

Jamie swallowed.

Why was Elliot calling there and what did it have to do with this case?

She sat, asking that question over and over again as the night wore on, desperate to know the answer, but afraid to answer it herself.

WHEN DAWN FINALLY BROKE, SHE FIGURED SHE'D probably snatched another hour or two of sleep in little stretches. But she was by no means rested.

As light crept into the sky, she walked through the quiet house and into the kitchen to fix some coffee. She poured yesterday's grounds out of the filter basket and into the bin before heading for the sink to wash it out. She turned on the tap and put her fingers under the water until it ran hot, glancing up through the window in front of her.

There, standing at the edge of the courtyard was a man clad in black.

Jamie blinked and he disappeared.

Her blood suddenly pulsed rapidly as she searched for him, eyes sweeping the treeline. He'd been there, hadn't he? She hadn't imagined that? Couldn't have—

'Fuck!' she yelped, pulling her hand from under the scalding water. She hissed and shook it off, running the tap cold now and putting her burned skin back under it.

Her eyes went back to the treeline, looking for him.

But he wasn't there. And as she kept looking, the likelihood of him never having been there rose sharply.

'Jamie?' Alina said from the doorway, rubbing her eyes. 'What's wrong?'

'Nothing, just burned myself,' she admitted. 'Tired, is all.'

'Uh-huh. Is there coffee?'

'There will be in a minute.'

She leaned against the door frame and closed her eyes. 'You want to talk?'

'About what?'

'About what's going on with you,' Alina said, cutting and direct as always. 'Another woman who looks like you died, Elliot's gone, Nasir's gone. You're on your own and you're seeing things.'

'I'm not seeing things,' she said defensively.

'So how'd you burn your hand? I was standing here

watching you. Looked like you'd seen a ghost through the window.' She yawned. 'And I know you *didn't* see something because otherwise you'd be out there waving a gun around.'

'You know that someone strung a wire across the path through the woods and almost killed Hati yesterday, don't you? Someone is *after* us. After *me.*'

She frowned. 'They've actively tried to avoid you, haven't they? Kept their distance every time you got near? Why do you think they're doing that?'

'They're playing mind games,' Jamie said. 'It's all psychological.'

'Right,' Alina said, shooting Jamie a quick finger gun, 'but they're not trying to kill you. But do you know who's actually been targeted? Who's disappeared? Who we can't find?'

Jamie just stared at her. 'Elliot?'

'Bingo.' She shrugged. 'Maybe you're not the target at all.'

Jamie's mouth just sort of flopped open.

'Shout when the coffee's ready, I'm going to check on Hati's stitches.'

And with that, she walked out of the room, leaving Jamie standing there with the sudden realisation that maybe, just maybe, this whole thing ... wasn't about her at all.

CHAPTER
TWENTY-SEVEN

I t was the longest morning Jamie had ever experienced.

The time ticked by painfully, but eventually it was midday and she was sitting at the kitchen table, the number already keyed into her phone, waiting for the minute hand to hit twelve.

She pressed the call icon the second it did and waited for it to connect. It rang for a little while, with that dull tone it always had when you called out of country, and then someone answered.

Jamie didn't know if she'd expected someone to be there or not, but when they answered, her mind seemed to go blank.

'Hello, Penhurst House, how may I direct your call?' came the somewhat formal, east-coast American voice.

'Uh ...'

Alina, sat opposite her, gestured for her to speak.

'Hi,' she said then, 'my name is Jamie Johansson, I'm a special investigator for the National Crime Agency here in the UK—'

Before she got any further, the woman cut in. 'I'm afraid we're not able to divulge any information to any law enforcement agencies, domestic or foreign, without a signed court order. Thank you for calling Penhurst House.' And then she hung up.

'Well, that was shit,' Alina snorted. 'What a bitch.'

Jamie hummed with frustration and didn't even bother to tell Alina off for her language. 'Let's try that again, shall we?'

She rang the number a second time, and once more the woman answered with the same greeting. 'Hello, Penhurst House, how may I direct your call?'

'Hi, me again,' Jamie said quickly. 'A person of interest in a case I'm investigating called your facility a few days ago, and I'm just looking to find out why—'

'I'm sorry, we're not able to divulge any information to any law enforcement agencies, domestic or *foreign,* without a signed court order from a US court, mandating us to break confidentiality. Thank you for your call.'

She hung up for a second time and Jamie just put her head in her hands. This was going nowhere, and fast. The US was a shit-show when it came to this kind of thing, and the red tape she'd have to hack through to get the information she needed was insurmountable.

Her phone began buzzing then, blocked number.

Jamie answered. 'Nyx,' she said, 'I couldn't—'

'I heard.'

'You *heard*? As in, listening to my phone calls?'

'Just that one. Your life is of no interest to me,' she said coldly.

Jamie didn't know whether to be relieved or offended by that.

'Brick wall,' Nyx said. 'Not a surprise, but it was worth a try anyway.'

'Is there anything you can do?'

'I'm doing it. Their site isn't linked in to their intranet, but their internal databases back up to the cloud, so there's vulnerability there. I managed to get in this morning and started pulling their patient and personnel records, but nothing's sticking out to me.'

'Nothing like ... No one who could be involved in these killings?'

She scoffed. 'No, the place is nothing *but* killers and unhinged psychopaths. Nothing's sticking out like I have no idea why Elliot called there, whether it was about a patient, an employee, or for some other reason.' She sighed. 'If there's anything you can do through your *proper channels,* I'll keep going on my end, see if I can't connect any of these people with Elliot, see if there's anything else I can turn up. I'll scrape their emails too, and send you anything I find.'

'Okay, thanks.'

'I'll be in touch.' She disappeared into her digital

rabbit hole once more and left Jamie sitting there facing Alina.

'She's so cool,' Alina said. 'So badass.'

'Well if you're thinking about changing career paths, I don't know what I'd prefer – career criminal and hacker, or detective.'

'Both sound cool. I could do both.'

'You'd be a force to be reckoned with,' Jamie said, laughing just a little.

'Pshh,' Alina said, getting up and heading towards the coffee machine. 'I already am. Just you wait, I'm gonna do big things.'

'Oh, I know it,' Jamie said, watching her pour a coffee. Just don't grow up too fast, she thought.

While Alina sipped her drink, Jamie called Radcliffe. He answered quickly.

'Jamie, you have something for me?'

'I do. I'm trying to zero in on Elliot—'

'Elliot Day?'

'Yes, he's been missing—'

'You do realise there's a killer out here dropping bodies like there's no tomorrow, and you're worried about Elliot Day?'

'Yes, but—'

'Have you turned on the news today? Do you know what's happening?'

Jamie had not turned on the news, and it was exactly because she *didn't* want to know what was happening. Radcliffe's words had stuck with her, and she was in no hurry to see her face plastered all across the television.

'I haven't had chance ...'

Alina was already back at the table and hunting down the headlines. In seconds she turned her phone towards Jamie, whose blood ran a little colder at the sight. Five pictures of five women, all of whom could have been Jamie if you squinted a little, filled the screen. The phone was on mute, but the headline riding the bottom of the page was pretty clear. *Serial killer targeting women across the UK. Police and NCA paralysed, not providing comment. Public outcry and backlash at fever pitch. People demanding answers, demanding progress ...*

Jamie stopped reading as the five women disappeared and her own photograph appeared on screen. The one from her Met warrant card. She was five years younger, brighter-eyed and determined.

Alina tapped the screen to enable subtitles and the words of the presenter appeared. '... Jamie Johansson, former Detective Inspector of the London Met. Each murder bears an unmistakable resemblance to one of her former cases. We have not been able to find or reach the former detective for comment, and ask, if she sees this, that she reaches out with any information she may—'

Jamie pushed Alina's phone down and cleared her throat. 'I know this sounds crazy, but if we find Elliot, I think we'll find our killer.'

Radcliffe didn't seem convinced. 'You seriously want me to pull resources from this investigation and redirect them to finding Elliot Day?' Every time he said his name, his voice dripped with contempt.

'Yes. He made an outgoing call to a Penhurst Wellness House, a privately-owned mental institution in New York state, and then disappeared right after. He ditched his phone, or it was taken from him - I don't know which. But what I do know is that phone call and this case are linked. I already called them and they threw up a brick wall. The kind that these places do when they're hiding something. I'm working on it this end, but if you can make some calls, see what shakes out ... ?'

He took a second to think about it. 'You said *Penhurst*?'

'Wellness House, yes.'

'New York,' he muttered, as though he was writing it down. 'Okay. I'll see what I can do. And Johansson?'

'Yes?'

'I hope you're right about this. Because between you and me, we've got nothing else.'

'I hope so too,' Jamie said, watching Alina watch the news. 'I hope so too.'

CHAPTER
TWENTY-EIGHT

Jamie did not like sitting around doing nothing.

It was getting late in the afternoon now and there was silence from both Nyx and Radcliffe. Alina's words were echoing in her head: this isn't about you.

If this was about Elliot, then maybe he wasn't gone, but *taken* instead. And if that was the case, Jamie had been looking in all the wrong places.

But what were the *right* places?

She didn't know. Mila hadn't known anything either, but then again, maybe Jamie wasn't asking the right questions. They'd not exactly ended on a positive note, but Mila had spent the most amount of time with Elliot over the last few years. So if anyone was likely to know how he was connected to Penhurst, then it was her.

'Hey,' Jamie said, standing in the living room doorway. 'We're going to head back to Elliot's, I need to speak to Mila again.'

'You think that's a good idea?' Alina asked, not peeling her eyes from the book she was reading on the sofa. Hati was lying across her lap, looking like he was feeling pretty sorry for himself.

'I can't just sit here and do nothing. She might know more than she realises.'

'Ooooh-kay,' Alina said, drawing air between her teeth like she thought it was a bad idea. 'I'll hang here—'

'You're coming.'

'But Hati—'

'He's coming too. I'm not leaving you alone. Not now. Not with all this going on.'

Alina looked up, and though it was clear she thought they weren't really in any danger from the killer, she still agreed. 'Alright, let's go.'

They drove out there, and on the way Jamie caught herself chewing her thumb nail on two separate occasions. She only did so when she was nervous, and realised quickly that she'd not been doing it when she thought the killer was coming for her, but now that she was fearing for Elliot … Jamie wasn't sure if she wholly believed that yet. But Alina was right, the killer had had plenty of opportunities to claim Jamie's life. And considering his efficiency and skill, if he wanted her dead, she'd be dead. Which meant that it probably wasn't his end goal, or at least not his immediate one. But what was?

And *who* was he, too? If he could best Elliot, what kind of man was this? Or worse, what kind of monster was this?

Before she knew it, they were pulling into his driveway once more.

The black Mercedes was just where it had been the last time, but Mila didn't run to the door now.

Alina plainly said, 'I'll wait here,' and sat in the back with Hati, the fierce brute now a sulking mess with his chin rested on her lap.

Jamie gave her a nod and climbed out, walking slowly up the driveway, replaying their last meeting in her head. How it had gone. How it had ended. And she was determined not to repeat it.

Whether their relationship was 'one of convenience' or not, Elliot and Mila seemed to be stuck together. And Jamie didn't like the idea of her and Mila being enemies in a love triangle that, as far as Jamie was concerned, didn't exist. Sort of. She let out a long breath and knocked on the door.

It took a while but Mila eventually answered, this time without a look of surprise. She was in a pair of jeans and knitted jumper, and despite having her hair tied up and no make-up on, she still looked amazing. It was no wonder really that Elliot had gravitated towards her. Even Jamie had to admit she had a magnetism, and she didn't even like the woman.

'You find him?' she asked in her perfect English, just a hint of her Russian accent bleeding through.

'No, but we're getting closer.'

'Thanks for the update,' she said, trying to close the door.

'Wait,' Jamie called, putting her hand out and stopping it. 'I wanted to talk.'

'What about?'

'I wanted to clear the air.'

Mila scoffed. 'Clear the air? That's one way of putting it. But unless you want to come inside, throw back ten shots of vodka and have a bare-knuckle fight, there's nothing to be said.'

Jamie didn't know if that's how they solved differences in Russia – maybe they did in her household – or if she just wanted to punch her in the face, but either way the words, 'I don't drink,' spilled out of her mouth reflexively before she could stop them.

Mila scoffed again. 'Of course you don't.' She narrowed her eyes. 'No wonder he's obsessed with you.'

'That's what I wanted to talk about really,' Jamie admitted. 'If we're going to be working together, I don't want there to be any animosity between us.'

'This the part where you say we could be friends, paint each other's nails and braid each other's hair?'

Jamie gestured to her head. 'This is technically a plait, and I don't even paint my nails.' She held her hand up, hoping a little lightness would be a welcome addition to the conversation.

Mila snatched her hand from the air. 'Or look after them, it seems,' she said, not hiding a grimace at the state of Jamie's freshly chewed fingers.

She pulled her hand free. 'Any chance I could come in? I'd rather not do this on the front step.'

Mila looked out at the car, at Alina.

'She's fine,' Jamie said. 'Headphones, YouTube. She'd be there forever if I let her.'

Mila huffed now, as though disappointed in Jamie's parenting, and then motioned her inside without a word.

As Jamie stepped in, she regretted coming, and had seemingly lost sense of why she wanted to come at all.

Inside, the place felt even more alien. Like when you went into the house of someone who had died and all their things were left behind. This was someone else's life that Elliot had bought into. The books on the book-shelves, the ornaments, everything. Jamie only now noticed that all of the picture frames around had been emptied and just stood blank. Mila had taken all the photos from them, but she and Elliot didn't have a life they could put in their place.

Mila turned in the hallway and folded her arms. 'You wanted to talk, talk.'

'Do you want to sit?' Jamie looked into the living room at the sofas.

'No, I'll stand,' she said. 'Say your bit.'

'Okay then. The first and last time Elliot kissed me I kneed him in the testicles.'

Mila didn't flinch.

'I have no romantic interest in him.'

'No?' Mila didn't seem convinced. 'Then why do you keep crawling back to him?'

'I wouldn't say *crawling*.' Jamie's brow crumpled. 'Not sure I like that word, or that it's apt.'

'I think it is.'

'Elliot's unique skillset and connections in the criminal underworld make him an indispensable asset.'

'Ah, so he's an asset you're using for your own personal gain. Now I feel much better. You can leave—'

'God, you want to stop being such a bitch for like five minutes?' As soon as Jamie said it, she regretted it. The words could have come from Alina's mouth, but not hers. She'd been so worried about Alina turning into her, she'd not even realised she might be turning into Alina – if only a little.

Mila bristled. 'Now you're on to insults. Ungroomed, boyish, short, *and* rude. I can really see why he likes you now.'

'I'm the average height for a woman, thank you,' Jamie snapped. She couldn't really argue with the other three.

'Maybe for this stunted nation,' Mila clapped back.

'You're a fucking Russian beanstalk, I get it. You're pissed at your husband, I get it. You think I'm trying to steal him, I get it. But I'm not. I don't love Elliot, for the longest time I wanted to kill him.'

'So did I. But that's how he gets under your skin.

Like a botfly. He burrows in, lays his eggs, and then it propagates. Spreads. Multiplies.'

'What propagates?'

'Your inability to see who he really is. *What* he really is.'

Jamie didn't need clarification on that. 'But you love him anyway? Why?'

'My hands are not clean. Far from it,' Mila said plainly. 'I have done things. Because my father wanted me to. Because I wanted to. We are not innocent. None of us. Me. Him. You. But what I won't stand for is disloyalty. Not to me. Not after he promised.'

Jamie steeled herself. 'I don't believe this is disloyalty. Not him bringing you here, and not him disappearing now. Elliot and I are ... I don't know. Friends? I know our relationship is far from normal, but I could never be with him. I don't ... I don't know if I could be with *anyone*.' Images flashed in her mind. Thorsen. Church. She could have stayed with Thorsen on that island in Greece, forever. He gave her everything she wanted. Patience, unconditional love, compassion. And Church? Church was ... Church was a mast she could lash herself to in a storm. He wasn't what she wanted, but he felt like what she needed. He wasn't afraid to tell her what he was thinking, exactly how he was thinking it. And that night they'd spent together? It was good. As good as Jamie had known. Though she didn't have much to compare it to.

But Elliot? No, she couldn't imagine it. Not in any

way. And yet … she needed him too. He was her dark reflection. He was the thing that convinced her she could go on, that she was okay. That she wasn't alone. He was the only one who understood her. Really understood her.

How she could articulate that to Mila, Jamie didn't know. Hell, she didn't think she could articulate it to herself.

'He's not being disloyal to you. He's in trouble. And we're trying to find him.' Jamie let out a slow breath, trying to calm herself and the situation. 'Shortly before he disappeared, he made a call to a Penhurst Wellness House in the US. Does that ring a bell?'

'Should it?'

'I don't know. Did he ever mention it?'

'No,' Mila said tiredly.

'Did he ever mention any contacts in the US, anything that could give us an idea of who he might have been trying to contact?'

'No. As I said, he keeps me separate from his work.'

Jamie racked her brain for any other questions that might help. She even would have asked to search the house if she thought it would be of any use, but she didn't think it would be. This wasn't their home, nothing of his would be here, nothing of value. If there was anything to find, it would be—

Her phone buzzed in her pocket and she pulled it free quickly, seeing Radcliffe's number.

Mila gestured for her to answer it and she did, stepping away to take the call.

'Yeah?'

'Jesus Christ, Johansson, the company you keep.'

'I assume the news isn't good,' she replied.

'Not if you're right and what I just found out about Penhurst has anything to do with this case.'

Her heart beat harder. 'What happened at Penhurst?'

'A friend of mine at the bureau said that eight weeks ago there was an incident. A patient who'd been there for three years, a model prisoner for lack of a better word, attacked his psychiatrist, strangled him to death in his office, bit his thumb off, and escaped through the biometrically locked doors wearing the doctor's clothes. He was stopped by two orderlies, murdered them with a fountain pen, then abducted one of the nurses, stole her car, broke her neck, dumped her body on the side of the road, and disappeared.'

Jamie didn't quite have the words to respond.

'You there, Johansson?'

'Just, uh ... just taking that in.' She cleared her throat. 'Who is this guy, do we know?'

'I don't have that information yet, private hospital and all that. It's all tied up with the insurance companies and the investigation is closed, being handled by the FBI so it's *need to know*. Though I sincerely hope you're wrong and whoever this guy is hasn't landed in our lap.'

Jamie still didn't have anything to say.

'You want to weigh in here with any keen observations? You're not really providing your money's worth right now.'

Jamie couldn't shift the lump in her throat. 'I'll, uh, I'll get back to you ...'

'Don't hang up—'

But she did, lowering the phone, thinking about how this had to be the guy they were looking for. But who was he, and what connection did he have with Elliot?

'Nyx?' Jamie asked aloud. 'If you can hear me ...'

She held her phone up and waited.

On cue, it rang again.

'That's a neat trick,' Mila said, hovering a little closer than before. Her cold air of superiority seemed to have been replaced by one of nervousness, the gravity of the situation setting in. Jamie had no doubt she'd overheard what Radcliffe had said.

Seemingly as had Nyx.

Jamie answered quickly. 'You hear that?'

'Much to Radcliffe's chagrin, I bet,' Nyx said, snorting. 'The guy you're looking for is Julian Voss.'

'He even sounds like a psycho.'

'He's not just a psycho, he's a Fields medallist, doctor of physics, chess grandmaster, and brain surgeon.'

'You're joking?'

'I wish I was,' Nyx said gravely.

'And you're sure it's him?'

'His patient notes stop eight weeks ago, on the same date that the head psychiatrist's name stops appearing on any of the patients' notes and is replaced by his number two. So yeah, I'd say he's the guy.'

'Fuck. And he's really a fields medallist?' Jamie didn't know anything about maths, but she knew the Fields Medal was awarded to mathematicians under the age of forty who'd achieved or contributed significantly to the field.

'Yeah, for his work on something called the Ising Model? I don't know, it's over my head. But he graduated MIT, worked in a physics lab, got his medal, then went back to med school and graduated from Duke before going on to work as a brain surgeon. A bloody good one.'

'That's not surprising,' Jamie said. 'Highly intelligent psychopaths are often drawn to the medical field. Case in point: Elliot. Power over life and death, that kind of thing.'

'The God complex,' Mila offered dryly.

'Exactly.'

Nyx went on. 'I haven't found the link between them yet, but both he and Elliot attended multiple conferences in both the US, UK, and all over the world. It's not a far shout to say they crossed paths at some point.'

'But that doesn't really explain why he'd come here, why he'd do all this, why he'd come after Elliot?'

'I don't know,' Nyx said. 'Public record for the arrest

and conviction of Julian Voss is for first degree murder. They charged him with sixteen other counts of murder, but only one stuck. A young man by the name of Stephen Farrow in New York City. The DA prosecuted with a mountain of evidence including voice recordings of Voss discussing the murder at length with an unknown third party.'

'Elliot,' Jamie said, the word forming before she'd even really thought about it. 'Elliot sold Voss out?'

'It's within his nature,' Mila said, her dryness now dripping with disdain. 'It wouldn't be the first time he'd betrayed someone close to him.'

She was right, the action wasn't out of the question, but reason still escaped her. 'Were they enemies? No, you don't divulge your darkest secrets to your enemy,' Jamie said. 'They were friends. But ... that makes even less sense.'

Mila shrugged. 'You're only Elliot's *friend* until it's no longer convenient. Then ...'

'But why didn't he just *kill* Voss if he wanted him gone? Why go to all the trouble of getting him arrested, convicted?'

No one answered Jamie this time. She supposed she'd have to ask him when she saw him.

Nyx chimed back in now, putting the cherry on top of it all. 'Voss's lawyers managed to strike a deal, pleaded down to an insanity charge, and by the looks of it paid out a huge sum to Stephen Farrow's family on the proviso that Voss went to Penhurst. His lawyers cited his years of public service in both the medical and maths fields, and said the murder was committed in a *temporary state of mental unrest.*'

'And the DA went for that?' Jamie scoffed. 'Fucking American legal system,' she muttered.

'From the looks of these notes while he was in Penhurst, he was a model patient. Mostly played chess, the piano, helped in the garden, the library ...'

'Biding his time.'

'Looks like.'

'And now he's here,' Jamie said, 'exacting his revenge on Elliot. He's ...' And then it all snapped into place. 'He's holding him, making him watch as he comes after me, torments me. He's taken everyone away – Elliot, Hassan, Hallberg even. He wanted me alone. He wanted me to suffer. For Elliot to watch it all, help-less. And then ...'

'He kills you,' Mila said with a sigh. 'Big shock. But where is he now? A dungeon somewhere?'

'His phone last pinged along the A40,' Nyx reminded them. 'That narrows down the direction at least.'

Mila's lip curled into a small smirk. 'Ashwood Court.'

'What's that?' Jamie asked.

She unfolded her arms and put her hands on her hips. 'It's Elliot's house,' she said, a small sadness coming across her face. 'It was *our* house.'

CHAPTER
TWENTY-NINE

J amie wasn't sure if she thought that Elliot was created in a government laboratory, or that maybe his ship crash-landed on earth when he was a child, but she didn't expect him to have been raised in a house called *Ashwood Court.*

It was a twelve-bedroomed country home on the edge of the Cotswolds that the Day family had owned for as long as there'd *been* a Day family.

Nyx didn't have any trouble digging up his family history, even if he had seemingly wiped his own from existence. He didn't seem to have a birth certificate, national insurance number, university transcript, or even medical licence anymore. Nothing digital, anyway – Nyx checked.

The house itself was now owned by a family trust and was overseen by a board of trustees working under a shell corporation registered out of Luxembourg, whose counsel was a Swiss firm of accountants. The upkeep and management were being paid for by them; which was clearly just Elliot giving HRMC and the government the runaround. But Nyx was impressed – and a little annoyed that he hadn't used her to set all this up. Though she admitted it was all before she'd known him.

Though beyond the layers of legal protection and anonymity, there was no record of Elliot even existing. All that remained of the Days were his parents Henry and Evelyn Day – deceased, father by heart attack, mother by cancer – and sister, Victoria, also deceased. Drug overdose.

As Jamie drove the A40, heading for the house, she listened to Nyx talk. Mila was in the passenger seat, and Alina was in the back with Hati the dog.

Night was on them, and the lights of the old Toyota cut weakly through the darkness.

Jamie thought about Elliot, about what lay ahead. And about his family, his sister. He'd never talked about his parents, only mentioned in passing that his father had been a cold, vicious man. Her first thought on recalling that was whether his heart attack had been a heart attack at all.

Had Elliot always been like he was? Or was he made that way? Had his father been the same? From what Nyx said, he'd been a ruthless business man, someone without mercy or scruples. Who could say? Elliot had told Jamie the story of what happened to his sister and she did her best to recall it now, wondering as she did whether it was true. She thought it was, that it had been told to her at a time when everything else about Elliot's life was a lie, a thin veil draped over the truth. But that story, that night ... in that other life, so long ago. It had felt like truth.

She could picture him now, the way he bit his lip, the way he wrestled over it. 'My sister,' he'd said, as though the words pained him. He leaned forward, rubbing his hands together slowly. 'She was seventeen when she went missing. I wasn't there, my father put us both in boarding school. Separately. We weren't at home much, and when we were there ... she and my father had a troubled relationship. "Difficult" my mother called it. She was expelled from boarding school and I found out afterwards. At the time, I didn't know. I was eleven, too young to understand, to do anything about it. She'd snuck a boy into the school and was caught. Of course, if that had been the end of it, it wouldn't have been a problem. Not really. That sort of thing happens a lot. And a sizeable donation from a parent will make something like that go away.' He'd shaken his head, disgusted by the power of money. Disgusted by his own family. 'But she got pregnant. I never knew that either, not until much later. That was why they expelled her, said she couldn't be there, around the other girls. And when she came home, she refused to tell my father who the boy was. I don't blame her. He could be ...' The word came to Jamie now as it had then. *Violent.* 'He told her that she had to get rid of the baby. He scheduled for a doctor to come to the house. She refused of course – she was as stubborn and strong-willed as he was.' She pictured Elliot smiling there, at the strength of his sister. At her courage to stand up to her father. 'He gave her an ultimatum. Either she got rid of the baby, or she left the house. A stupid thing to do really, but neither of them would back down.' Jamie slowed for a turn and guided them around it. Nyx was still talking, but Jamie had tuned out, replaying the conversation in her head, hunting for some clue, some sort of insight into what to expect. Though she knew that was a lie. She was looking for something human in Elliot, maybe holding on to the only human part of him she'd known. The part when she didn't know him at all. 'I didn't come home for Easter that year – so it was July by the time I got there. My sister had been gone for nearly four months by that point.'

'Where did she go?' Jamie asked, playing her own part in her head.

'I don't know,' Elliot continued. 'My father, in his infinite wisdom, called her friends' parents, told them not to offer her a place to stay. They all knew each other of course, and they wouldn't cross him. No one would.'

'Did she come back?' Jamie asked, knowing the answer now as she did then.

'No.' Elliot had laced his hands together and started cracking his knuckles at that point. The noise was low and sharp. Like the clink of his metallic surgical tools.

She'd not been able to read him at that moment, but she'd sensed a coldness in him, the first hint of his truth. Though she'd not seen it then, not wanted to see it. 'She contacted my mother about six weeks after she left – said that she'd sold all of her jewellery, everything she had, and had run out of money.'

'What did your mother say?' Jamie had asked.

'She was as scared of my father as I was. She told her to come home, to get rid of the baby, to go back to school. But she wouldn't.'

'What about the father of the baby?'

'I don't know. She never told us who he was. And I think she was too afraid to go to him in case my father found out. He had reach. Influence. And we all knew what he would have done to him if he knew who he was.'

Killed him, Jamie thought.

Maybe he did.

'What happened then?' Jamie had been afraid to ask.

He'd considered his words, his answer. 'Nothing. We never heard from her again. We never found out who the father was. She disappeared. Her body was found less than a year later. Heroin overdose.'

'And the baby?'

'It looked like she miscarried because of the drugs. Late. The report said that she had overdosed almost immediately after. The police said there was evidence she had been prostituting herself to survive. And I never knew any of it. Not until my mother told me, two years later.'

Jamie let him finish his story, remembering how they'd come on to the topic. They'd been talking about Grace Melver, a young girl hooked on drugs herself. Sixteen or so. Almost the age that Elliot's sister had been at the time.

Jamie felt a pang of something sharp in her chest and looked in the rear-view, watching Alina.

Grace had been almost the same age as Alina was now. Alina met her eyes then and Jamie glanced away, unable to look at her.

Her grip tightened on the wheel.

She couldn't imagine doing something like that to her child; shutting her out like that. Condemning her to death. Family was ... hard. Jamie knew that as much as anyone. But there was always a way back, wasn't there?

Is that what Jamie was doing now? Finding a way back to her family? To Elliot?

His voice rang in the darkness of her mind once more, the end of his story dredging itself from the depths of her memory.

'I do what I can,' he'd said, 'for the people who need it. Some throw their lives away. Some can't be saved. But some can.' He looked at her, his eyes intense, a hot, glowing fire burning behind them. A fire with the heat and the violence to burn the whole world. A violence that his father never could have produced, never could have dreamed of. 'You understand that, don't you?' he'd asked. 'Some lives can be saved. And some should?'

Jamie had tried her best to smile. An echo of it played on her lips now, forced as it was years ago. 'Yeah, Elliot. Some people can be saved. Others ... can't. No matter how hard you try, or how much you want to. You understand that, don't you?'

She didn't know if he did.

'But we should still try,' he'd said.

'We all have the power to try. And sometimes, that's all you can do.'

'Hmm?' Mila asked from the passenger seat, turning her head. 'Did you say something?'

Jamie cleared her throat, not realising she'd said the last part aloud. 'No, no,' she said, adjusting in her seat and driving on. 'Just talking to myself.'

CHAPTER
THIRTY

They left the main road and wound into the country, coming up on the gate to Ashworth Court at a crawl.

Jamie killed the lights on the Toyota and eased along by the glow of the moon and stars, sparse as it was.

Mila seemed to know the way regardless, giving orders in a hushed and harsh tone.

'The gate is right here,' she said, gesturing left.

Jamie wheeled up to it.

'Wait,' she said.

Jamie stood on the brake and the whole car rocked. 'What is it?' she asked.

She narrowed her eyes, and they glinted with the reflection of the instruments on the dashboard. 'It's open. It's never open.'

'Guess that's a good sign,' Jamie muttered, squinting

into the darkness ahead at the hulking silhouette of the house. 'Means we guessed right.'

Mila let out a slow breath, the reality of things setting in.

Jamie let the Toyota idle, looking up the long driveway. 'Tell me about the house.'

Mila shrugged. 'It's old. What do you want to know?'

Jamie looked around the car, lamenting not having Hassan, or Church, or even Elliot there. Someone with the experience needed to infiltrate a building and sweep through it with prejudice.

'Layout, entry points, exits. What are the grounds like? Where are the staircases, bedrooms, anything like that. Is there somewhere we really don't want to find ourselves?'

'I never liked the laundry room, it was always cold,' Mila offered.

'Not what I meant.'

'There's the front door, and a back door too – servants' entrance is to the left, and to the right is the solarium which opens into the statue garden.'

'Statue garden? Solarium?' Alina scoffed. 'I knew Elliot was rich, but *shit* ...'

'Language,' Jamie reminded her. 'Alright, so front, back, servants', and solarium,' she said, pointing to either side of the building. 'The solarium is going to be a no-go for entry.'

'Why?'

'Because it's made of glass and he, or they, could see us coming.'

'They?'

'I don't know how many people are in there. It could be one killer, it could be fifty.'

'So shouldn't we call someone?' Mila asked, as though it were an obvious question.

Jamie had thought of that. Had thought of calling lots of people. Everyone. But this killer had been so smart, so well connected, and had anticipated every move they'd made. She thought that if they had any chance of getting to Elliot, it would be by moving slowly and quietly. Images of Jillian Jones being joisted into the air and out of her reach flashed before her eyes.

'It's likely that Voss is holding Elliot, and I already saw what he's willing to do to the people he takes. The longer we wait, the longer he has to prepare. I want to get the drop on him. And I want to do it now,' Jamie said firmly, 'but I'm going in alone.'

Alina made a sound of protest, but then rethought her position. This wasn't kids' stuff, it was real. And she knew it.

'So, the front, the back entrances,' Jamie went on. 'They open into hallways? Multiple doors in each?'

'Yes.'

'Okay, and the servants' entrance, that opens into ...'

'The laundry room.'

'And that goes into?'

'The servants' quarters.'

Jamie tried to recall what she knew about houses like this – not a lot – but she was aware that servants often had their own staircase so that they could move up and down to tend to the bedrooms without crossing the owners.

'And there are stairs there?'

'There are. They lead to the upstairs corridor – runs the entire length of the house left to right,' Mila offered, drawing a line through the air.

Jamie thought on that. She'd want to be upstairs if she was in the killer's shoes. Easier to fortify, and stairs meant choke points that were easily defended. She honestly had no real clue what to expect, but she hoped that at least she'd have the element of surprise.

The killer had homed in on the personal elements, had recreated Jamie's cases, had taken Elliot and brought him to his own home. So if he was going to be keeping Elliot somewhere, it would be somewhere personal to him.

'Did Elliot have an office, or a favourite place in the house?'

'Yes,' she said. 'It's on the upper floor, overlooking the garden. Last door on the left when you're upstairs.'

'The *furthest* from the servants' staircase?'

'Yes,' Mila said, almost reluctantly.

'Alright,' Jamie breathed, steadying herself. 'No point wasting more time.' She pulled her P229 pistol free of its position tucked in the small of her back and ejected the magazine, checking it was fully loaded. Thankfully it was.

'I'm going in on foot. Take the car, and go back down to the main road. Keep the lights off,' she instructed.

Mila nodded affirmatively. 'Here, you'll need these,' she said, pushing a set of keys into Jamie's hand, 'for the doors.'

Jamie looked down at them. She hadn't really considered how she was going to get inside, but this would be much easier than breaking a window or finding a way to lever the door open. 'Thanks,' she said, offering a brief, unsteady smile before reaching for the door handle.

Alina's hand found her shoulder then and Jamie paused, looking back at her.

'Do you want me to come with you?' she asked, her voice small. She didn't want to come, Jamie could tell that, but the fact she was offering meant a lot. Still, Jamie wasn't going to let her. Not in a million years.

'You look after Hati,' she said, her eyes falling to the mutt, his one eye shining in the darkness. 'He needs you more.'

She smiled softly. 'Be careful.'

'Always,' Jamie said, reaching up and squeezing her hand. 'I'll be right back, I promise.'

Alina's grip tightened on her shoulder and then released, allowing Jamie to slip from the car.

She waited until Mila climbed across to the driver's seat and started reversing down the road, the gentle whine of the gearbox ringing in the dark. Luckily it was a quarter of a mile across the grounds to the building, the lawns lined and dotted with fruit trees Mila had said.

Thick enough foliage to swallow the sound. And to mask Jamie's approach.

When the Toyota was out of view, Jamie approached the gate, standing between the massive stone pillars, weapon hanging loosely at her side.

It wasn't just the element of surprise that was guiding her here alone. She felt like she was supposed to be by herself. Voss had gone through all the trouble of getting rid of everyone else, of singling her out. He'd had chances to kill her, to hurt her, to confront her ... but he hadn't. He'd left her alone and well, going after the others instead. And she wasn't about to let anyone else get hurt. She knew that he wanted her and only her. And whatever lay in wait wasn't going to be good. But it would be worse for anyone else.

And as she began the journey towards the house, she knew that there was no element of surprise. Not really. She was either coming here exactly when Voss wanted her to, or he'd wanted her to come earlier and she'd just failed to figure it out.

Either way, she expected him to be waiting. And watching.

But she still had to be careful, because maybe this was it. Maybe this is where it was supposed to happen, and he was just holding Elliot so that he could lure

Jamie here to kill her right in front of him. Was that his punishment? To watch Jamie die?

A part of her wanted to stand in front of the house and scream his name, demand he came out. Demand he faced her. But she still hoped, waning as it was, that she could get inside and find him before he found her.

As she neared, the house rose above her, dark and cold. She shrank under its size, its heft, thinking about what it would be like to grow up in a place like this. How empty it must have felt. She'd never wanted to know more about Elliot, never wanted to know him better. And she'd never felt more conflicted, either. He'd done so much to gain her trust, and it felt like they'd come so far. And now this – another layer peeled back to reveal what festered beneath it all.

Jamie followed Mila's directions, tracing her way around the building, being careful to stick to the trees and the grass, avoiding the stone-chipped paths and the noise they would create.

The driveway led to the front of the house, splitting at the foot of a stone staircase and running in two directions. As Jamie continued to skirt the left-hand one, she saw that it led to a parking area and a bank of garages attached to the house, and there, in front of them, was a wooden door to the main building.

She breathed a little sigh of relief, taking a minute to assess the situation, to make sure she wasn't running into a trap. Nothing moved and no lights burned. The entire place was as quiet as a grave. She just prayed it wasn't about to be hers.

Being careful to step over the chippings running along the edge of the lawn, she stole across the tarmac and approached the door, pulling out Mila's keys.

She pressed herself to the wood, and began thumbing through them, squinting in the darkness to see if she could match key to lock. She tried three or four before one fitted and turned, the old, heavy bolt clunking as it did.

She cursed and held the handle, listening.

She pulled the door open slowly, and mercifully it didn't squeak.

And then she was inside, her weapon unholstered, her sweating hand flexing around the grip.

She left the door ajar and waited for her eyes to adjust to the pitch darkness inside. There was no moonlight to guide her here. Just her outstretched hand, fumbling along the smooth stone walls.

'Fuck,' she dared to whisper. She couldn't see shit, which meant she could be walking into anything. Something Alina said came to her mind – an axe rigged to swing down into a doorway right into her chest. It was an easy decision to take her phone out and risk the torch after that.

CHAPTER
THIRTY-ONE

The beam cut through the air, lighting up the room Jamie was in.

As Mila had said, it was a laundry room. Across the back were two pairs of laundry machines - washers and driers - and to their left, a huge drying rack and empty shelves that would have no doubt been filled with sheets and towels at one point. Now they just lay vacant and abandoned, like a skeleton of a once living creature.

Jamie's eyes continued to move, finding the door that led to the upper floors. She breathed a little sigh of relief and started towards it, not wanting to waste any more time. Though as she got close, the light from her phone caught a chunk of shining steel. She closed in on it, lifting the heavy laser-key padlock, inspecting it, along with the lock that had been installed on the door.

With rivets, not bolts or screws, so she'd have no chance removing it.

It was all brand new, done just for her, to stop her going up there. Too big to smash, impossible to pick.

She looked around instinctively for another message; "Right where I want you". But she didn't see one, just a clear path through the house. One she had to follow.

Might as well be a yellow brick road, she thought sourly, swooping back towards the doorway to the kitchen.

She approached cautiously, weapon raised, and moved through it, listening for any hint of movement ahead, anything to suggest she wasn't alone.

As she passed under the frame, she felt something brush the strands of hair on the top of her head and ducked instinctively, turning back to look. A spider's web?

She saw nothing, holding the light up, moving it around to see what she was missing. And then it glimmered, the thinnest strand pulled taught across the opening.

She moved closer, holding the phone so the light played down its length. It was like a hair, so minute she was barely even sure it was there. But it was.

She reached out and rested her thumb on it, getting the same sensation you did when you checked the sharpness of a knife.

For a moment she didn't know what she was looking at, but then her mind went to the wire across the path at the farm. Same thing, except this was finer, sharper. And set at the perfect height for Jamie to walk right under it, but for anyone else - for Hassan or anyone with her - to have their face sliced, their eyes. Another fail-safe to thin the herd.

She grimaced and lifted her pistol, bringing the barrel of it down on the wire. It twanged, the metal line whining before it ripped free of the frame and hung limply at one side.

She needed to be careful now. Expect this sort of thing around every corner.

She carried on, turning back and heading through the larder, another empty room lined with shelves that would have once been full of food. There was an old feather duster on one of them and she grabbed it, waving it through the doorways to check for any other traps.

This one was clear and she stepped up into the kitchen, pushing the door open slowly.

Mila and Elliot had moved out months ago. So why was there a smell of fresh food? How long had Voss been here, making himself at home?

Something kindled in her memories, the smell familiar, dragging something from her past to the front of her mind.

The door swung wide to reveal the kitchen, an old wooden table in its centre. A single chair was pulled out, and in front of it, a plate of steak, fried onions, and potatoes.

Jamie stared at it, and then remembered. When Elliot had *let himself in* to her apartment in London, he'd cooked this exact meal for her.

But how the hell would Voss know that? It was waiting for her now as it had been then. It was during the trafficking case she'd worked, after she found out who Elliot really was.

She'd thought it was poisoned. But it wasn't, he'd simply been trying to do something nice, or at least Elliot's version of nice. Which wasn't quite the same as anyone else's.

Jamie blinked a few times, trying to regain a sense of the present. Of what she was here to do.

It's all a trick, she told herself. Made to mess with you.

She stepped forward, waved her hand over it. Jesus, it was still warm.

Guess that meant she *didn't* have the element of surprise.

She moved to the counter, swapping the feather duster for the chef's knife lying there, the one that Voss had used to prep her meal. She picked it up, holding it in her left hand along with her phone, and used it like a probe to check the next doorway which led through to a sitting room containing old, wooden-backed sofas and chairs. Ahead, she could see that it opened into a dining room and then, beyond, the main entrance hallway.

She steadied her breathing, feeling oddly calm about it all, like there wasn't anything to be afraid of. Not yet at least.

The rooms moved by in a blur, her eyes aching from focusing so hard as she circled the twelve-seat dining table and moved into the hallway. She paused there, looking left and right. The house was dark. Silent.

The stairs loomed ahead, stretching upwards into darkness.

She let out a little breath. What she'd find at the top she didn't know, but she knew it's where she had to go.

They creaked under foot as she ascended, not worried about the sound her weight made on the staircase any more. Voss knew she was here.

As she crested the stairs she froze.

There in front of her was a single chair. On it, a pair of thick zip ties.

She looked at the thing, wondering what the hell it was for.

And then her wrists burned a little, and she remembered when she'd been trying to gather evidence on two corrupt detectives working at the Met - Brock and Amherst. How they'd shown up at her apartment seemingly at random and taken her. How they'd zip-tied her to a chair, questioned her, threatened to beat her, to kill her. And how Elliot had swept in at the last moment and saved her life. She'd always counted that in his *for* column. But she never did quite know why Brock and Amherst had chosen that moment to take her, or how

Elliot knew where she was, and right when she needed him. She'd always had an inkling that it was him. That it was all his machinations. That she was, and always would be, just a pawn he moved around the board at will, putting her in front of the queen to bait her, or sacrificing her to create a greater opening.

Jamie grimaced and moved past the chair, not appreciating this latest trip down memory lane.

She kept going, the silence in the house deafening. She expected everything to be covered in white cloth, preserving it, but the place was pristine, not a lick of dust anywhere. It smelled like it was being cleaned daily, despite the emptiness. Had this been where Voss had camped out? Where he'd been plotting and planning and scheming? How he'd got all the way here, Jamie didn't know. America was a long way away. But Elliot seemed to have no trouble scurrying through the cracks, and if they were as close friends as Jamie feared, then they probably ran with the same crowd, had the same contacts. The same modes and methods of transportation and infiltration.

Jamie slowed, the first noise breaking the quiet ahead.

She listened, pricking her ears, trying to discern what it was. The sounds of a piano, of violins filtered back to her. The gentle rise and fall of classical music. She didn't know what piece it was, but the sounds were all too familiar, echoing down this long corridor, mournful and cold. Ahead, a tiny shard of light punctured the darkness from beneath a doorway, beckoning her.

An acrid smell burned her nostrils then, harsh and chemical-like. She grimaced, turning away from it, pushing her nose into the crook of her elbow as her mind wrestled with it. She knew that smell. It was familiar, like everything else here. What was it? When was it from?

As she looked up again, her mind betrayed her for an instant, the corridor gone, replaced with the platform in Halliday Station, the disused underground stop that Aaron McElroy, the killer who'd harvested the hands of musicians, had used as his base. The smell was formaldehyde, the preserving chemicals he'd used to do his work.

Jamie shook her head again, her mind swimming from the sudden onslaught of the odour. She stifled a cough, trying to get it out of her throat, but it wouldn't budge.

Halliday Station faded and she came back to reality, the memory of what happened down there replaying in her head. They'd caught McElroy, Hassan dealing him a vicious blow that had put him down but not killed him. Though someone did die that day: Mimi Paganelli. Jamie had been operating under the assumption she was dead, but she was very much alive, and when she rushed Jamie with a knife, she had been forced to put her down. To shoot her.

She'd collapsed in front of her, the life draining from her right before Jamie's eyes.

That was her first kill.

The one that started it all, the first ripple in what had now become a storm of death, swirling around her.

Jamie blinked again and realised she was right in front of the door with the light coming from it.

The last on the left.

Elliot's office.

Her hand stretched out. What awaited her? Alina's axe to the chest? No, she didn't think so. She half expected Elliot to be sitting there, a cup of tea in hand, awaiting her arrival. That this would all be some great trick of his and she was once more led on a merry chase, a pawn moving in his game.

She touched the knob, hesitated for just a second, and then twisted and pushed the door inwards.

It swung freely, smoothly on the hinges, revealing the scene within.

Elliot's office was cavernous, like all the rooms here, she suspected. The walls were lined with huge book-cases stretching to the ceiling, filled with volumes and volumes, ranging from ancient to new, covering every topic that teased his brain she thought.

Great artworks hung on the walls, no doubt care-fully curated and all meaning something to him. Repre-senting some great, unknowable thing to mere mortals.

And yet, the god that Elliot thought himself to be … had been brought low.

A huge desk dominated the centre of the room, a single lamp burning atop it, throwing light over Elliot's bare shoulders.

He was on his knees, naked, his hands bound behind his back, lashed to his bound ankles so that he could only double forward. Except he couldn't even do that. Fastened around his throat and attached to the ceiling by a chain was a spiked collar, the barbs facing inwards, drawing blood from his throat. It dripped down his chest, his stomach, onto his thighs. His bare skin was slick with sweat, shining in the meagre light as he struggled to stay upright, to stay conscious. If he didn't, if he gave in and sank forward, the collar would puncture his windpipe, sever his carotid. He'd drown in his own blood if he didn't bleed out before that happened.

Elliot shuddered under the strain of it all, his eyes lifting from the floor in front of him to Jamie. For the first time in her life, she saw fear in them. The icy, cold blue was now weak and watery, bloodshot and unfocused.

His teeth showed between his lips as he bit down on the fabric gag pulled tight into his cheeks.

He made a small, pained groaning noise and Jamie stepped forward instinctively, moving to untie him.

'I wouldn't,' came a voice from the darkness behind him.

Jamie's eyes jumped to the silhouette leaning against the bookcase. She squinted through the glow of the lamp, seeing it only illuminating him from the knees down. His large frame was familiar, his accent unmistakable. American. Julian Voss.

He didn't move. Stayed perfectly still, arms folded easily.

Jamie's pistol lifted, levelling his head between the sights.

'Shoot me,' he said easily, his voice echoing around the room, smooth and cool, like Elliot's always was, 'and you'll be killing him. You see that neat little collar I made him? Well, it's attached to my wrist. My arm falls an inch, and he'll get his throat cut. So I'd stay that trigger finger. At least until I'm done talking.'

Jamie's eyes went to the chain, seeing now, just like at the energy park, it was run through a pully, the other end indeed attached to Julian Voss's wrist. Had she not already seen it in action she might have risked it, tried to shoot the chain, or done something else. But she already saw what happened when she tried to play by her own rules. This time, she had to play by his. This was Voss's game. It always had been.

'You want to talk?' she spat, looking him in the eye, pistol still raised. 'Then talk.'

She didn't want to hear what he had to say, but she needed time to think. Time to figure a way out of this. A way to save Elliot. That was all that mattered now.

'Don't sound so unenthused,' he drawled. 'It's a story you'll like. I promise you that.' He chuckled softly and

Jamie shuddered. Was this the man she'd seen at the hospital in York?

The American drew a slow breath, still unmoving, and then began.

'Elliot and I used to be friends. Good friends, in fact. Isn't that right, *buddy*?'

Elliot winced slightly and Jamie didn't know if Voss had given the chain just the gentlest tug.

'We got on very well. Saw something in each other that we both recognised. It's rare in this world to find that, isn't it? Someone you can just be your true self with.'

Elliot looked up at Jamie and she stared back. How many times had she said those exact words to herself when justifying his actions?

'Though you know all about that, don't you? It's a shame, really,' Voss went on, 'that I have you at such a disadvantage. I know all about you, and you don't know me at all.'

'I know who you are,' Jamie said, still keeping her gun firmly raised.

He chuckled through closed lips. 'Of course you do. Or you think you do, at least. I am Julian Voss, surgeon, intellectual, chess grandmaster, friend to many, foe to some—'

'And a fucking serial killer,' she spat, not able to help herself. Who the fuck was this guy? Did he think *that* highly of himself?

Elliot's pleading whimper said that he did. Don't poke the bear, it seemed to say.

'If you like. But no worse than the one kneeling in front of you. Better, even. I've killed fewer people. By a long stretch. Your Elliot here is quite prolific.'

Jamie swallowed, not looking at the man on his knees. 'Is this your big story? I'm getting tired already.'

'Oh no, this is just the preamble. An aperitif. A little witty repartee to get us in the mood. Some verbal jousting. Like you and Elliot are wont to do, hmm? He told me all about that. Your sharpness, your ability to thrust and feint and wound so deeply. You think he doesn't feel, but he does ...'

'Any time this millennium,' she urged him.

'You know,' Voss went on, unperturbed, 'that when Elliot first met you, he reached out to me. He told me about you. I suppose we were about as close as friends could be at that time. He said that there'd been a *mishap* with his work, and a young determined detective was on his trail. And he thought you might be smart enough to figure him out.'

A mishap? Oliver Hammond escaping. Is that what it's called when one of your victims slips through your fingers? She let Voss keep going.

'He thought the best way to ensure that you *didn't* figure him out was to get close to you. Was to ... *befriend* you. I suggested, rather uncouthly, that he should seduce you, bed you, fuck you so silly that you wouldn't have the mental capacity to see through him.'

Jamie's eyes flitted to Elliot again. He watched her unflinchingly, breathing slow.

'But he wasn't amenable to that. It's a tried-and-true method, but he seemed to actually *like* you. Which I found odd. Especially given your positions on opposite sides of the board. But the heart wants what the heart wants, doesn't it? And he thought he had you, that he was safe. That he'd pulled the wool over your eyes. That letting you in, just a little, would be enough to persuade you of his humanity, that once you saw that little glimmer of warmth flickering in his soul, deep down in that endless, dark pit inside him … that you'd convince yourself, oh dear and real *friend* of Elliot Day, that he wouldn't, nay, *couldn't* have committed such vile acts. That was his plan. It almost worked, didn't it? And despite himself, his desire to, and my advice to, keep an even keel, keep you at arm's length … he just couldn't. Couldn't resist. Just couldn't help but fall in love with you.'

Elliot's gaze fell to the ground for a moment, and then slowly raised to Jamie once more.

She looked back at him.

'What a touching moment,' Voss boomed. 'Is this how you imagined it? Finally hearing that word aloud in each other's presence? You've tried so hard to resist it for so long, haven't you? But I'm getting ahead of myself here. There's more to this story. Where was I? Ah, yes. Elliot thought he'd got away with it, that you'd lost the trail. But then, much to his chagrin, the watch.'

Jamie remembered. It was the watch. The watch that had pointed her at Elliot when there was nothing else. A watch they found in the tent of a homeless girl. A watch that she'd stolen from Elliot. It was as small a detail as a mismatched outfit that had niggled at her. Enough to burst the illusion he'd created.

'He told me about that. I thought it was hilarious. Undone by matching a silver watch with brown shoes. His sloppiness of course was the thing. Careless even.'

Elliot bristled as best he could without slitting his own throat.

'I thought it was a great piece of deductive work,' Jamie said flatly.

'It was. Or maybe it was a shot in the dark and you got lucky. Who knows? Who cares? That's not the part of the story I like the most.'

'And what is?' Jamie asked, narrowing her eyes slightly and adjusting her aim. She wondered if she could confidently blow a hole through Voss's wrist. Whether she could sever the chain in a single shot.

'That despite Elliot's affection for you, his blossoming love, and that he thought he got away with it, the night that you finally *cracked the case,* the same night you were supposed to meet him for dinner, to see where it would all go ...'

Jamie glanced at Elliot once more, but he wasn't looking at her. His eyes were lowered, as though he couldn't face her.

Her skin erupted in gooseflesh, as though knowing what Voss was about to say before he even did.

'That night,' he said, 'Elliot was going to kill you.'

CHAPTER
THIRTY-TWO

Jamie's mouth went dry all of a sudden.

Elliot was going to kill her?

'It's alright,' Voss said. 'Take your time to process that.'

Jamie needed to. She looked down at Elliot, feeling the gun waver and begin to sink in her grasp. This man, the one in front of her … the man she *loved*? He'd wanted to kill her. And had she not found him out, just hours before they were due to meet, he would have. That thought rang in her head. An alarm bell she couldn't ignore.

'I admit,' Voss continued, though Jamie wished he wouldn't, 'I may have moved the needle a little. Encouraged him to take care of the problem. Egged him on, so to say. From all he told me about you, about how smart, how tenacious, how damaged you were … we both knew that any kind of relationship would have a timer on it. Would count down to the inevitable slip up. You'd be too curious, too questioning ... *Dear, why are you home so late and whose blood is that all over you?* That sort of thing. So I suggested that he simply take care of you before that happened. And, well, he agreed it was for the best. Self-preservation and all that,' Voss sighed, 'but then, somewhere down the line, after you ran him out of house, home, *and* country, he changed his mind.' Voss's frustration was palpable. 'And I didn't see it coming. You see, you not only figured out Elliot's *dark secret*, you also cost him his life, his livelihood, every-thing. You made it so he could never go home, never be himself, never walk free with his head held high ever again. And that ... that hurt him. Made him want to hurt you.'

Jamie held firm, watching the American.

'And he had plans, unfinished business in London. He knew he could use you. And he did, didn't he? Came back, got you involved in things you didn't understand, got you doing his bidding for reasons you couldn't even fathom. You know that, don't you? Remember that? How he manipulated you, lied to you, coerced, groomed you ...'

Jamie did remember that. She remembered it all.

'All for his own amusement. His own enjoyment. It was the beginning of his revenge. To take everything from you. Slowly, piece by piece. Gain your trust. And then drive a knife between your ribs. Metaphorically, of course. That would have been too quick. Too kind. Oh, in those days we dreamt up so many ways to kill you. To skin you, to maim you. To slaughter you like an animal, or to torture you across days, weeks even. To really revel in it. To enjoy it. But then, somewhere along the way, Elliot lost his nerve. He changed his mind.' The words dripped with contempt. 'I began to gain an inkling of it. That he was getting cold feet. That his heart and his stomach weren't in it. But I never thought that he would do what he did. Betraying me like that. I didn't realise it at the time – this was my best friend! A man to whom I told all my deepest, darkest secrets. A man I thought held my confidence. And yet it couldn't have been anyone else.

'I suppose it was shortly after he came to visit you in Scotland, after you killed that girl, what was her name? Mimi Paganelli? How did that feel, your first? Is it still fresh enough that you remember? It's been so long for me. Alas, I digress. It was just after that when he said he wanted to come to America, to stay with me, to lay low because there was too much buzz about him in Europe and in England. And I welcomed him. Little did I know he was a Trojan horse. He said he was all twisted up with what had happened, that he needed a palate cleanser. A fresh kill in a fresh place to stoke his fire for murder. To get him ready for … you.'

'Stephen Farrow,' Jamie said.

'Oh, you have been busy.' He gave the same easy, chilling chuckle. 'Yes, Stephen Farrow. Elliot said he wished to watch, to study my methodology, my selection process, the way I conducted myself before, during, and after. And I, the fool that I was, fell for it. We selected Farrow together, talked at length about how we'd do it, when, where. And we carried it out. Flawlessly. And it was the most enjoyable kill of my life. I hadn't considered working with a partner before, but oh how sumptuous it was, how liberating! And then, from nowhere, a knock at the door. Who could that be, I thought. I rose from my chair, Elliot sitting opposite with an innocent, dumb look on his face, lowering his book with complete nonchalance, and I walked to the door, opening it to find two FBI agents and a fleet of police officers standing on my stoop. And when I turned and looked back into the living room, the chair was empty, the book laid neatly on the coffee table. And Elliot? Elliot was gone.'

He was looking up at her again, as close to crying as Jamie thought he was capable of.

How like him. To betray, to stab in the back like that. Every friend, everyone that trusted him, he betrayed.

Her weapon fell lower, and lower, and then hung at her side.

'There it is,' Voss said.

Jamie hung her head.

'Now do you see? Do you see what he really is? What *this* really is? What it's all about?'

'It's for him,' Jamie said. 'It's about Elliot.'

'Yes! And you. It's about him, and you, and me. And it's about him finishing what he started.'

'Killing me ...' Jamie said, the words barely forming on her tongue.

'When it started, when *I* started, Elliot understood. He understood very quickly, and he found me. Pleaded for it to stop. Well, more like *demanded*. But I told him, there's only one way it stops. That the killing stops. And that's to do what he promised he would. And kill you. Finally, finally kill you.'

'But he wouldn't,' Jamie muttered, not looking at either of them.

'No, he wouldn't. Rather disappointingly. So the killing went on. And it will go on ...'

Jamie's eyes snapped to Voss.

'... that is unless ...' He took his time, languishing in it. 'Unless you kill Elliot instead.'

She froze, her heart beating hard in her throat.

'You have a gun, and he's on his knees. You know what he did, what he's done. And now you know the whole truth. That he was going to murder you. Like one of his *donors*.' He tutted disapprovingly, as though calling them that, giving Elliot's victims a *reason* for dying other than simply the pleasure of the killer somehow cheapened it all. 'So I serve it up on a plate. Your revenge. Your recompense. Your ... liberation. From his stranglehold. From his dominion, his influence, his crushing grip on every facet of your life and being. Just raise it up, Jamie, raise up that gun and point it at him. Put it between his eyes and pull the trigger. Do that, and it will all be over. I will stop. I will not kill any more. I will simply melt away, disappear, and you'll never hear from me again. It will be done. You have my word on that. Don't, and the killing will go on. And on. And on. And I can promise it won't get better. It will only get worse.'

Jamie looked at Voss, then turned her attention to Elliot.

He looked back at her, breathing slow. And then he nodded. Do it. She could practically hear his voice. Do it, Jamie. Kill me and save them. Save yourself. From having to go through that. From having to live with that.

She raised her weapon slowly, shakily, until it was level with Elliot's forehead.

'Do it,' Voss said. 'Kill Elliot Day and be done with him forever.'

Jamie couldn't say she hadn't thought about it. Hadn't threatened it. A hundred times. Hadn't dreamt about what it would feel like to finally be rid of him. To finally be without him. To finally be free. To finally be ... alone.

She let out a slow, rattling breath.

Elliot closed his eyes.

She rested her finger on the trigger, taking one last look at Elliot Day.

Kill him, and the killing stops. Voss disappears. That is the end of it.

But then ... those women. Julie Johns, Judith James, Jana Jelinek, Jillian Jones ... they all died, for what? For

Jamie to stand here and kill Elliot? And for Voss to just get away with it all? No. As terrible as Elliot was, letting Voss walk free? That was worse than anything else.

In a flash, Jamie's gun lifted over Elliot's head, finding Voss in the darkness.

She pulled the trigger three times. Three shots. Close grouping. Centre mass. No fucking around. No risks. Heart shots.

Muzzle flash lit the room, the reports echoing, deafening. Elliot let out a long, stifled howl.

Voss convulsed, tipped back, and then sprawled forwards.

The chain quickly snapped tight around Elliot's throat, but Jamie was quicker. Her hand leapt out, snatching the chain from the air, stopping it from ripping into his throat.

The barbs bit his skin and fresh blood ran down his chest.

The American fell straight into Elliot's desk and Jamie waited for the crack. The crack of a skull on polished wood, the dull thwump of a dead body hitting the floor. The shake as his weight shook the boards.

But it didn't come. A hollow thud echoed, and Voss's stiff body bounced off the corner of the desk and dropped to the ground behind it, the end of the chain swinging freely in the air above the lamp.

'What the fuck?' Jamie said aloud, yanking on the chain so that it flew through the pulley and fell to the floor next to Elliot's knees.

He keeled forward, exhausted, and laid on his side, mumbling frantically through the gag as Jamie walked around the desk to finally lay eyes on Voss. But he wasn't there. The only thing she found was a mannequin. Dressed in a suit, a sinister, bloody grin smeared across its featureless face.

'How disappointing.' Voss's voice echoed in the room and Jamie saw now that a speaker was fixed to the wall behind the spot where the mannequin had been standing. Voss's voice piped in from who knew where.

Her eyes went upwards then, looking for and finding the camera hidden in the gloom above them.

Voss was watching it all.

'I should take some joy in the fact that you were willing to risk killing Elliot to get to me I suppose ... but it wasn't what I asked. It wasn't the deal. And now, Elliot, you know what's coming next. You have your life, but at what price? The ghosts of your past are coming back to haunt you. Say hello to them for me.'

The voice disappeared and a low, thin static rang in the air.

Jamie stared at the speaker for a moment longer, then the camera. And then she lifted her pistol once more and blew it to pieces. Then the speaker.

On Elliot's desk she could see a shining letter opener. She grabbed it and went to him, finding the rope between his wrists and ankles and cutting through it without much care.

He groaned with relief as he unfurled, twisting

around and bringing his hands under his feet. They were still bound, but at least now he could move them independent of each other. She didn't much feel like untying him just yet. She didn't much feel like doing anything – except maybe shooting him after all.

What had just happened? And what had she unleashed?

Elliot pulled the gag from his mouth and pushed himself to his hands and knees, still fighting to catch his breath. 'Jamie—' he started.

'Save it,' she replied, raising her head and looking through the open door. 'He could still be listening.' Her voice was hollow, emotionless. This was his work, his doing. He'd emptied her out once again. A knife between the ribs, metaphorically. He'd done what Voss had said he would, what he'd done to everyone else.

He'd betrayed her.

For the last time, she promised herself.

'Please,' he said, forcing himself to a shaky stance before her. 'Just let me explain—'

'I don't want to,' she said coldly, looking right past him. 'I'm going home.' She steeled herself. 'I suggest you do the same. Your wife is waiting for you.'

Numbly, she stepped past him and out into the hall-way, retracing her steps back down the corridor.

She could feel him watching her from the doorway as she went, kicking over the chair at the top of the stairs as she reached them, descending at speed. In the kitchen she picked up the plate of food and hurled it into the wall, shattering it into a thousand pieces. She flew past the limply hanging wire and out into the laundry room. She pulled the door wide, throwing it into the wall, and then stepped out into the night and walked away from Elliot Day's house.

And she hoped, really, really hoped, away from Elliot Day too.

But she knew that wasn't possible.

That whatever had happened in that room tonight ... that it would have reverberations that would shake her life to its foundations. That it would begin a storm unlike any she'd faced before. And that at the centre of it, with chaos and death and destruction swirling all around, would be her and Elliot.

As Jamie walked, she wiped tears from her cheeks with the backs of her hands, wishing she'd taken that deal.

That she'd killed Elliot Day.

And that it could all just be over.

EPILOGUE

The time between Jamie walking out of Elliot's house and her climbing into bed was a blur.

She knew she'd shoed Mila into the passenger seat and then driven back to her house. She knew she'd asked what happened, what was going on, was Elliot okay? Was he alive?

Jamie offered curt answers. Yes. He's fine. Ask him yourself.

Mila seemed to glean that all was not right, and that any explanation would need to come from the man himself.

She climbed out and disappeared into the house without a word and then Alina clambered into the front seat.

She seemed to talk a lot on the way home, not asking about what had happened, but rather filling the silence. Jamie suspected, now, lying in bed the following morning, that she'd sensed Jamie had gone through something, and knew she didn't want to talk about it. Alina had likely experienced the same thing. And the silence that followed, that festered, was worse than anything. Even if talking was just white noise, it kept the darkness that came with the quiet at bay.

Jamie smiled a little, thinking of that. Thinking of her. How wonderful she was. How strong. How caring. How smart. And how fragile. How Jamie's life could so easily spill over, and had, to Alina. How she could be caught in any crossfire at any time. And how terrifying that was.

There was a knock at the door, timid almost, and then it cracked open and Alina appeared in the gap, smiling.

The sun streaming in through the window told her it was still early. She wondered how long she'd slept. How long Alina had slept. She nudged the door open with a tray in her hands and came towards the bed.

Jamie pushed herself backwards so she was sitting upright, the covers over her legs, and crossed them to make room.

Before Alina got there Hati loped in and leapt up on the bed, slumping down awkwardly right in the middle.

'Make yourself at home,' Jamie said, shifting more to get out of his way.

He fired her a sideways glance and then rested his chin on his paws.

Alina knelt at the bedside and laid the tray on the duvet.

There was a silver cafetière, a thin stream of steam curling from the spout, the plunger not yet pushed down. Two cups with milk already in them sat next to it.

Alina was staring right at Jamie.

'Thanks,' Jamie said, almost shyly. 'Guess I must have slept in ...'

'You didn't,' Alina said, still staring right at her. 'You never do. Which means, if you're in here, you're hiding. And you only do that when there's something you don't want to talk about.'

Jamie stared back at her now. 'Sure you want to be a detective? Sounds more like you've got a future in psychology.'

'They're pretty much the same, aren't they? Reading people is job number one?'

'I guess so,' Jamie said, reaching out and pushing down the plunger, knowing she'd need coffee for what they were building up to.

'Not yet,' Alina said swatting her away.

'Holding it hostage until I tell you what happened last night, are you?' Jamie asked, trying to lighten things.

'No, I'm just letting it steep properly. Hassan was very particular about the method, but he wasn't wrong,' Alina answered. 'And I wouldn't do that – wouldn't try to blackmail you into talking to me. I hope by now that you'd *want* to talk to me.'

Jesus, when did she become an adult? Jamie thought. She was so mature, so sharp. Too sharp to hide anything from anymore. And she was right, Jamie shouldn't want to hide anything from her anymore. They were ... mother and daughter, Jamie supposed. Though that still seemed so strange to her. She wondered if, as Alina grew older, she'd see her more as a sister, more as a friend, than the girl she rescued ... She didn't know. Time would tell, she supposed.

Alina, seemingly happy with the coffee now, slowly pressed the plunger down, a mirror image of Hassan when he did it. Flat of the palm, even pressure. Work *with* the coffee, not against it, or you get sediment above the filter.

It was one thing Jamie had to credit Alina with; her ability to mimic, to mirror, to pick things up quickly and perfectly.

She carefully measured out two cups of coffee, moving slow so Jamie had enough time to stump up the courage to speak. But she knew Alina wouldn't wait forever. And to let her go without telling her everything wasn't fair. Elliot was too much to her for her to not know the truth, and, hell, Jamie could do with the advice.

But how to put this?

'Elliot is alive, he's fine,' Jamie said, almost as a throwaway remark, as Alina handed her her coffee.

'I guessed. Anger meant he was alive. And that what

you found out wasn't … good. He was involved with the killer somehow? This whole thing was about him?'

'You were right, yes. The killer was targeting him all along. And was … punishing me, I suppose, to get at Elliot. They were friends. Good friends from what he said.' Jamie readjusted herself in bed, making enough space for Alina to climb in next to her. And she did so without invitation, causing Hati to promptly roll over so she could scratch his neck. Which she did so without invitation.

Jamie went on, 'How much did he tell you about how we first met? About how we got to know each other?'

'Not a lot. He said you'd tell me when you were ready. Just that he was on the other side of things to you, that he did things that were technically wrong, but for good reasons …'

Jamie snorted a little at that. 'Of course he'd package it that way. Elliot was a killer.'

'We're all killers,' Alina said, almost gravely.

'Out of necessity,' Jamie reminded her.

'We always have a choice, don't we? Necessity is just a shield we hold up when the light shining on us is too bright.'

Jamie blinked a few times. 'Add philosopher to your careers list, why don't you.'

She smiled sadly but didn't say anything else.

Jamie sipped a little more coffee and went on, keen

to skip to the relevant part, keen not to paint Elliot in *too* ill a light. He'd betrayed her trust more than once, but he'd been good to Alina, and her own mother had done a great job of turning Jamie against her father when he'd only tried to do his best for her. She was determined not to do the same thing. Not to be that cruel. Especially not for her own gain. If there was one thing she was not, it was her mother.

'I was working my first murder case, and he was helping me. But he was also the person I was looking for. We grew closer, and ...' Jamie hesitated. She was about to admit something she'd never done so before. But after last night, it seemed pointless not to. 'I liked him.'

'Like *liked him* liked him?'

Jamie nodded. 'I think so. Which is rare. For me. But he understood me, it felt like, when no one else did.'

Alina nodded now, as though that was all the explanation she needed.

'But then I found out the truth, and what I felt meant nothing. He lied to me, he deceived me, and he turned out to be guilty. If I saw him, I needed to arrest him, to put him in prison for what he did. So he ran.'

'But he came back, right?' Alina asked.

Jamie had told her little bits. That they had a habit of separating and then coming back together. Alina had remarked it sounded like Elliot was a comet, and Jamie the sun. That she pulled him close and then pushed him away. But he was always in her orbit, whether she could see him or not. She didn't like how apt that sounded.

'He did,' Jamie went on. 'But not before he went running to Voss. He needed to be with someone he trusted, somewhere he could *lay low.'*

'And that's why you're so angry at him? Because he was friends with Voss and he didn't tell you?'

'No, it's not that,' Jamie said, searching for a way to make this not sound horrible. 'It's …' She let out a sigh. 'There's no other way to say it, really. Elliot was going to kill me.'

Alina spat out the coffee she was drinking, choking, then laughing, then coughing when she realised Jamie was serious. 'Really?'

She nodded. 'Yes. He'd discussed it at length with Voss, and they'd agreed to it. Planned it all out. All the ways they were going to hurt me. To cut me. To make me bleed. In recompense for discovering Elliot's truth, for ruining his life, Voss said.'

'But he obviously didn't,' Alina said defensively. 'He never tried to kill you, did he.' He it wasn't a question so much as an accusation.

'It's still …' Jamie began before checking her tone and making it less sharp. 'It's still that he lied. That he planned to, at some point, do it. That he was going to murder me.' She couldn't believe she had to re-explain that for effect.

'So says some psycho serial killer,' Alina said, shaking her head. 'Did you even ask Elliot if that was the case?

And anyway, if Voss was in jail, like he was, convicted for murder himself, and he was after Elliot when he broke out, then he likely had a hand in putting Voss away, right?'

'Right,' Jamie said, almost begrudgingly. 'Astute as always.'

'So Elliot was on your side, as usual. He didn't kill you, he betrayed Voss instead. So I really don't see why you're angry at him at all.

Jamie set her jaw. The simplicity of her reasoning was annoyingly sensical. But she was also overlooking a fact. A fact that Jamie always knew but never admitted to herself. That she ... loved Elliot. And that finding out he intended to murder her, whether he did it or not, was more devastating to Jamie than she could ever explain.

'And I'm guessing Voss is still alive?' Alina asked.

'Yes,' Jamie said.

'And Elliot is going to go after him, right?'

'I don't know. I would assume so.'

'And you're going to help him, *right?*'

'Uh ...'

'Right?'

'It's not that simple.'

'It is that simple. Elliot's done *everything* for you. Everything. Helped you whenever you've needed. Whenever you've asked. And now that he needs your help with something, you're just going to turn your back on him?' The scorn in her voice was clear.

'Alina ...'

But before she could say anything else Alina got up from the bed and walked out of the room.

Hati stared after her, than looked at Jamie.

'You understand, don't you?' she asked hopefully.

He chuffed once, then got up and went after Alina, disappearing through the open door.

Jamie let out a long sigh, and then closed her eyes and put her head back, the coffee already going cold in her hands.

SHE DIDN'T SEE ALINA FOR THE REST OF THE morning. She locked herself in her room, her music turned up.

But that was okay, because Jamie needed time to think, to regroup, and to plan her next move. Because this thing was far from over. And Voss's words were ringing in her head. The ghosts of Elliot's past coming back to haunt him. She had a sinking feeling that it wasn't some abstract metaphor, but rather something far more literal.

All of which meant that Jamie needed help. And she needed to make sure Radcliffe knew what was going on. He was her boss, and this was work after all.

He picked up quickly. Jamie was outside, walking the courtyard with her pistol in her hand – just in case – seeking a little privacy for the debrief. And with Alina inside and no one else here, it was the only place she could find it.

'Johansson,' he said. 'What have you got?'

'Julian Voss,' Jamie said. 'He's the man you're looking for, our escaped prisoner from Penhurst.'

'And how exactly did you come by this information?' The tone of his voice conveyed the fact that he was frustrated he didn't get there first.

'Friends in high places,' Jamie offered dryly. 'But it doesn't matter. What does matter is that he's got a bone to pick with Elliot Day – the biblical kind. And last night I pulled Elliot's head out of a noose. Literally.'

Radcliffe was silent.

Jamie bristled at his lack of response. 'You might have told me the terms of the NCA's deal with Elliot, by the way. Thanks for keeping me in the dark.'

'I'm sorry, I didn't realise it was part of your job description to know every facet of my private business.' The tone was enough to put Jamie in her place. 'This Voss,' he went on after a moment. 'You know where he is?'

'No, not yet,' Jamie said.

'You know what he's planning? Outside of putting Elliot's head on a pike?'

'No, not fully. But people are going to die. Going to keep dying. That much I can pretty much guess.'

'Guesswork. Fantastic,' Radcliffe muttered. 'You're in over your head, and you're drowning. That much is clear as day. But, the problem is, Johansson,' he said, slowly, 'you've backed me into a corner here. You and Day, your histories, the people you've pissed off ... And seeing as I'm the one who brought Elliot into this, and brought you into it, too ... well, if I go crying for help, it's *my* mess that needs cleaning up. So tell me, how big is this going to be? The ripples? It's my job on the line, I need to know.'

'Your job? It's our *lives,'* Jamie practically spat.

'Your lives *are* my job. And your lives are your job too. You are the thin line between people like Voss, people like Day, and the rest of the fucking world. That's what you signed up for, what you wanted. So don't cry to me now that you don't like it.'

Jamie was the one who was silent now.

'Answer me truthfully: can you get this done? You, Day, your little team? Or do I need to call in the cavalry? This is need to know as of right now, but if I make a phone call ... it's out of my hands and I can't control what happens. What happens to you, to your little ward, your protective bubble ... and I certainly can't help what happens to Elliot Day. This neat little house of cards you've built. It all comes crashing down. So tell me, can you get Voss?'

Jamie hoped it would be that simple. 'Yes,' she said. 'But I need Hassan.'

'He's with his family in protective custody. And I can hardly call and give the all-clear now, can I? Who else?'

'Hallberg?' Jamie asked.

'A little busy with her day job.'

'Uh ...' Jamie said.

'There no one else you haven't burned a bridge with?

'No, it's not that,' she said, 'I know someone, someone we can rely on. It's just ...'

'Just what?'

Just that last time we worked together, he didn't exactly take kindly to Elliot's presence, Elliot's personality, or Elliot and my relationship. So, if I bring him in and he finds out the truth, he might be liable to shoot Elliot in the head. And also, we slept together, and I was hoping it would be longer before I saw him again, and kind of hoping I'd *never* see him again ... Instead, Jamie just said, 'Nothing. I'll call him.'

'Good. Let me know if you need anything. Stay in touch, and stay safe.'

The line went dead and Jamie let out a long breath, pulling her phone away from her ear and looking at the screen. She navigated to her contacts, scrolled to the name she wanted, and let her thumb hover over it.

'Alright, then,' she muttered. 'Here we go.'

And then she called Solomon Church.

———

THE CONVERSATION LASTED ALL OF TWENTY seconds.

'Hello?' he asked, his deep voice a reminder of just how large he was.

'Church,' Jamie said, feeling herself smiling as she said his name. She'd been nervous before she'd called, but the thought of him coming did ease her angst some.

'Jamie? Is everything alright?' he asked cautiously, maybe reading the urgency in her voice.

Where to even begin? There'd be a lot to talk about, but over the phone wasn't the right way to handle it. 'No,' she said. 'I need help. Can you come?'

He processed that for a few seconds, and then simply said, 'Okay. I'll leave now, be there in the morning.'

Jamie barely got the word, 'Thanks,' out before he hung up. But despite the abrupt end to the call and whatever it was he was doing that she'd probably really inconveniently interrupted, she felt betting knowing he was on the way.

She'd thought about it, sought comfort in the knowledge that he was going to be there soon and she wouldn't be alone, as the day drained away.

She went for a run, trained a little in the barn, drank too much coffee, read too much about Julian Voss's life; or at least what she could find of it, and thought about everything he'd said. Everything that was to come.

And then it was night and she was in bed, still thinking about it.

Morning broke after an age and Jamie rose, knowing everything would be better that morning.

She heard the sound of a car coming down the drive

before she saw it and by the time she made it down the stairs, he was already at the door.

As she went towards it, her heart beat harder, her palms sweating. Alina wasn't up yet, but that was good. She needed some time alone with Church, to explain, to catch him up on everything that had happened. To work out what they were going to do next.

Just like ripping off a plaster, she thought. Open the door.

But as she did, the relief she felt all just fell away.

Because it wasn't Church.

It was Elliot.

And his wife.

He put his hand on the door as though Jamie were going to throw it shut in his face. She might well have.

'We need to talk,' he said, stepping forward.

Her kneejerk was to tell him that they didn't, but she thought they probably did. She'd just hoped to have a bit more time to mull things over before he arrived at her door.

Jamie let go of the handle and stepped back, going for the kitchen. Coffee. She needed coffee for this.

Elliot followed her inside. 'Jamie, please slow down,' he said. 'If you'd let me explain—'

'I think Voss did plenty of explaining,' Jamie replied coolly, fixing herself a cup. 'Or was there something important he missed?'

Elliot stopped in the doorway, Mila at his shoulder. 'I

don't expect you to forgive me, but I hope the fact that I didn't go through with it counts for something.'

Jamie tried not to think about Alina telling her the same thing. So she said nothing at all.

'But that's not the most pressing issue right now.'

'Voss,' Jamie said, leaning on the counter, a half-filled cup between her. 'He's still out there.'

'He is.'

'So how do we find him?' Jamie closed her eyes, feeling the easy warmth of the sun on her face. Winter was almost here now and the days were shortening quickly.

'We don't,' Elliot said. 'I do.'

'You're going after him alone.' It wasn't even a question. 'So why are you here?'

'Because Voss isn't our only problem.'

'The ghosts of your past?' Jamie asked. 'Voss didn't seem like the cryptic sort.'

'No, he's not,' Elliot said. 'Please, sit.' He offered her the table and she reluctantly agreed. If things were about to get worse, she needed as much information as she could get.

Before she even sat, Elliot was speaking.

'Julian and I didn't see eye to eye on a lot of things, as you saw last night.'

'Yeah, I kind of gleaned that from the fact that you were stripped naked and about to get your through cut.' Jamie leaned on the counter, sipping her coffee rather than sitting.

He cleared his throat a little. 'Yes, well, during our friendship, he was determined to get me into a little *club* that he was a part of. I was never keen on the idea, never liked it. The boastfulness of it, the arrogance. But ...'

'Jesus Christ,' Jamie muttered, shaking her head. 'Please don't tell me it was a club for serial killers?'

Elliot clasped his hands in front of him. 'Julian spent a lot of time on the dark web, surfing the deepest corners.'

'Oh my fucking God, it is. You were in a serial killer chatroom, weren't you?'

Elliot didn't deny it, and went on. 'Voss and several other prolific individuals would convene every now and then to ...' He seemed to fidget over the words. 'To discuss their work, and—'

'You mean killing people,' Jamie said flatly.

Mila looked down at the table but remained quiet.

Elliot let out a long breath. 'Yes,' he said. 'They were serial killers who got together to boast and brag about their killing. To discuss methods and tactics, and to generally wave their supremacy at others. One giant pissing contest,' Elliot said.

'And that's why you didn't like it? Couldn't measure up?' Jamie asked cuttingly.

His eyes flashed to her and she almost flinched. 'No,' he said, voice cold. 'I didn't like it because they were brutes. Animals. And they enjoyed killing in a way that I did not, that I don't, and I never will.'

Silence hung in the air for a few seconds and then Elliot seemed to soften a little. 'But regardless of what's already happened, we should be focused on what's coming next. And judging by what we saw at Ashwood Court, I know what that is. Or *who,* I should say.'

Jamie raised her eyebrows, waiting for her revelation.

'He goes by Mister Mannequin.'

'Mister Mannequin?' Jamie confirmed.

'His screen name,' Elliot said. 'In real life, they call him, The Mannequin Man, or at least that's the rough translation from Kashmiri, where he does most of his ... hunting. He's been active for about thirty years, give or take. And killed more than a hundred people.'

Jamie recalled the mannequin with the grim grin, and had wondered. Though she was hoping it wasn't going to be something like this.

'This Mister Mannequin ...' Jamie asked, almost afraid to do so.

'So the story goes, he used to be a night guard at a mannequin factory and warehouse—'

'Already not a good start,' Jamie said, folding her arms. 'Go on.'

'A massive factory in Northern India, north of Srinagar in the foothills of the Himalayas, makes them. Around four percent of all the mannequins on earth. Which is a lot, trust me,' Elliot said. 'In ninety-two, it was the worst winter storm in their history. A blizzard came in, and all but buried the factory entirely.

Overnight the doors were blocked, and across the week of the storm more than thirty feet fell, burying the warehouse almost entirely. It took weeks to dig the village free of the snow, and the factory came last. They expected him to be dead. His name is Bashir Amad, and he was not dead. But nearly a month in darkness with nothing but mannequins for company ...'

'I can only imagine.'

'He's quite mad. And his methods are quite ... brutal. He takes his victims and injects them with a paralytic agent mixed with a nasty concoction that stiffens muscles, thickens blood ...'

'So he takes them, injects them, poses them, and then they get stuck in that pose and die,' Jamie said plainly, finishing Elliot's explanation. 'Fucking great. So you made friends with this nutcase, all these nutcases, and now that you've stabbed Voss in the back he's gone ahead and flown them here first class to wreak havoc? That about the sum of it?'

Elliot glanced at Mila and then back at Jamie. 'I don't know for certain, but I suspect so.'

'Great,' Jamie muttered, pinching the bridge of her nose. 'So you want to go after Voss and leave me to deal with the psychotic mannequin-making super killer?'

'Divide and conquer,' he said, as though it would be some sort of consolation.

'What makes you think you can even get to Voss? He already captured you once before.'

'Last time, I went to talk to him.'

'And what's different now?'

'This time, I'm going to kill him.'

Jamie stared at his cold, surgical expression. It wasn't some claim. It was just fact.

The sound of another engine filtered through the glass behind her. Church. Thank God, she thought. She was sort of coming around to the idea of him shooting Elliot now. But having him here at least would be a barrier, someone else to make her feel a little more sane for all the anger she was harbouring right now.

The engine disappeared, a door opened and closed. Footsteps on gravel.

Jamie pushed off from the counter and headed for the door, Elliot watching her go.

'Two on one now,' she whispered to herself, grabbing the handle and twisting, pulling it open to welcome him before he even knocked. 'Church—' she started, the word dying in her mouth.

There was a man standing there. A man about as tall as Church. But it wasn't him, either. No, standing there, knuckles raised, ready to rap on the wood, with an expression displaying more rage than surprise, was the last person Jamie expected to see.

Kjell Thorsen.

She would have taken a *hello*. Even an *oh*. But not what he said.

'Fuck.' He lowered his hand and let out a long, unabashedly disappointed breath, and then turned around to reveal a woman standing behind him. She was petite, with short, dark hair, big eyes. Pretty features. And on her left hand, third finger, a diamond ring.

Jamie's eyes seemed to go there and stay there and all three of them stood in silence for a few seconds. It was only broken when a low growl emanated from behind Jamie.

She turned to look at the stairs and saw Hati standing there, halfway down, looking over her shoulder out of the open doorway.

'Hati?' Thorsen asked, blinking a few times to make sure he wasn't seeing things. 'How did you—' But before he could finish, the dog bounded down and leapt at him, all but knocking him over.

Thorsen grabbed the mutt by the neck and wrestled him back to earth, petting him roughly, just how he liked, while the dog licked vigorously at his face.

Alina's laugh punctuated the air and she stepped down next to Jamie. 'He likes you,' she announced, looking at Thorsen and the mystery woman behind him.

'I like him,' Thorsen said back without looking up. 'I missed him. Didn't think I'd see him again. Didn't think you would, either,' Thorsen added, looking up at Jamie. She couldn't help but detect some derision in the tone.

'Yeah, well ...' She didn't know how to finish that.

'Hi,' Alina said, putting her hand out to their visitors. 'I'm Alina.'

The woman stepped forward, first, glad to be doing

introductions and not just standing in the cold. 'Pleasure to meet you. I'm Nathalie.'

'Nathalie?' Jamie said aloud. That was Thorsen's nurse who answered the phone the last time she called, said that Thorsen didn't want to talk to her. To see her. To ever hear from her again. And now they were … engaged?

'Yes, that's right. And you are?' she asked, offering her hand to Jamie now.

'I'm … Jamie,' she said with some confusion. This was her house, right?

'Jamie?' Nathalie's grip tightened for a fraction of a second and then she pulled her hand away quickly. 'Jamie Johansson?'

Kjell put the dog down and stood, brushing the hair off his jeans. 'Unfortunately,' he said, the cold radiating from him.

'Unfortunate that I'm Jamie, or unfortunate that you're here?'

'Haven't decided yet,' he replied gruffly.

'Speaking of which, why are you here?'

He hesitated. 'It's, uh, a long story.'

'And one you should probably tell me? I'm guessing this isn't a social call. Unless you're here for …'

'For what?'

She shook her head. 'I don't even know.'

'I'm sorry,' Alina cut back in. 'Who are you?'

'Kjell Thorsen,' he announced, offering her his hand.

She shook firmly. 'Thorsen? This is Thorsen?' she asked Jamie.

'You told her about me?' Thorsen asked.

'Of course, you were my partner.'

'Partner, right,' he said, chuckling a little.

Jamie couldn't help but feel the anger there.

'We just got back from Kurrajak,' Alina said. 'Jamie told me all about *Krakornås Kang* – am I saying that right?' she confirmed.

'Yeah,' Jamie said, not taking her eyes of Thorsen.

'You went to Kurrajakk?' He looked from Alina to Jamie and back. 'Not to be direct, but who are you?'

'This is my … daughter,' Jamie said, unsure how he'd take it.

He laughed. Loudly. 'Daughter? Jesus, did I miss something when we were together? Gotta say, you move fast.'

'I could say the same about you,' Jamie replied, not appreciating the confrontation. She raised her chin at Nathalie and then realised it probably wasn't the best peace-brokering move.

Thorsen puffed. 'Careful,' he warned her. 'You don't know shit. You weren't there.'

'Oookay,' Alina said loudly, jumping in. 'Why don't we all go inside and have a cup of tea or something?'

'Yes,' came another voice from behind Jamie. 'I'll get the kettle on,' said Elliot, cheerfully.

Jamie closed her eyes, wishing so badly for the day to be over.

'Charlie?' Thorsen said, stepping back off the porch. His hand leapt to his empty hip, looking for the weapon that wasn't there.

'Kjell, I know you must have lots of questions ...' Elliot said, raising his hands in a show of amnesty. 'But let's go inside and talk.'

'I have questions,' Alina said. 'Primarily: who the fuck is Charlie?'

'Language!' both Jamie and Elliot snapped at the same time.

Alina shrank a little.

'He's Charlie,' Thorsen said, pointing at Elliot.

'He's Elliot,' Alina corrected him.

Elliot extended his hand. 'We haven't officially met. Elliot Day.'

Kjell looked at Jamie, stunned. 'What ... Who ... What the fuck is going on, Jamie? A daughter? Your brother, here? In Wales? How ... What ...' he stammered.

'Brother?' Alina parroted back. 'Elliot's not Jamie's brother, he's—' But she didn't get to finish before Elliot put a firm hand on her shoulder, cutting her off. She seemed to get the message that the situation was delicate.

'Seriously, Jamie – what the fuck is going on here?' Thorsen asked.

Nathalie took his hand, squeezed for support.

Jamie just put her face in her hands. 'Honestly, I wish I knew. Why are you even here?' she pleaded now.

'I'm here because ...' He settled himself a little, Nathalie's other hand on his arm now, calming him. He looked good. Better. Like he had when Jamie knew him, before the injury, before Gotland. His hair was shorter, but otherwise he looked like him. Like how she remembered him. Like how she missed him. 'I'm here because Lena Viklund broke out of the hospital.'

Jamie lifted her head. 'What did you say?'

'Lena Viklund is loose. And it looks like she's fallen back into old habits.' He took a deep breath, steadying himself, but this was clearly proving to be a lot and the way he was screwing his eyes closed made it seem like he was in pain. Maybe he was. Headache, Jamie thought. Maybe he wasn't quite as healed as he looked. 'She managed to spike a handful of staff members with a hallucinogen, and got them to throw themselves out of a second-story window. Lena climbed out afterwards,' he said with some difficulty, 'and used their bodies as a crash mat.'

Jamie processed that, and was about to ask why now when she answered the question herself. 'It's connected to our case,' she said. 'It can't be a coincidence.' The ghosts of our past, she thought.

'Our case?' Thorsen asked. 'To the King Of Crows?'

'No,' Elliot said. 'To *our* case. One we're working now.'

'You're working with your brother?' Thorsen asked.

'He's not her brother,' Alina reminded him.

'Right,' Thorsen said, shaking his head. 'Sorry, I'm still a little fuzzy, and this is all a little … *fucked.'*

'Isn't it just,' Jamie said.

It was Nathalie who spoke now, her English lilted with a northern Swedish twang. 'It has been a long journey,' she said, 'and we've been up all night. So if it's still on offer, I'd take a cup of tea.' She smiled broadly and Jamie felt a little pang of warmth. She was so damn likeable. It faded, replaced but something far more petty. Jealousy.

'Tea, yes,' Elliot said, disappearing towards the kitchen.

Alina seemed to read the tension, and offered a hand to Nathalie. 'Come on, I'll show you to the kitchen.'

She glanced at Thorsen, who was staring at Jamie, gave his arm one more squeeze, and then went with Alina, leaving them alone.

'It's, uh, good to see you,' Jamie said, barely able to get the words out.

He didn't say anything back. And he clearly didn't feel the same away.

'But I can't believe you came all this way … To tell me? To see me?'

'I didn't come to see you,' Thorsen said. 'I had no idea you lived here. I thought you were in Sweden, working with the NOD, with Dahlvig. When I rolled down that track, you were the last person I thought would open the door. The last person I wanted to open that door.'

'So what are you doing here?' Jamie tried to hide the hurt she felt at that.

'Lena Viklund was visited several times over the last few weeks but an unknown male with what we now realise are forged ID documents. He claimed to be a family member of hers, but we now know that to be a lie.'

'Julian Voss,' Jamie said.

Thorsen seemed to take that on board and then just went on. 'After she broke out, her room was searched and among her things was a piece of paper with a set of coordinated on it. Coordinates of this house. We thought he might have given it to her, that she might be coming here, or already be here. That it might be a safe house or something like that.'

'So you're working again, working the case?' Jamie was glad of that.

'No, not quite. I'm not fully on active duty yet, but I'm assisting. I wanted to come here, to investigate, but they wouldn't let me. Said she'd have no way of getting here alone, a child. That it meant nothing. So I took time off to ...'

'Come here of your accord. Which explains Nathalie,' Jamie added, hearing her laughing in the kitchen now. Elliot doing his charming thing. Alina doing her ... *Alina* thing.

'Yes, well ... No Lena Viklund. Just ... you.'

'Sorry to disappoint.'

He fell silent again.

There was so much to say. But it didn't seem like either of them wanted to say any of it.

'You look good,' Jamie began after a few awkward seconds. 'You look like you've healed—'

'Don't do that.'

She stopped speaking.

Thorsen filled his chest and stood straight, towering over her. He looked around at the place, the house. 'Tell me,' he said. 'Was any of it true? Or was it all bullshit? Did I ever really know you at all?'

Jamie swallowed, a hot lump of iron in her throat all of a sudden. 'It was all ...' she started, unable to say the word *true*. Because it wasn't. There were lies. Too many in the end to keep track of. So she said the only thing she could, the only thing that *felt* true to her. 'It was real. Everything between us was real.'

He took that in, nodded slowly, and then stepped past her and into the house without another word, heading for the kitchen.

Jamie just stood there, holding her breath, knowing if she tried to inhale she cough, splutter, probably sob. That the tears would roll.

It felt like there was electric in her hands. They fizzed and vibrated painfully as she stood in the doorway.

For a third, and Jamie hoped final time, she heard the sound of an engine in the morning air.

A black Land Rover Defender rolled into the farm yard and circled, parking alongside the other cars.

The door opened, the whole vehicle jostling, and Solomon Church stepped out, mountainous as he was.

He smiled at first, but it broke as he laid eyes on Jamie, on her expression.

Leaving the door open, he came forward.

Jamie did the same, not waiting for him to say a word before she threw her arms around him and hugged tightly.

He took a step back and then swept her up in his embrace. 'Is everything okay?' he asked, resting his chin on her head.

She pushed her face deeper into his chest. 'Not really,' she said, laughing sardonically.

'What's wrong?'

'Everything,' she said, pulling away and looking up into his dark, slate-coloured eyes. 'Everything's wrong.'

'It's okay,' he said back, smiling again now. 'I'm here. We'll figure it out.'

'I don't know that we will,' she said back. 'But I am glad you're here. You brought a gun, right?'

'Yeah ... why?'

She stared back at the house, the kitchen window, and the figures inside. All her favourite people in the world – at one time or another, at least. So why didn't she want to go in there? It didn't take a detective to figure that one out.

'So you can shoot me,' she said.

'What?' Church laughed.

'Seriously,' Jamie said. 'Just kill me now, please. It's one of those days, and I really don't want to go in there.'

He looked up at the house now. 'You didn't call me because of some weird social thing, did you?'

'No,' Jamie said, 'of course not. I called you because there's seemingly a team of vicious serial killers being unleashed on us and we need all the help we can get.' She looked at the house once more. 'But what's going on in there? Hell,' Jamie said, swallowing hard. 'I think it might be worse.'

AUTHOR'S NOTE

Goodness me, hello for the first time in a while! – I didn't seem to realise with everything going on, but I didn't include an author's note with *The Hiss Of The Snake!* It came out right before we moved from Canada back to the UK and things were hectic, to say the least. But this is a good opportunity to share some of that, some of what's gone on, and a little about this book and what's ahead!

My partner and I moved to Canada in 2021 during the pandemic to get away from the UK and see some more of the world. It was a really eye-opening experience in so many ways, and allowed us to grow and change as people. But, now, with family getting older, careers taking form, and our priorities changing, we found ourselves missing home in a way we never did before. So we made the extremely difficult choice to leave the life we'd built behind and come back to the UK, to Wales, specifically.

It's crazy to think that it was only following the release of *Old Blood*, the third Jamie Book (in the main series) that we moved away from the UK, and everything that's happened after took place in the time we were in Canada. I wanted to do something a little new after that book, and ultimately, the switch to a more psycho-thriller-esque style with *Death Chorus* set the series down a new path. It was after *Ice Queen,* though that things got more difficult. We bought a home in the town we were living in that needed some work, but after we completed, it turned out the house needed to be gutted and renovated from the studs up.

We had to completely drain our bank accounts, beg and borrow to scrape together enough to make it into something livable, and that took so much time and energy that there was a full eight month gap before the next book, *Black Heart*, released.

Sadly, this big gap meant that a lot of the momentum of the series was actually lost, and far fewer people ended up reading that book than *Ice Queen*. Which was really, really hard to take. All the work I'd put in to building this series was just falling away, and I didn't know what to do.

It wasn't long after this that we made the difficult decision to leave. The stress of the renovation and of being away from family and familial support, especially with the intention of getting married and having kids, made even more difficult by the constantly rising cost of living in Canada, was all just too much for us. So we decided that we were home-bound, however that looked.

The sale of the house was more than difficult, and done at a really difficult time. And we ended up losing some of the money we'd invested just to get out of it. But we knew it was for the best, whatever happened. We felt like it was the right path for us, finally. That we were swimming with the current instead of against it.

During that time, I also had to plan what to do next with the series, because we were seven books into it, and there wasn't much light at the end of the tunnel. Keep going, or try something different? I had to take a chance, and I decided to move the Jamie series back to the UK, to Wales, to make it more ... *me,* I guess.

The book was received well and did okay in terms of sales, but it didn't take off like *Angel Maker* did, and running two series concurrently without either of them doing particularly well, as a pure indie author investing their own money into it ... It was bleeding me dry, slowly but surely.

Honestly, through all of this, I've had more months were I've lost money than made it, and there've been some real highs, but also a lot of lows. And upon finishing and releasing *The Hiss Of The Snake,* I came to realise that the new Wales-set series, wasn't going to breathe the new life into Jamie that I hoped it would. So, again, I had to think, to figure something out. And that was to bring them all into a single series, and hope that it would help with people reading *all* the books, rather than getting to *Black Heart,* and then stopping, as seemed to be the case.

All in all, it's been a rough journey with lots of stress and pressure, and though I've loved it, it's been hard. Jamie has been my rock, my hero, but as much as I love writing her stories ... I can't keep doing it at this volume, this pace, for no reward. Hearing the reviews and the kind words fills me, fuels me, but, gosh ... House prices now, the cost of a wedding, the cost of kids. And I'm still working a full-time job, too. Something has to give. And though I hoped I'd never say these words: it has to be Jamie.

There is another book coming, don't worry! But, I have to do something else, to try something else, to try and get me from where I am now, to where I want to be. Writing full time, earning enough to support my family. Four or five novels a year (six this year among everything else!) is not sustainable, and I'm burning myself out chasing a goal that's always just out of reach.

So I've got to turn my attention to other things. To other stories and other opportunities, to try and create some magic somewhere. And I wanted to share this story with you because I think it's important for readers to know what it's like on the other side. So many authors are doing fantastically well, but the majority of us are just fighting to keep our heads above water, regardless of whether there's a bestseller tag on our books or not.

So what comes next? Well, the next Jamie is up for pre-order, and if you want to support me (and any author!), the best way to do that is by pre-ordering their next book. It helps *so* much. It really does. It's currently slated for June next year – which is not very wintery, considering the title, I know – but I reserve the right to bring that forward if I finish the manuscript early and have the ability to do so. You can read more about it on the next page here and follow the link to go find it on Amazon!

But before you do, I just want to promise you that I'm always going to keep writing, keep fighting, because this is something I've always wanted to do. The only thing I've wanted to do. And the only thing I'll ever want to do. So I'm going to keep doing it. And, hopefully, before the next Jamie book comes out, there'll be lots of news. Another self-published series. More US-set standalones. UK-set psycho-thrillers. And maybe some other projects in totally different genres. Who knows! If you're just here for Jamie, I get that – and if that's the case, I'll see you in a year with some good news, I hope! If you're interested in what else I'm doing and what's going on, come find me on Facebook. We have an excellent community of readers and friends and that's where I share all my news and updates, let you know what I'm working on and what's going on behind the scenes …

So, yeah. Come on by. Drop a comment. Send me a

message. Or, find my website by searching my name online, and join my mailing list or drop me an email and stay in touch. I'd love to hear from you. Seriously, I respond to everyone so just send me a little message if you want to chat, it's the highlight of my day hearing from readers.

But, for now, that's about it. Hope you enjoyed this one, I really did. Bringing back so many old characters and taking Jamie (and you) on a trip through the years has been brilliant fun. And bringing Thorsen back in at the end? Well, it's going to be great having him back in the mix going forward. It's a bit of a wait until the next leg of the adventure, but hopefully more than worth it.

Thank you, reader, for sticking with me and Jamie through it all. Here's to many more in the years to come.

All the best,
Morgan

ALSO BY MORGAN GREENE

<u>Standalone Titles</u>
Savage Ridge
A Place Called Hope
The Trade

WHAT'S NEXT FOR JAMIE?

Read on to discover *The First Snow Of Winter*, the next thrilling instalment of the Jamie Johansson Series.

Mister Mannequin claims his first victim, and the reality of their situation becomes starkly apparent.

Jamie, Church, Thorsen, and Elliot forge an unlikely alliance to hunt a devious killer that's leaving them bloody breadcrumbs all across Wales, working up to a gruesome grand finale.

But with Julian Voss still on the loose and working the puppet strings from the shadows, they can't afford to keep their focus so narrow. And now, with Lena Viklund on a revenge-fuelled ramapage, too, and strange reports of abnormal behaviour and suicides trickling in, there's no doubt that she's arrived on ther doorstep to stake her claim, too. But with Church pulling her one way, Elliot another, and Thorsen in a third, who will Jamie Choose? And what will the consequences be?

Jamie has hunted serial killers before, but never three at once.

Has Jamie finally met her match, and with the stakes higher than ever before, can she put her trust in her team to do what needs to be done?

The First Snow Of Winter is coming in 2025 on Kindle, Paperback, and Audio! Pre-order your Kindle copy today to read it on release day.

See it now on Amazon.

LOOKING FOR MORE JAMIE?

Thank you so much for joining Jamie and me on this adventure. I sincerely hope you've enjoyed it and are looking forward to the next one. You can find the entire catalogue of Jamie novels on my Amazon page, and stay up to date with all my new releases by following me on Facebook or signing up for my mailing list on my website.

Printed in Great Britain
by Amazon

44316562R00192